CHANTAL ROOME

To that little voice inside us that says we can't be the best at
something so we may as well quit.
Screw You.
We're doing it anyway.

Not today, Man-bun. Not today

Rhea

"I'm sorry, Sir? I don't think I heard you correctly. Did you say *suspended*?" I can't be suspended. I follow all the rules. Out of every officer in the precinct, I'm the only one who does every single thing completely by the book. "Are you sure you're talking to the right person?"

"Unfortunately, yes, I am talking to the right person. I don't agree with it, but I can't do anything about it. You are being suspended for excessive use of force. Turn in your badge and gun. You're suspended without pay for thirty days pending adjudication by the Police Commission."

"I understand, Captain Ross, Sir," I say numbly, removing my badge and gun and placing them on the Captain's desk. My movements feel jerky and stilted, and my voice doesn't sound quite like my own. "I take full responsibility for my actions, and I'm prepared to take whatever punishment the commission sees fit."

"Listen, Rhea." Captain Ross takes his glasses off and rubs the bridge of his nose with one hand. "This situation won't resolve itself easily. There is a good chance that you won't be allowed back on the force. Between you and me, the guy making the complaint, Frank Martin, is friends with the mayor. I'm already feeling pressure from higher up to just fire you and get it over with."

Frank Martin? The abusive husband Kaden and I brought in? "I don't understand, Sir." Why would they want to fire me? I do my job, and I do it well. "We were responding to a domestic disturbance call. He was screaming so loudly at his wife that the neighbors were concerned enough to call us. He pushed her down the stairs right in front of me. I couldn't just leave him there and risk him doing worse, could I?" What the hell did they expect me to do in a situation like that?

He heaves a heavy sigh. "No, you're right. You couldn't just allow it to continue. It's just that this is now a whole thing, and unfortunately, it's usually the person who *isn't* friends with the mayor that gets shit on in these situations. I'm only telling you this so that you spend your time wisely during your suspension. You may need to consider a different line of work when this is all said and done. You're a good cop, Rhea. You just got unlucky this time."

"Oh." All I've ever wanted to be was a cop. Every decision I made regarding education and extracurricular activities was made with that goal in mind. I don't even know what I would do if I couldn't be one anymore. Why the hell does it always have to come down to politics and popularity, even in police work? It seems like every day it becomes less about right and wrong and more about who knows who. I'd be lying if I said being a cop has lived up to my dreams of what it would be like.

"I'll do what I can for you. You're the best cop I've got, and I'd hate to lose you."

"Thanks, Captain. I guess... I guess I'd better get going then. I look forward to hearing from you when this is all cleared up."

I'm sure nothing will come of this. I did everything the right way. They can't fire me because someone doesn't like me. Can they?

"You too, kid. Take care." He grunts and shuffles some papers around on his desk. "Send Cross in here, would ya?"

I'm barely two steps out of the captain's office before my partner, Kaden Cross, jogs up.

"So, how did it go?" He asks.

I've been worried about this meeting since the captain's secretary booked it with me. I've never been brought in front of the captain before. If it's possible, Kaden has been even more concerned. I'm not one to step out of line, so the captain wanting to see me was big news around the precinct.

"Oh, not too bad," I say, my voice dripping with sarcasm. "Just off to start my thirty day, unpaid vacation now. Captain wants to see you, by the way."

What am I even going to do with myself for thirty days? I foresee a lot of trail runs in my future. Maybe I should get a pet? Like a cat. Or a snake.

"You're suspended? What the hell for?"

"Remember that domestic disturbance call we went on last week? When I arrested the older guy for pushing his wife down the stairs right in front of us?"

"Yeah, I remember. That guy was a dick. All 'Do you know who I am?' and 'You're going to regret this'. Such an asshole."

"Well, that asshole is friends with the mayor. And he's saying I used excessive force when I took him into custody. Now I'm suspended for thirty days, and the whole issue is awaiting adjudication by the police commission."

"What? That's bullshit. I was there. You barely even touched the guy. It was a textbook arrest. You were even gentle when you put the cuffs on. You're the most by the book cop anyone in this precinct has ever seen. I don't think you could break a rule if you tried."

"You know that, and I know that, but apparently it doesn't matter. It's okay, though. I'm sure it will all work out. There's no way they'll fire me for something that didn't happen. Right?"

"I guess." Kaden doesn't seem as confident as I feel. "What will you do if they do fire you, though? You've always wanted to be a cop."

"That's a damn good question. I guess I have something to think about while I'm on my unplanned vacation. That'll give me something to do other than run, at least."

"Well, worse comes to worst, I'm sure we can convince Xena to hire you at Bump & Grind. Maybe you could even get her to stop threatening people with that stupid foam sword she has behind the counter and save me some money." He shakes his head.

Here at the precinct, we have a sword jar instead of a swear jar and Kaden is the only one who has to contribute. Every time we get a call about his sister threatening her customers with a sword, he has to put money in.

"You gotta admit, though, it is pretty funny seeing her swinging that thing around and then seeing the looks on her customers' faces. And aside from you having to put five bucks in the sword jar every time it gets called in, it's not really harmful. We all know it's not a serious threat."

"Whatever. I still think it's unfair. It's not my fault my sister loses her mind any time someone calls her 'Warrior Princess'. If anyone should have to pay five bucks when she pulls out that sword, it should be our parents. They're the ones who named her after the character Lucy Lawless played, not me." He crosses his arms and frowns. "And besides, she really *should* be arrested one of these days. She's becoming a menace."

Kaden follows me into the locker room, where I empty my locker into my bag. No sense changing here. I'll just take off my uniform shirt and wear the tank I have underneath when I go.

No one could think I look like a cop while I'm wearing a tank top with Wonder Woman on the front.

"She's only bothering you, Kaden. Everyone else thinks it's hilarious. You probably just need to drop it. It's a lost cause."

"Gah!" He says, while shaking his fist to the sky melodramatically. "I know. It's just so damn irritating. I need to figure out a way to get back at her. That might make me feel better. At least for a little while, anyway."

"Alright, you keep me posted on that." I give him a little wave with my keys. "I'm going to head out. You should probably go see the captain now. He may need to assign you a new partner. Or maybe he'll make you ride a desk until I'm back, because you just made him wait so long."

"Oh, shit." He jumps and starts jogging away. "I'll call you later to check on you."

I shake my head as I walk out of the precinct. All those years I spent dreaming of being a cop, I never pictured my partner being someone like Kaden. He's got the muscular body I imagined a male cop should have, but that's where any resemblance to my imaginary partner ends. I always thought my partner would be incredibly smart and serious, and Kaden is... well, Kaden is smart enough, but he's rarely serious. But we've been partners since the beginning and I wouldn't have it any other way. He's the brother I never had.

Really, he's the brother I do have. When he found out I grew up in the foster system and don't have any real family, he made me a member of his. His sister is one of my best friends. I get invited to every holiday dinner and every birthday. His parents fill a stocking for me on Christmas, for crying out loud. I might as well me Rhea Cross instead of Rhea Ryan. The third, unrelated, Cross sibling.

And that's how I know, no matter what happens with this suspension and adjudication, I will be fine. Even if I'm not

Kaden's partner, I will still be part of his family. And family takes care of family.

Stepping out into the sunlight to get to my car leaves me blinded for a moment and before I acclimate to the brightness, someone has walked up beside me and started talking.

"Diana Prince, just the person I was hoping to see," he says to me, using the name of Wonder Woman's secret identity. Maybe wearing this tank wasn't such a good idea after all. "I was hoping to ask you something the other day after you arrested my friend's ex-boyfriend over at Peaceful Pines, but I didn't get the chance. And I haven't been able to get in touch with you since then, either."

It's the hippie-looking, long-haired guy who was with Devon the day I arrested some idiot who got himself tied up by two little old ladies while attempting to take them hostage. As if today wasn't bad enough, now I have to deal with this random guy who keeps trying to ask me out. He was trying to talk to me that first day, and he's been around the precinct a few times since. What's it going to take for him to get the hint that I don't want to go out with him? I mean, he has a nice-looking butt, but get a clue man. I don't have time for this.

"Oh hey... you," I say, already walking away. I don't even know the guy's name, I've just been referring to him as 'Man-bun' in my head, because of the way he always wears his long hair in a high bun. "Can't talk now. I'm swamped. So many things to do. Catch you later." I speed walk to my car, arms and hips swinging, unlocking the door with the fob before I'm even close to it. Without a single look back at Man-bun, I throw my bags in, jump in the driver's seat, and start it up, already speeding out of the parking lot before I've got my seat belt on.

"Not today, Man-bun. Not today." I whoop, turning my car toward home, leaving him standing in the parking lot with his mouth hanging open. "You and your exceptionally nice ass are just going to have to find someone else to date."

2

Back to my Roots

Aiden

THREE MONTHS LATER

Sometimes I find it hard to believe this garage is where it all started. When we were just starting out with Sleeping Dogs, the guys and I would jam here pretty much every day. We all had other jobs to work around, or school, but we made it work. The neighbors can attest to how much we rehearsed, I'm sure. They sent me a fruit basket when I finally ramped up the soundproofing. It's a good thing I did, too, because this is still where I come when I just need to blast music and practice my craft.

Some people don't realize how extremely physical playing the drums is. There's a reason the drummer is usually the sweatiest guy in the band at the end of the show. At least in our band, that's the case, anyway. With drumming, I take all the anger I feel at the world and put it into practicing drum techniques. And it has the added bonus of wiping me out so thoroughly that I can sleep for more than a few hours at a time, something I'd never done before I started playing.

Since the beginning, I've practiced for at least two hours a day, regardless of circumstances, whenever I'm not touring with Sleeping Dogs. Even after all these years, I still need the physical and emotional release I get from playing to get a mediocre night's sleep. Wearing myself out drumming, and delighting in the fact that my asshole dad is long dead, has me sleeping okay most nights.

Last night's sleep was worse than most, so I've set out to exhaust myself completely today. I'm just getting into hour four of practice when Johnny shows up, waving from where he's standing at the door to the house.

Leaning over to shut the backing music off, I grab a towel and start mopping up the sweat that's dripping down my body. When we play shows, I wear jeans and t-shirts but when I'm at home, I stick to just shorts. The other guys all take more time with their appearance, but I'm happy to blend into the background, both literally, given my position at the back of the stage during shows, and figuratively, given how I dress in a way that draws the least attention to me. I'm not interested in hooking up and I don't care if I impress anyone and my clothes definitely tell that story. The only thing that might draw attention to me is my long hair. And even then, I wear it up in a high bun when I'm not playing, so I look like any other man-bun-wearing asshole out walking around.

Speaking of assholes. Where did Johnny get to?

"What's up, man? What are you doing here?"

I find Johnny standing in my kitchen, looking through the fridge.

"Well, it's nice to see you too, sweetheart," Johnny says while blowing me a kiss. "I couldn't sleep last night, so I spent the entire night baking. I figured I'd deliver some for you to bring to the shelter when you go later." He closes the fridge and points to the stack of bakery boxes on the counter.

I volunteer at a local domestic violence shelter and I go in nearly every day. Whenever Johnny feels stressed and has one of his marathon baking sessions, he loads me up with treats to bring the women and kids taking advantage of the safety and support of the shelter. A lot of them have been barely surviving, living in fear, and the gift of home-baked goods is a small indulgence they've been missing in their lives.

"Hey thanks, man." I pull on a t-shirt that's hanging inside the door to the house. "The director messaged me earlier to let me know we had a few new intakes overnight. I'm sure some of Johnny's famous cookies will bring a smile to some kids' faces."

"Do they even believe you when you tell them I make this stuff?"

Johnny is the last person you would expect to see baking cookies and cakes when he gets stressed, or any time, really. He's covered in tattoos. Seriously covered. I'm not positive, because there are parts of him I don't want to look at that closely, but I'm pretty sure his face is the only part of him not tattooed. Yes, including his dick. But that's just a rumor I heard, because, again, I don't want to look that closely. And I only say that because his face is mostly uncovered. He has a couple of smaller tattoos on the left side of his face, some Latin word I don't recognize, and a little heart. So, yeah, to think of him in an apron, measuring ingredients, and covered in flour, it's a tough pill for some to swallow.

"They think I make them and am too shy to tell the truth. Apparently, I made you up to divert attention away from myself. One of these days, you'll need to come with me when I deliver them."

I pour each of us a coffee.

"But that's not really why you came here, is it? Got something on your mind?"

I'm the oldest member of Sleeping Dogs, which somehow makes me the go-to for advice when the other guys need help. And I'd much rather they come to me than go to each other. These guys could really get themselves into a lot of trouble with some of the ideas they've had in the past. They're all impulsive, jumping into things without thinking them through fully.

"Yeah, kind of. I mean yes, definitely. It's just this whole thing with Becca. She doesn't seem to be interested most of the time. It's getting me down."

"Doesn't she work, like, all the time? And she works for herself too, right? Photographers don't exactly keep regular hours. She has to be available when the clients need her. She might be interested, but just doesn't have enough time for relationships right now," I tell him.

"You think?"

"I mean, it's possible? But she probably just doesn't like you." I laugh.

Johnny just stares at me while I laugh. I really shouldn't take pleasure in what is clearly causing him pain, but the guy kind of deserves it. He's pulled the same hot and cold routine with lots of women. It's about time it came around to bite him in the ass.

"But seriously," I add. "Just relax. Maybe ask Alex? If anyone knows anything about what's up with Becca, it's her. Or maybe Ryder, but he's a little too busy these days, what with getting ready to be a dad, and reading all the baby books for Denise."

Since their wedding almost four months ago, Denise and Ryder have been spending a lot of time getting ready for their baby's arrival. In just two short months, we'll be welcoming the first baby to our Sleeping Dogs family. And somewhere around three months after that we'll welcome babies number two and three when Alex and Connor have their twins.

We're going to be overrun with kids before we know it. And it's about time, if you ask me. None of us is getting any younger. Not that I'm going to be having any of my own, mind you. That's a no go for me.

"I don't know how you've never had a girlfriend. Out of all of us, you're the most stable. And you're definitely the most mature. Doesn't it ever get lonely living here in this house by yourself?"

"Nah, I'm good," I say, cutting the conversation short. The guys know a little about my history, but they don't know the real extent of my father's abusive. It's better if they don't.

It's not something I like to talk about. But I do know having him as my father means I could end up the same way. I refuse to allow that to happen. In the interest of safety, I just stay out of relationships. No relationship and no kids means I will never need to worry about becoming an abusive asshole like he was. It's best this way. I may get a little lonely sometimes, but I can deal with that. What I can't deal with, though, is the thought I could ever do to my family what he did to his.

Nah. I'm more than happy to just be Uncle Aiden. I don't need to have a wife and kids to feel fulfilled in my life.

3

Pity Party Interruptus

Rhea

"So that's it then? Those bibbity bobbity bastards! How can they get away with that?" Xena is foaming at the mouth on my behalf, and when she's mad, she uses some incredibly creative language. "What about Kaden? Or the cuntwaffle's wife? Wouldn't their witness statements count for something? Prove you didn't use excessive force with that abusive dick weasel?"

The police commission took less than seven days of my initial thirty-day suspension to determine that I did use excessive force during the arrest three months ago. And I just got word they've denied my second, and final, appeal just like they did the first. It's official. I am no longer a police officer. My lifelong dream was destroyed because I dared to arrest a man who was friends with the mayor.

"His wife refused to press charges against him and recanted her witness statement. So it was only Kaden's word against theirs. There's nothing left to be done. It's time for me to start really thinking about what to do for work now."

I have a dual major in Criminal Justice and Social Work I could use when looking for a new job. I initially wanted to be a police officer so I could help kids the way a police officer helped me when I was a kid, but now I need to find another way. This will require lots of coffee and some quality time on the computer.

"Well, that sounds like a big wet puddle of septic system contents to me," Xena says, employing some of her creative cussing again. "What are you going to do?"

"Well, for now, I'm going to take home the biggest coffee you have. Then I'm going to go home and sit on my computer and see what I can find. Maybe this is a chance to do something totally different?"

Xena grabs a travel carafe and fills it with the dark roast I like. She fills a box with assorted donuts for me, too.

"Ha! That's funny. A cop getting donuts. Good one," a masculine voice behind me says.

I spin around to see Kaden's friend Devon standing there.

"Oh, shit." Xena eyes go wide. "I didn't even think of that. I'm so sorry, Rhea." She overreacts in typical Xena fashion, and before I can say it's no big deal, she's thrown the box through the little pass-through window that leads back into Bump & Grind's kitchen.

A laugh escapes me, sounding more like a snort than an actual laugh.

"I think I might be missing something," Devon says, looking back and forth between me, Xena, and the pass-through. "Is everything okay here?"

"It's fine, Devon," I tell him, even though things are not feeling fine at all. "I got the result of my latest appeal today, is all. For the excessive force thing? They turned it down again, so I'm off the force permanently. I'm not a cop anymore."

"Oh... oh shit!" Devon grabs my shoulders, shaking me a little. I have to look up to see his face, which is unusual for me since at five foot ten inches, I'm considered a tall woman. But Devon is another level of tall altogether. His six and a half feet of height makes me feel petite in comparison. "I am so, so, sorry, Rhea. I didn't know." He pulls me into a too tight hug, somehow squeezing my face down between his pecs, and I'm tempted to motorboat him just to see what he does. Something tells me Xena would lose her shit if I did that, though, and since she's pretty much my sister, I decide to just pinch him instead.

"Ow! Rude." Devon squeals.

"You were suffocating me with your man-boobs. I had no choice but to retaliate. It was feeling like life or death there for a second." I grin up at him while he rubs the spot on his side where I pinched him. "Besides, you've got a wall of solid muscle there. I could barely pinch anything."

"Right?! I am a pretty spectacular specimen." He flexes his biceps, kissing each in turn.

"Oh my god, get over yourself, Tiny Dancer." Xena rolls her eyes at him. He just winks back, making her blush.

That's interesting.

"Okay, well, as much fun as this has been, I'm going to go job hunting now. How much for the coffee?"

She scrunches her face at me. "Seriously? You're unemployed and you're practically my sister. Like I'm going to charge you for coffee."

"Ugh, fine. I accept. But only because I don't want to stand here and argue with you for another half an hour and then just end up accepting anyway, because you're impossible to argue with."

"That's wise of you. At least getting fired hasn't dulled your common sense. Yet." Xena laughs, and waves me off with my travel carafe. "Call me later and let me know how the search is going. You can always come work for me until you find something."

"Yeah, okay. I'll talk to you later. See you, Devon."

As I'm walking out, I hear Devon ask if he gets free coffee, too. Xena's uncontrollable laughter is the only response I hear before I'm back outside. They have a strange friendship, those two. Kaden's been concerned about it for a while now, but I don't think he has anything to worry about. If Devon and Xena get together, they're old enough to deal with any fallout on their own. But it's hard for Kaden to imagine his sister and his best friend being interested in each other. He's protective of both relationships.

He's protective of his friendship with me too, but luckily he doesn't have to worry about me starting a relationship with someone. I have no interest in becoming involved with anyone. Being involved with someone would require me to trust that person, and I have a hard time trusting anyone. Hell, it took me almost five years to trust Kaden, and he's the one who has my back when shit gets bad.

Shit. *Had* my back. I'm not a cop anymore.

I feel the weight of the last three months hit me all at once and my legs wobble as my vision blurs. I'm too far from any benches, so I just stumble to the edge of the sidewalk and slide my back down against the side of a building until my butt hits the pavement. I pull my knees up and rest my elbows on them, allowing my head to hang down while I get control of my breathing.

What the hell am I going to do now?

I have some savings to keep me going for a few more months, but it's not a lot. I need to find a job quickly if I'm going to keep my apartment.

Crying has never been my thing. When I was young, I learned crying was useless since my mom was always too drunk to hear me. But right now I let a few tears drop to the carafe sitting on the sidewalk between my feet. I just got fired from the only job I've ever wanted in my life; I think I'm allowed to throw myself a small pity party. Probably shouldn't do it here on the sidewalk, though. It would suck if one of my former coworkers had to arrest me for loitering.

"You alright?" A pair of beat up old Converse sneakers stops in front of me. I assume they're attached to whoever just asked me if I'm alright but I don't care enough to find out.

"Yeah, I'm good. Thanks," I say without looking up. It's bad enough I'm crying. I don't need anyone seeing me do it.

"Oh yeah, I can see that. I often see crying women sitting on a busy sidewalk in the middle of the day. It's a totally normal thing that always happens in this neighborhood," the guy says with a hint of sarcasm in his voice.

"Just got some bad news and needed a minute to wrap my mind around it. No big deal."

He reaches his hand down into my line of sight. "Well, can I at least help you up? I'd feel bad if I just left you sitting here. It's not exactly summer anymore, you know. Your ass might freeze to the sidewalk and then you'd have to chew it off to set yourself free. Then you'd be crying *and* assless. I can't have that on my conscience."

I choke out a weak laugh. "That's the most ridiculous thing I've ever heard. But sure, I guess you can help me up." I take his hand a feel a tingle shoot up my arm as he pulls me up.

"Oh hey, it's you," the guy says as he stares at my face with shockingly green eyes. They're light green but so vibrant they almost glow in the sunlight. He reaches up and cups my face, wiping a tear from my cheek with his thumb. Instinctively, I lean into his hand and a shiver runs up my spine.

Ah, shit. And here I thought this day couldn't get any worse. I was wrong, though, because who should find me in my weakest moment but Man-bun. The guy who couldn't take no for an answer and kept trying to ask me out after Kaden and I arrested a suspect in the Peaceful Pines retirement community. The one who followed me out to the cruiser when we brought the suspect out, and he even had the audacity to show up at the precinct a few times after that, too.

I mean, it's not that he isn't attractive, with his cute little sloppy man-bun, and his low-slung jeans, and his t-shirt that's so worn it's practically see through, showing a good amount of smooth, delicious muscle underneath. He is so not unattractive.

Whoa, get it together, Rhea. Keep it in your pants. You're definitely not interested in this guy. Even if he is a 'spectacular specimen', as Devon would say. But spectacular specimens can still be scary stalkers.

"Oh yeah, hi," I drawl. "I'm sorry. I didn't catch your name last time?" I'm going to need a name to put on the restraining order if this guy doesn't stop bothering me. But I'm sure that's what this even is. "I'm Rhea."

"Yeah, Devon told me who you are after you guys left Gran's place the day you arrested my friend's crazy ex. I'm Aiden."

That's good enough for me. I can get his last name out of Devon later, before I go to the precinct to process the paperwork. If I can bring myself to do it, anyway. He doesn't seem dangerous, so maybe he won't need an official restraining order? And I suppose, if he's friends with Devon, he might not actually be a scary stalker. Aside from him showing up all the time, my gut doesn't tell me this guy is dangerous.

I still don't want him to ask me out right now, though. I have way too much going on in my life for that.

"Nice to see you again, Aiden. But I really need to get going. I've got a lot to do today. Bye-bye now," I say, and start walking away a little faster than normal.

"Oh, I just need to ask you something real quick. I was wondering if—"

"Nope, sorry. No time. Gotta run," I interrupt him, and then I literally start running. Maybe he'll actually get the hint this time and just leave me alone. Even if he is cute, I don't have time to stick around talking to someone who can't take no for an answer.

4

Maybe I Should Do Something About That?

Aiden

"WAS THAT RHEA?" DEVON is standing beside me suddenly, as I stand watching the strangest woman I've ever met run away from me. Again. "Why is she running?"

"I don't know, man," I say, scratching my head. "I was just coming to grab a coffee at Bump & Grind and I found her sitting here on the sidewalk, crying. I helped her up, then she asked my name and ran away. It's totally bizarre."

"Oh shit, she was crying? I better let Xena know. Come on, maybe she'll give us free coffee if you're with me. Lord knows I can't get any on my own."

Bump & Grind is just a short walk from where we're standing. Rhea must've just left if the carafe she was carrying was any sign. I wonder why she needs so much coffee. Bringing it to the precinct, maybe? Or going on a stakeout?

I never understood the whole drinking coffee on stakeouts thing. Wouldn't that increase the likelihood you'd need to piss in a bottle? Plus, women can't piss in bottles. What would they do?

"Honey, I'm home," Devon calls out as we enter the coffee shop owned by Denise's best friend Xena.

I've been getting coffee here for years and I had no idea my band's manager was such good friends with the feisty little owner. I've even seen Xena swing her rubber sword at someone for calling her 'Warrior Princess' once or twice and that was some funny shit.

"Ugh, why are you back already? It's only been five minutes since I got rid of you last time." Xena wipes her hands on a towel. "Hey Aiden, the usual?"

"Please," I say, throwing five dollars on the counter. I just get regular drip coffee. None of those fancy drinks for me. Too sweet for my tastes. I'd rather eat Johnny's baked treats if I'm having something sweet. And I still have some left at home from the stuff he brought me yesterday. I accidentally missed a box when I brought the other stuff to the shelter. It's not like I purposely kept it for myself.

"So we have a minor situation." Devon puts five dollars on the counter beside mine. I guess Xena knows his regular order too, because she doesn't even ask before pouring another of what I'm having. "Aiden just ran into Rhea down the street. She was sitting on the sidewalk and crying, apparently."

"I knew it!" Xena yells, throwing the money into the cash register and slamming it shut. "I knew she was too calm after getting such terrible news. I need to call someone in to cover for me. Rhea needs tequila and a girls' night, not coffee and job searching." Xena pulls her phone out of her apron pocket and starts frantically swiping the screen.

"Job searching? Why would she be job searching?" Not that I care much. She's brushed me off more times than I can count. I keep trying to ask if she'd be interested in helping teach some self-defense classes at the shelter and she keeps avoiding me completely. She's been quite the bitch about it, too, if I'm being honest. Who turns and runs away from someone in the middle of a conversation?

I can't say I mind watching her walk away. The sight of her round ass is all the consolation I need.

Seeing her crying there on the sidewalk stirred something in my chest, though. Something I'm not willing to investigate.

"Well, she made a political mistake a few months ago. She and Kaden got called to a domestic disturbance and when they arrived, the dude shoved his wife down the stairs right in front of them. So Rhea arrested him."

"Good for her. She was right to arrest him. I probably would have pushed him down the stairs so he could see how it feels, but arresting him is good, too." I make a mental note to get the guy's name and address. It sounds like I'll need to visit him to dole out some of my particular brand of justice.

"Funny you should mention that," Devon says, stirring sugar into his coffee. "Apparently, the guy is friends with the mayor. Long story short, he claimed she used excessive force, and now she got fired."

"Well, the guy's wife and Kaden must have made witness statements, right? Or can't she appeal?"

"The wife won't press charges, and Kaden's word means nothing if the wife doesn't corroborate it. And Rhea's used up all of her appeals already. There's nothing else she can do."

I stir a little sugar and cream into my coffee, trying to think of another way Rhea could get back on the force. It doesn't seem fair that she was doing her job, and helping an abused woman, and now she's fired because the guy she arrested knows someone important. This just confirms my suspicions about the law enforcement system being flawed, and the laws rarely favoring the victims of domestic violence. It certainly never helped me when I was a kid. And even when the victims press charges, they frequently don't get justice. It's why I started my little side business. Well, my side hobby, anyway.

It's not like I get paid.

"So what's this guy's name, anyway?"

"Oh no, no way. If anything happens to him, who do you think will be the first to get blamed? You stay away from him." Xena covers the mouthpiece of her phone and chastises me in a loud whisper. "She has enough trouble in her life right now without being suspected of an actual crime."

I throw my hands up in surrender. "Okay, okay. It was just a thought."

I actually hadn't considered anyone would blame Rhea for it, so it's probably a good thing Xena talked me out of it. It's not like the guy would end up dead or anything. But a broken arm or two, so he had some recovery time to think about whether he wanted to lay hands on his wife again? That could be a good thing for him.

Not that I deal in that sort of revenge. Instead, I tend toward the petty vandalism type. As much as I would love to dole out physical punishments, I'm just not comfortable with that. No matter how much the assholes deserve it.

I wouldn't be doing it for Rhea, either. After how my dad terrorized my mother and me when I was growing up, it's kind of my calling to help as many victims of domestic violence as I can. I volunteer with the women's shelter as much as possible. I donate money to tons of different initiatives aimed at eradicating domestic violence. Whether they be education, support, or crisis-based. One of the main reasons I'm in Sleeping Dogs is to make the money I need to do what I need to for people who've been affected by violence in this way. Whether that's the legal and monetary help I provide or the slightly less legal ways I go about encouraging offenders to rethink their ways.

"Okay, Tanya is going to be here in about twenty minutes. Tiny Dancer, I need you to go buy tequila. Get the good stuff too. None of that gasoline-flavored donkey piss, okay? Take Aiden with you. His thoughts are too loud and he's getting on my nerves. I need to think of what I'm going to do to help cheer up Rhea. I don't need Captain Serious over here harshing my vibes."

"Ha! Captain Serious, that's a good one. I'm going to have to remember that." Devon looks at me and laughs.

"You do that, *Tiny Dancer*. I don't mind at all." I jump out of the way as he attempts to punch my arm.

"Princess, look what you started," he says to Xena. "Pretty soon everyone is going to be calling me by that stupid name."

Xena just grins and winks at him.

Devon grunts in response. "Come on, let's go buy this stupid tequila before she gets really demanding."

I grab my coffee and follow Devon outside. The store we're going to is only two blocks away, so we're there before my coffee has even cooled.

Once inside, Devon goes straight to the register and asks to have the manager meet us in the tequila section.

"You need a manager to buy tequila?" I ask as we walk over to the tequila to wait.

"I need whoever has the keys to get the good tequila out of the locked cabinet." He points to a fancy looking blue and white bottle and one that's got 'dangerous' in the name. "Xena likes these two. They're sweeter than other tequilas and don't have that 'gasoline' taste she hates."

The manager comes over and gets Devon's two bottles, then walks us to the register. Devon pays and we're back outside in no time.

"You sure know a lot about her tastes in tequila. You two spend a lot of time drinking together?"

"Nah, nothing like that," Devon says, but his cheeks get a little pink. "I've been friends with her brother for years. She's used me as an errand boy many times. This store helped me pick out tequila that met her requests the first time, and I just keep buying the same ones."

"You just spent over three hundred dollars on tequila. That's a lot of money on alcohol for your friend's sister."

"You guys pay me a lot more than what I need to live comfortably. I'm happy to buy it for her. Plus, she only asks for it a couple of times a year. It's not like I'm spending thousands of dollars buying her expensive gifts or anything." Devon is looking a little uncomfortable. I wonder if Kaden knows about the tequila arrangement? My instincts tell me no. "She might still have some left of the last bottle left at home. But Rhea lives close to the coffee shop, so Xena is probably going to head straight there when her replacement shows up at work."

Suddenly a flurry of tiny arms and legs is careening in our direction. Xena crashes into Devon instead of stopping before she gets to us.

"Did you get the good one?" She asks while her eyes roam Devon's body, looking for the bags from the store.

"I got one of each of the ones you like. But you still need to pace yourself and make sure you eat something first, okay? I don't want you calling me later to come hold your hair while you puke your guts out."

Xena laughs. "Nice try. My hair is short enough I can handle any vomiting all by myself. I might have to call you to drive my drunk ass home, though. So keep your phone on. I need to go pick up some clothes for Rhea, too. I think some forced dancing might be in order." She shakes her butt a little to show us what she means.

She grabs her bottles of tequila, giving us a wave as she turns and walks away.

"Well, what are you up to now? Want to come over and play some video games while you wait for that call?" I ask, taking a drink of my coffee.

"Yeah, why not? I haven't kicked your ass in Mario Kart in a while."

I laugh. Devon's never beat me at any game, ever. "Sure. But I get to pick which system we play on."

5

Time to Shake our Asses

Rhea

"Knock knock knock. Special Delivery."

I'm not expecting a delivery, but I bet I know who is at my door, and why she's here. She has her own key, so I don't even bother leaving my desk to open the door.

During my online search, I found an interesting job posting at a local women's shelter I'm thinking of applying for. I've been trying to figure out the best way to word my reasoning for leaving the police force ever since. Somehow, fired for arresting the wrong guy doesn't seem quite right.

"Bitch," Xena says from the doorway. "My hands are full and you made me open the door myself? Rude."

She juggles several bags as she walks over to set them on the couch.

"I'm busy here too, you know. I found a job I might want to apply for, but I can't figure out what to say about getting fired. It sounds so bad to say I got fired from being a cop." Not to mention it's totally depressing, considering it's the only thing I've ever wanted to do with my life. I liked it, even though it was never quite what I expected it would be.

"Tell the truth. You arrested someone who had a well-connected friend, and they made you pay for it."

I sigh, rubbing my eyes with the heels of my palms. "It all just sounds so ridiculous, you know? I feel like I'm in an awful movie where a cop gets on the wrong side of the city's dark underbelly, and has to become a private investigator. I'll be spending all my time staking out motels and dive bars, trying to get proof of infidelity in people's marriages."

"Well, whatever puts food on the table, right? It probably beats stripping."

"I guess. Stripping seems more honest than trying to catch people cheating, though. Too bad I can't dance, or I'd at least have that to fall back on." I flop back in my chair and lock my hands behind my head. "I just never pictured myself as anything other than a cop. It's all I've ever wanted to do with my life. I don't even know what else I might be good at."

Xena makes herself at home in my kitchen, banging around in my cupboards, pulling out glasses, ice, salt, and a cocktail shaker. Ah, I guess it's to be margaritas tonight. That's good. I saw the two bottles of tequila she had and I was not looking forward to drinking it straight. She always insists she buys 'the good stuff' but I can't taste much difference between the good stuff and the not so good stuff. Tequila is not my favorite. But Xena is like a sister to me, so I usually go along with her impromptu tequila parties. They don't happen too frequently, so it's not that big of a hardship. I guess.

"Should I order us some dinner?" I ask. "I've barely eaten today and if you're going to be mixing up margaritas, I probably should get some food in my stomach."

"Already taken care of, Rhea. Little sister Xena is taking care of you tonight."

I watch as she pours way too much tequila into the shaker, not even pretending like she's measuring it. You know it's going to be a rough night when she's already free-pouring and it's only the first drink. Maybe I can dump some of it in the sink when she's not looking?

"What did you order?"

"Tacos, obviously." She looks at me like I'm nuts for even asking. "Tacos and tequila. Too bad it's not Tuesday. The alliteration would be outstanding. But taco and tequila Friday is cool, too. We get to go out dancing later this way. If it were Tuesday, our options for getting up to no good would be much more limited. Westborough just isn't big enough to have a big middle of the week club scene."

"Oh no, Zee. I'm not really in the mood for dancing. I kind of just want to lie low at home for the night." I know I've already been off work for three months, but at least I had hope during that time. Now that I know I'm never going back, it feels so much worse, so much more real.

"Tough titty said the little kitty. We're going dancing. You're going to shake your ass, maybe grind on a couple of cute guys, and just have a good time. You don't have to be a serious cop anymore. It's time to cut loose and have some fun."

I sigh. Xena just doesn't get it. I *enjoyed* being a serious cop all the time. I felt like I was helping people. Protecting people the way I wished someone would protect me when I was a kid. How it was a police officer who finally protected me when she got me away from my mother for good.

I guess she was lucky my mother didn't know the mayor, or she might have been in the same position I'm in now, instead of being a little girl's hero.

"Okay, fine. You win. Give me the margarita." I close my laptop and get up from my desk. Taking the glass from Xena, I add, "And then you can help me find something to wear when we go out dancing. You've seen my wardrobe. Nothing about it screams 'I'm having a good time.'"

Xena snorts a laugh. "No, it certainly does not. It screams a combination of, 'I'm really a farmer' and 'can I talk to you about your life insurance needs?'" Xena finishes making her own drink and joins me in the living room. "Now, let's get some dance music on while we get ready."

She connects her phone to my stereo and puts on what she calls her 'dirty girls' party hard' playlist. I can't deny the first song choice makes me want to shake my ass. Any song with the word *Booty* in the title is bound to have that effect on a person, I'm sure.

After we've had a few drinks and eaten our tacos, we are back in my room again, looking through the dismal selection of clothes my closet offers.

"What about this one?" I ask, holding up a knee-length dress with a floral print and a peter pan collar. "I wore this one to one of my foster brothers' high school graduations."

"Ew, no," Xena says, holding her nose like she's trying to avoid an unpleasant smell. "That was over ten years ago. And this dress was ugly even then."

"What about this one?" I hold up a cute yellow sundress with thin straps, buttons all the way up the front, and, most importantly, pockets.

"That's cute, but not for our purposes this evening. Put it back."

I hang the yellow dress up and flip through the hangers in my closet again. Button up blouse with frilly cuffs? No, definitely not. Bridesmaid dress with seven ruffled layers of skirt and a long train? Maybe if we were going flamenco dancing. Shit, maybe we are? Where did I put my castanets, though? Never mind, we can worry about accessories after we get the clothes figured out.

I hold up the dress with a laugh. "Are we going flamenco dancing?"

"No, but leave that dress on the bed. We can bring it in case we need to perform a magic show. I would make an amazing cape." She makes some vague gestures with her arms, looking more like Vanna White turning the letters on *Wheel of Fortune* than a magician. "And for my next trick, I will remove the stick from this woman's butthole."

I throw the flamenco bridesmaid dress at her. "Shut up. I do not have a stick up my butt. I'm a fun person. I have fun... things... I do things... of fun... things that are fun." I shake my head, trying to get my thoughts in order. "Things." I squint at her and shoot her with my finger guns. "Pew pew. Nailed it."

How many of these margaritas have I had already? And when did it get dark outside? Exactly how long have we been digging around in my closet?

"How drunk are you?" Xena asks with a chuckle. "Hold on, I know how we can tell. One sec. Where's my phone?" She digs through a pile of discarded clothing options until she finds her phone. After a few passes and a *lot* of giggling, she finally finds what she was looking for and then makes a big show of pressing something on her screen.

And then it happens. The bass pumps. The music flows. And I am free.

"Oh, shit. This is my jam!" I yell, throwing my arms up in the air, and start dancing around.

"Yup, I think you're drunk." Xena laughs as I rap along with the lyrics. How she doesn't get excited over Sir-Mix-A-Lot's *Baby Got Back* is beyond me. This song is brilliant.

"I forgot I brought something for you," she says before running from the room. "I can't believe we wasted all this time in your closet."

She comes back in with a big t-shirt and a pair of scissors and gets busy laying it all out on the bed. She starts cutting the shirt, but I'm too busy declaring my love for big butts to even care about finding something to wear anymore. I could happily stay in my apartment and dance to this song all night.

I suppose it's a good thing the store I live over is closed right now. I doubt the cute older lady who runs that place is as excited about big butts as me and my pal Sir-Mix-A-Lot.

"Okay, I've got it," Xena says proudly. "Put these on."

She thrusts a pile of clothes in my arms and leaves the room. The crazy girl has even picked out my underwear. At the top of the pile sits a dark purple lace thong with a matching bralette that I have never seen in my life. Did she buy these for me? Has she had this planned all along?

I strip and slip on the underwear and inspect the other items she's chosen for me. The denim shorts are a little shorter than I'd normally wear, but she's also thoughtfully added a pair of fishnet tights to go underneath them. Adding those over the underwear on my body, I pick up the only item left of the pile she'd given me. It's a black t-shirt from which she's cut out the arms and part of the sides (so that's what she was doing with the scissors), turning it into a tank top. On the front is the picture of a drummer, his long hair flying, sweat making his shirt stick to his body, and his arm muscles flexed and visible. I turn the tank around and written across the back in huge letters are the words *Sleeping Dogs*. It's the band Devon works security for. He must have a ton of these things lying around for Xena to have stolen this one.

Once the entire outfit is on, I only see one minor problem.

"Xena," I call through the open bedroom door. "This shirt is way too long. What am I supposed to do with it?"

She comes running into the bedroom and skids to a stop when she sees me.

"You look amazing!" She yells, her eyes wide. "Just tuck in the front like this."

She comes to me and shoves a little of the shirt into the front of the shorts. I turn to the mirror. That actually looks pretty good. A lot less buttoned up than I normally look, anyway.

"Now for makeup," Xena says. "Come with me."

I follow Xena back to the living room where she's set up what looks like a little makeup and hair studio on my coffee table. She instructs me to sit on the couch and then immediately gets to work. I don't even recognize half the things she uses.

I tend not to wear makeup at work. At least, I didn't when I was a cop. Who knows what I'll do at my next job. If I decide to wear it, no doubt I'll need Xena to teach me how to put it on.

"There. Perfection." She hands me a mirror and I get my first peek at my fresh look. Well, my look for tonight anyway. I'm wearing more makeup than I've ever worn before, but the way Xena's done it just makes me look mysterious. Everything is dark, but it somehow makes my eyes look bigger and greener than their normal hazel color. And she's used a dark red lipstick to make lips where there were none before.

"Holy shit, Xena. What did you do? I barely recognize myself." I turn my head from side to side, admiring the vaguely Viking-esque hairstyle she's done for me. She's done assorted messy braids on the sides and teased the top into a mohawk, leaving the rest loose in my natural waves. "Are you sure Bump & Grind is what you want to do with your life? Because you could make a ton of money styling people. You really have a gift." I gush. "I can't even see the old cop me in the mirror. Like, if anyone on the force saw me now, they wouldn't even recognize me."

"Let's find out," she says. "Put these on then stand up." She hands me my pair of beat up old combat boots. I used to wear these with my uniform until they were too worn looking to be presentable. They're hella comfortable though, so I kept them anyway.

I stand up and put a hand on my hip, cocking it out to the side. "How's this?" I say with a laugh. "Am I sexy now?"

"You look gorgeous, darling. Work it, work it. Yasss!" She snaps picture after picture with her phone while I laugh and vogue my way through a bunch of ridiculous poses.

"Okay, that's enough." I sit down with a huff. "If we're going dancing, then let's get going. I think I'm ready to shake my ass now. Whoever the Rhea is who wears outfits and makeup like this," I gesture up and down my body. "She really loves shaking her ass."

Xena laughs. "Well, what are we waiting for, then? Let's go shake our asses."

How Do I Keep Getting Into These Situations?

Aiden

Devon did not beat my ass at Mario Kart like he intended, and he was called over to Connor's place for something before he had the chance to redeem himself with a rematch. Why he thinks he could beat me, I'll never know. I live and breathe these games and systems when I'm not drumming, and choosing a classic, well-known game when you challenge me is just about the dumbest move you can pull.

A close second in the dumb move department is showing up where the person you're interested in is going to be with their date. Yet that is exactly what Johnny is doing tonight, and because I'm an idiot, I am going with him.

"I just need to see what this dude looks like and then we can leave," Johnny tells me as I throw my hair up in my usual man-bun.

I always have my hair up when I'm home and down and loose during shows and press. It's almost like a disguise, really. The fans don't seem to know what my face really looks like, and that's how I like it.

"Why can't you just let it be, dude? This is stalker level behavior."

"Right, but it's totally fine for Connor to creep around Alex's neighborhood looking for her when he didn't know where she lived?"

"No, that wasn't completely okay either," I say, even though when it originally happened, I was all for the idea. I must've been lost in the romance of it all, I guess. "But at least Alex had seemed interested before she disappeared. Becca is on a date. With *someone else.* I'm not sure how much less interested she could be."

Johnny thinks for a minute, fussing with his own hair for a second. "I get that. But I *know* there is interest. Something is holding her back and I need to figure out what it is. I'm out of ideas, so I'm hoping seeing what this guy looks like might help me figure it out. So just be my friend and come with me. And stop me from doing anything stupid. I don't want to interrupt her date, just see what the guy looks like. And then we can go. Okay?"

"Okay, let's go then. I'll drive." I grab my keys from the table near my front door and head out, waiting for Johnny to follow. His car isn't even here, so I guess I'm driving whether I like it or not. "How did you get here?"

"Travis dropped me off on his way to meet a date or something. I can't believe you still drive this old thing," Johnny says, pointing to my 1980 Volvo 265. "It's not exactly the type of classic car you'd expect a famous rock star to drive."

"That's exactly why I drive it," I tell him, getting in and reaching over to unlock the passenger door. No automatic locks on this baby, but at least I don't have to roll down the windows manually, too. "Who would expect me to be driving around in a station wagon, wearing this man-bun, dressing like any slob on the street? No one, that's who. I'm as anonymous as I can be. Plus, I love this car."

"Fine," Johnny sighs. "But you know this car isn't going to get you any chicks, right?"

I give him a look; he should know better.

"Oh yeah, right. Aiden doesn't date. I forgot."

"I don't want a relationship because it's going to interfere with my life. I like being in the band, I like all the volunteering I do, and I like giving away most of my money to charity. A girlfriend would definitely have opinions about those things." Not to mention having a girlfriend increases the risk of passing on my asshole father's genes to another generation, what with the regular sex and all that. I don't want there to be any chance I could be like him, or that any kid of mine could be like him.

"Well, that makes it a lot harder to get your dick wet," Johnny says. "You should try to find yourself a friend with benefits."

"I'm good, thanks."

"Whatever you say, man. All I'm saying is your hand must get tired."

"Maybe I have one of those super-advanced sex robots?" I do not. "I keep her in a drawer under my bed." Nope. I don't do that either.

"Fuck off, no you don't." He laughs. "We would all know if you had something like that."

Yeah, he's right. They probably would know that. There aren't many things I keep secret from these guys. Other than the reason I don't date, that is. That is one thing that's just for me. If they wanted to, it wouldn't be too hard to find the reason. There was a ton of news coverage back when my family died in the accident. It would be easy enough to work it out from articles in the paper. At least, it would be for anyone who is as paranoid and suspicious as I am.

"Okay, so am I just going to keep driving around, or were you planning to tell me where we're going?" It's been a few minutes since we left my house and we've been talking the whole time about my lack of a love life. He still hasn't told me where we're headed.

"Oh, it's that new dance club downtown. I think it's called Redemption, or something?"

"Yeah, I know where it is." I actually assumed we'd be headed downtown, anyway, so we're almost there. Dates at this time of the night require a nightlife that only downtown Westborough offers. All the best restaurants and bars are downtown, so I guessed if Becca was on a date, this was where she'd be.

I pull up and park on the street opposite the club. The line for Redemption goes right down to the end of the street, but the bouncer at the door has done work for us before and we get right in.

I hate dance clubs. I have a professional distaste for music that uses primarily drum tracks as opposed to real drummers, and most of what you hear in dance clubs seems to be of that variety. I can't deny it's catchy, though. I can see why other people would want to be here, though. It has two dance floors filled with writhing, sweaty, twenty-somethings all trying to dry hump someone into coming home with them tonight. If you were looking to hook up, this is the sort of place you'd look.

Makes me wonder why Becca would be here on a date. That girl fits in with this crowd almost as much as Johnny does. Meaning she doesn't fit in at all. I think the two of them have more tattoos between them than all the other people in this building combined. If she's on a date right now, I'm pretty sure it wasn't her idea to come here.

"This place is packed. What's your plan?" I ask Johnny while I scan the people surrounding us. "Even with how much she'll stand out in this crowd, it's going to be almost impossible to find her."

"She's right up there," he says, pointing to the second floor. Sure enough, there she is, standing at a table along the glass wall, keeping the second level separate from the first. Oddly enough, she's looking right back at us.

"Dude, how did you know she was there?"

"No idea." He shrugs. "I just knew."

Johnny watches as some guy joins Becca at the table and she turns to face him. He looks like every other guy in here.

"Okay, you've seen him. Ready to go?" Somehow I know he's not coming with me right now, regardless of what he said earlier.

"I'll be right back," he says, waving me off and heading for the stairs. "I need to get a closer look."

Yeah, sure. I have a feeling he's not coming with me tonight at all now. Might as well just go home.

I'm about to turn and go when I spot Devon in the crowd. He's on the dance floor, dancing with two women. One of them is clearly Xena, but it's the other who surprises me. Is that Rhea? Holy fuck, she looks hot. Unexpectedly, my dick stiffens in my pants as I take in the way she moves to the music, bouncing and thrusting her hips into nothing. She certainly doesn't look like a cop now. She doesn't look like much of a dancer, either, but my dick doesn't seem to mind. My body tells me to get over there and give her something to grind on, but my brain argues that it's obviously a terrible idea. This woman has been nothing but bitchy to me, yet there's still something about her I find intriguing. Does finding her intriguing mean I should talk to her, though? I can't seem to decide either way, so I just stand there watching her dance.

It's not until I notice the shirt she's wearing that I make up my mind to talk to her. I mean them. I need to go talk to all three of them.

Plus, it would probably be rude of me to leave before I know for sure Johnny isn't coming with me, right?

7

If He Follows Me Home Can I Keep Him?

Rhea

IT FEELS LIKE WE'VE been dancing for hours. I'm not sure when Devon showed up, but ever since he did, I've been feeling like a third wheel. Plus, I'm not nearly as good a dancer as he is. Also, thanks to Xena's makeover, I've been fighting off guys half my age. Good for the ego, but annoying as fuck. They all smell like cheap cologne, desperation, and bad choices to me.

I motion to Devon and Xena that I'm getting a drink and shove my way through the crowd to the bar. I've been pacing myself better since we left my apartment, but I'm still a little past tipsy. I order a double margarita and turn around to look over the crowd.

Everyone here looks so young, but I suppose that's probably because I'm well beyond the age of dance clubs. Of course, the young guys who've been attempting to grind on me this entire night don't seem to care. Either they're looking for a cougar or Xena did a better job making me over than I thought. The bartender taps me and hands my drink over. I suck it back in one gulp, feeling the burn of tequila all the way down my throat, and head back to the dance floor to resume my third-wheel activities.

The tequila warms me from the inside, and I'm feeling pretty good, shaking my ass with the rest of the sweaty masses. I'm feeling so good, in fact, I let a guy dance with me. Of course, *that* turns out to be a bad idea. He pulls my back to his front, rubbing his body against me, trying to get me to grind against him, and just as I'm about to turn around and tell him he's gone too far, when suddenly he's pulled away. Before I can turn to see what's going on, the body is replaced by someone who feels familiar in a way I can't define. One that, for some strange reason, I have no intention of pushing away.

"You're wearing my shirt," a man says in my ear, his lips brushing my hair, his hands on my hips as we continue to sway to the music. "It looks good on you."

I spin around and discover Aiden. Is this guy seriously stalking me or what? I guess I know why he felt familiar, but why was I thinking I didn't want to push him away?

"No, I'm pretty sure Xena stole this shirt from Devon." I put my hands on my hips and tilt my chin up at him, daring him to argue with me. I know where this shirt came, and it wasn't from this guy.

He laughs and leans in again. "I mean, you're wearing a shirt with me on it."

"What?"

He runs his finger down the image of the drummer on the front of my shirt, sending a pleasant rush of heat to my lady cave of wonders. Maybe he wants to go exploring? *Damn it, Rhea. Stop it. He's following you. I demand you stop being attracted to him.*

"I am on your shirt. I'm the drummer for Sleeping Dogs. You are literally wearing a picture of me across your chest right now."

The way he whispers to me about my chest makes me really wonder if maybe he does want to go exploring, but I still don't believe it's him on the shirt. I try to hold it out from my body to get a better look at the drummer on the front, but it's impossible from this angle.

I must be more than a little tipsy because what comes next is so far out there from anything I would normally consider doing, there's just no other explanation.

I pull off my shirt in the middle of the dance floor, turn it around, and hold it up close to his face.

"Yeah, I still don't think that's you," I say, closing one eye to help me focus and looking between him and the shirt. "But I guess if you want the shirt, you can have it. Your arms would look amazing in this, with all those muscles." I grab his bicep and squeeze.

"No, that's okay," he tells me, his head on a swivel as he looks around a little frantically. "You can keep it. Why don't you put it back on?" He looks around some more, squinting a little. He must be drunk too if he has to squint to see.

"Really? Don't I look okay? Xena bought me this bralette, to go under the shirt because the arm holes are so big. She didn't want me wearing one of the sturdier bras I used to wear when I was a cop. I guess she thought they'd be too ugly or something. Did you know I'm not a cop anymore?" I reach out and run my hands up inside the front of his t-shirt, telling him way more information than I should be. "You should put the other shirt on. I'll help you with this one. Wow, you have some muscles under here. I'm impressed. You must work out a lot."

He laughs a little. "Tell you what, let's trade shirts for now. I'll wear yours, you wear mine, and then I'll tell you all about my workout. How's that?"

"That is such a good idea. Best idea ever." He's being really nice and literally giving me the shirt off his back. My heart does a little flip-flop in my chest. No one besides Kaden's family has ever been this nice to me before.

I watch as he peels off his shirt, but I don't remove my hands from his abs. This guy is scorching hot. I wonder what he'd look like with the rest of his clothes off? Maybe I should see if he'll follow me home? Why was I so hesitant to go out with him before? I mean, he shouldn't have tried asking me while I was in the middle of arresting someone, and he definitely shouldn't have tracked me down to the precinct after that, but... He's a hot guy. Like, he's probably the hottest guy I've ever seen.

"Here you go," he says, slipping his shirt over my head and helping me get my arms through the sleeves. I tuck the front of this shirt in like I had the other one.

"Your turn," I say, holding out the tank. "Bend down a little."

He complies and I slip the tank over his head. I was right. He looks amazing in it. I can't stop myself from running my hands up and down his arms.

"Hey, that's a good look for you. I'd rather look at you shirtless, but this will do." He raises an eyebrow at me, like no one's ever said they want to see him shirtless before. I find that hard to believe.

Devon and Xena materialize beside us. Well, I guess they didn't materialize, but I certainly haven't been paying them much attention since Aiden showed up. His hotness has distracted me. Why was I ever upset he kept asking me out, and why did I keep saying no? Or did I never even give him a chance to ask? My memory is a little fuzzy, but I have a strange feeling I've done a lot of running in the opposite direction where Aiden is concerned. After feeling his abs and arms, I just don't know why I would even run away anymore. And his shirt smells amazing. Like soap, musk, and some sort of subtle cologne.

"What's going on, guys? We're just getting naked in the middle of the dance floor now?" Devon asks with a laugh.

"Rhea here didn't believe me when I told her she was wearing my face so she stripped her shirt off to compare. I convinced her we should trade shirts because she had way too many weird dudes staring at her in her bra."

"No, that's a lie. He didn't like how I looked in my bra and he wanted me to cover up. It's okay though. I know I'm not as hot as he is. Pretty sure my panties melted right off me when I felt his abs."

Aiden's eyes go wide. What? Like he's surprised he melts the panties off unsuspecting females? This man seriously underestimates his hotness. I bet if we polled the women on the dance floor right now, at least ninety percent of them would be suffering from melted panties, thanks to Aiden. It's practically a melted panty epidemic.

"Why did you feel his abs?" Xena laughs. She's swaying on her feet a little. She's had more to drink than I have, and it shows.

"She was trying to get my shirt off for me, and I think she got a little distracted." Aiden laughs too.

"It's true. I did get distracted. So very distracted," I admit, licking my lips before turning to face just Aiden. "Hey, you promised to tell me about your workouts if we traded shirts. So come on, then. Spill it."

"You won't like it," he says. "I play drums for a couple of hours, sometimes more, every day. Then I do a little weightlifting. That's it really."

I look around, confused. "Why do you play drums so much? And isn't that a little excessive? When do you find time to work?"

Devon and Xena both burst into laughter, and Aiden smirks a little.

"He's the drummer for Sleeping Dogs," Devon says. "He plays a lot because he's rehearsing and constantly learning. That is his work."

"No." I look back and forth between the three of them. "You guys are all just fucking with me. Aren't you?"

"They're not," Xena says. "He really is the drummer for Sleeping Dogs. Why do you think he was there that day when you arrested my friend Denise's ex? Or why he knows Devon so well? It's hilarious how you've got him wearing a shirt with a picture of himself on the front of it."

"You look like such a dickhead, dude." Devon laughs, and Aiden replies by flipping him off.

Xena and Devon dissolve into giggles again.

Well, shit.

Now I feel dumb. And I hate feeling dumb.

"Screw you guys. I'm getting another drink," I say, as I turn and walk back to the bar. If I have to feel stupid, I'm going to do my damndest to not remember it.

8

Just Take Her Home

Aiden

RHEA IS A LITTLE unsteady on her feet as she walks away from us, but fuck if I can look away from her ass as she goes. Those little shorts she's wearing barely cover it and I find myself itching to run my hands up her legs to the curve of her ass where they end. I wonder what it would feel like to spread her thighs and shove my cock in her as I fuck her against a wa—

"Whatcha looking at?"

I jump as Xena's voice cuts through my increasingly dirty daydream about the woman she considers a sister. Thank god for that too, I can't get involved with anyone. I know I can't make anything of it, so there's no sense in even letting my mind go there. Something about Rhea tonight, though... She has me thinking all sorts of dirty things I have no business thinking.

What is it about her that has me all fucked up like this?

"Nothing. Just making sure she gets to the bar alright." I run my hand down the back of my neck. "How much has she had to drink, anyway?"

"Too much," Xena says. "This ought to be her last one. She needs to get some water into her soon, or she's really going to regret this tomorrow."

I can only imagine. I've never been a big drinker, even back in the early days of the band, when we did a lot more partying. The other guys got into way more trouble than I did. They thought it was because I'm older, but it's really because I need to always be in control of myself so I can be sure I'll never act like my dad. The few times I've gotten really drunk in my life, I could feel my temper flare and I hated it. That or I was so worried I'd wind up in bed with someone I couldn't trust to be in charge of contraceptives, I couldn't even have any fun. Because we all know how I feel about passing on my shitty genetic material.

Nah, it's just easier for me to stick to one or two drinks, if I have any at all.

"Hey, listen. I need to get Xena home. She just told me she has to work the early shift tomorrow. Do you think you can make sure Rhea gets home safe?" Devon asks. "She lives close enough to walk, but I don't want her walking alone at this time of the night." Devon has his arm around Xena, and she's suddenly looking pretty rough. I'm sure she's exhausted from getting up too early and drinking a little too much tequila.

"Yeah, sure man. No problem. I've got my car here. I can give her a ride."

"Okay, great. You don't have anyone you need to wait for?"

"Nah, I came here with Johnny because he wanted to spy on Becca, but he ditched me as soon as we walked in. That's when I saw you guys and came over to talk." Plus, something keeps drawing me to the woman wearing a picture of me on her chest, but he doesn't need to know that part.

"Perfect. Get her out of here before she drinks anything else, and see if you can make her drink some water before she goes to bed. Those tequila hangovers are monsters." He chuckles and leads Xena to the exit.

Rather than wait here for Rhea to come back, I walk over to meet her at the bar, where I find her talking to some guy. My chest burns when I first catch sight of them. Am I jealous over a conversation she's having with a guy at a bar? That can't be right. I may think she's gorgeous, but that doesn't mean I want a relationship with her. She can talk to whomever she wants to. If she enjoys talking to this guy, then maybe I should leave her to it. I'm sure I'll get over that burning in my chest eventually. But then again, I promised Devon I'd make sure she gets home safe so I can't leave. I can give her some privacy, though.

I stand back and watch their conversation; the burning in my chest gets worse the longer Rhea talks with him. Actually, it looks more like he is talking at her, and she is trying to lean away without being too obvious. My breath catches in my throat at her visible discomfort. Can't this guy tell he's freaking her out, getting into her personal space when she obviously doesn't want him to? Good thing I didn't leave. I close the distance between us in three long steps, wrapping my arms around her when I get there.

"Hey babe, I missed you. Sorry I'm late." I kiss her on the temple. "Who the fuck are you?" I say, turning a steely glare toward the guy.

"I was talking to this chick here. She didn't mention a boyfriend. Sorry, man. Then again, since she didn't mention you, maybe she'd rather stay here with me?"

My temper flares, my hands becoming fists at my sides, my body preparing to fight. This guy needs to get the hell away from my girl—I mean, get the hell away from me—before I make him.

"I'd love to go somewhere and talk," Rhea says from my side, pulling my arm back around her. "Aiden, baby? Should we go somewhere private and *talk*?" She slides a hand into the side of my shirt, rubbing my abs like she can't get enough of me.

The rage I'm feeling for the asshole in front of me suddenly shifts until all I feel is a desire for Rhea coursing through my veins. She's doused the flames of my temper, just like that. *Isn't that interesting?* Now if only she could douse the lust she's ignited in me as easily. I'm barely able to resist her as it is. Her touching me like this is almost too much for me to handle.

"That is the best idea I've heard since I got here. I've been wanting to talk to you all night." I know this is an act, but the way she's looking at me through her eyelashes, and the way her hand feels resting against my stomach, I sort of wish it wasn't.

As though she can read my mind, she slides her hand down to rest at the top of my jeans, fingers slipping inside the waistband to trace one of the muscles making up my Adonis belt. A jolt of lust shoots right to my dick, making me instantly hard. I pull her to face me, using the cover of her body to adjust my cock so I don't make too much of a spectacle of myself.

"You're playing a dangerous game," I growl softly in her ear. She's too good at this act. If she keeps this up, she'll have me believing she's actually interested, and it will be that much harder for me to deny my attraction to her. "Let's go."

She giggles as I take her hand from the front of my pants, lacing her fingers with mine, and walk us to the exit. I take a quick look around for Johnny, but I don't see him. No big deal. He can find his own way home if he's even still here. I have a sneaking suspicion he left with Becca shortly after we arrived, anyway.

"Off so soon?" The bouncer who let us in is still working the door.

"Yeah, man. Just came to drop off Johnny and pick up my girlfriend from her girls' night. See you around."

"Aww, am I your girlfriend, Aiden?" she asks once we're out of carshot of the bouncer. "I'm honored."

"No. You're not my girlfriend," I tell her. "I don't date. Ever."

"Relax," she says with a laugh. "I was just messing with you."

I feel a little sick when she says she's messing with me, which is clearly stupid. It's not like I want her to be my girlfriend, so why should I care if she doesn't want to be?

Rhea holds my hand while I walk her across the street to my car. I unlock the passenger door and open it for her.

"This is your car?" She asks, inspecting my Volvo with a curious gaze. "If you're really a rock star, why are you driving this station wagon? Seems a little suspicious to me. It's one step away from a windowless van with 'free candy' written on the side." She snorts a cute little laugh.

"Haha, you're hilarious," I deadpan. "Get in and I'll tell you while I drive you home. Devon had to take Xena home, and he asked me to make sure you got home safely, too. There's nothing safer than a Volvo."

"Right. But is that still true when the car is older than you are?"

"Har-har, you've got all the jokes tonight, don't you? Since when are you a comedian? I'll have you know this car is barely older than I am. In fact, we're almost the same age."

"So, you're saying you're old too, then?" She laughs.

"Never mind, smartass. Get in." I can't stop the smile from creeping up on my face. Rhea's funny. I kind of wish she wasn't, because it makes her so much more appealing. I'm having enough trouble keeping my mind off of her with adding funny to the list of her attributes.

She slides into the passenger seat and I close the door before making my way to the driver's side. I take a few deep breaths before getting in, though, because Rhea is really getting to me. This sassiness is adorable, and she's so fucking hot I can barely stand it. I need to get her home safely, get some water into her, and then I'm home free.

With one last deep breath, I open my door and get in. Once I start the car, I realize I still don't know where she lives.

"What's your address?" I ask.

"Oh, it's really close. Just start driving and I'll tell you when to pull over."

I pull away from the curb and drive. Not even three minutes later, I'm pulling up in front of a small store down the street, only a few blocks from Bump & Grind.

"You live in a store?"

She laughs. "No, I live in the apartment upstairs," she says as she unbuckles. "It's creepy enough living upstairs from a vintage doll store. I can't imagine ever being able to sleep again if all those dolls were staring at me all night. It took me months before I could get a proper night's sleep just living upstairs from them."

"Oh. Yeah, I guess that makes more sense." I lean past her and look at the store window. Dozens of creepy dolls stare back. The shudder rolls through my body before I can stop it. I doubt I could sleep at all, knowing so much nightmare fuel was downstairs waiting for me to let my guard down. "They look fucking terrifying."

"Shit," Rhea says as she feels around her pockets. "I gave my keys to Xena to carry in the little fanny pack thing she was wearing. The pockets in these damn shorts are way too small."

I swallow hard, remembering how short those shorts looked while she was dancing. I'm surprised they had enough space in them for pockets at all, even small ones.

"That's okay, we can go get them. Call Xena and tell her to have them ready for us."

Rhea groans and lets her head fall back against the seat. "I can't do that either. I gave her my phone, too. And before you ask, no, I don't have her number memorized."

I grab my phone and pull up Devon's contact information. I don't have Xena's phone number, but Devon might still be with her. I press the call button and it doesn't even ring, instead it goes straight to voicemail. That's weird. He must have it turned off.

"Well, let's drive by her place and see if she answers the door." I pull away from her place and start driving again. "Assuming you at least remember where she lives?"

"Give me your phone," Rhea says, holding out her hand. "I'll put the address in your GPS. Thank god I have *that* memorized, because I get lost every time I try to get there on my own." She laughs and shakes her head. "For a cop, you think I'd have a better sense of direction. I mean... for someone who used to be a cop." That's going to take her some getting used to, I'll bet. She frowns for a moment before shaking herself out of it.

Shortly after she takes the phone from my outstretched hand, the GPS voice begins telling me directions.

"So, tell me about this car. There has to be a good story behind why a famous rock star drives a vintage station wagon."

"Uh, well, it's nothing special. It's just... When I was a kid, everything was shit at home. I'd see families in cars like this and imagine their lives were perfect. When it was really bad, I'd lay awake at night picturing myself as part of one of those families." Why am I telling her this? I could have made something up instead of giving her a glimpse into my shitty childhood. What is it about her that makes me want to open up like this?

When I was a kid, I used to imagine the all the families with station wagons like this were perfect and happy. They'd eat dinner around the table every night, the dad would read them a bedtime story, and the mom and dad loved each other and the kids more than anything. I would lie in my bed at night and imagine they were my family, and that we were all loading up into the Volvo to go do a group activity, like bowling or camping. In my family, my dad was more likely to call me a stupid fucker than to read me a bedtime story. And forget loving us. And there was never any mention of family activities. This station wagon is my way of remembering something good about my childhood, even if it is only the dreams I had about other people's families.

She sits quietly for a moment, and I hope she doesn't ask what I meant about things being shit at home. I didn't even mean to tell her this much. So I'm certainly not ready for that conversation yet. It's not something I've ever told anyone the whole truth of. No one could ever forgive me if they knew the truth.

"So you bought this car and what? You're going to make your own perfect family to fill it?" She asks. "You and the wife, and your two kids going on family road trips and stuff? Go see the world's biggest ball of twine?"

"Ha! No, I'm not planning on having a family at all. I like the things the car makes me remember." It's a reminder that I can't risk having a kid of mine laying awake at night, imagining he's part of a different family to get a brief glimpse of happiness. It's more like a reminder of the things I need to stay away from, than the things I want to have for myself. A lot of possessions in my life serve that purpose.

And that's the main reason I can't pursue this attraction I'm feeling to Rhea. I can't allow myself to get too close to anyone or I risk hurting them the way my father hurt my family.

I need to get her home, go back to my place, and take a nice, long, cold shower.

9

Great, We're Having a Sleepover

Rhea

AIDEN DRIVES THE REST of the way to Xena's place in silence. I don't think he told me everything about why he drives this car, but it's not my place to push it. We barely know each other. He doesn't owe me explanations for anything. Plus, it's not really a big deal. I'm not *that* interested in why the drummer for a famous band drives a really old station wagon. Even if it is super weird.

"Here we are," Aiden says, pulling up in front of Xena's little house. "I'll go check if she's here. Be right back."

I watch him as he walks up the path to her door. His butt flexes in his jeans as he moves, and a little groan escapes my throat. That ass is so gorgeous I suddenly feel a desire to sink my teeth into it, and I'm not normally a biter. Does he seriously not work out much? Every part of him I touched tonight felt like solid muscle, and his ass looks like it's no exception. I have a hard time believing drumming could be responsible for all that. And if it is, it's the best kept workout secret of all time.

Maybe I can convince him to teach me to play so I never have to work out again? No, that won't work. I like my trail runs too much to stop them altogether. But some extra time around a sexy man wouldn't be a bad thing, would it?

All the lights are off in Xena's place, and Aiden is waiting on the step. I have a sinking feeling I'm not getting my keys. Even if she is home, she's probably asleep already and can't hear the doorbell. He must be cold standing there in only that tank.

I can't believe I pulled it off in the club, and that he traded me his own shirt. *His super amazing smelling shirt*, I remind myself, and pull the neckline up over my nose and take a deep sniff. How does he smell so good? The combination of his soap and some light cologne reminds me of the smell of running through a forest trail after a rain. Fresh. Clean. Earthy. It calms me, almost like running a trail does.

I'm still not one hundred percent certain the he is the drummer for Sleeping Dogs, though. Of course, Xena and Devon have no reason to lie to me about that, and I have no reason to doubt them. He doesn't look much like the picture on the shirt, though. Maybe I can get him to let his hair down? That could have something to do with it.

I look up just in time to see him walking back to the car. I pull my face out of the shirt as he opens the door before he slides into his seat. That would've been embarrassing to explain. *'Oh, don't mind me. Just smelling your shirt because I find you incredibly attractive and your smell is so relaxing. Nothing weird going on here.'* I'm sure he wouldn't find it weird at all.

"She's either out cold, or she's not home. Let's take a quick drive by Devon's place. If they're not there, you can crash at my place tonight and I can bring you to Bump & Grind in the morning to get your keys."

"Oh, um yeah. Okay." It's not okay. I'm more attracted to this man than I've been to anyone in a long time. Or ever. I can't be alone in a house with him. Who knows what I could do? The last thing I need with how my life is going is to throw myself at a guy who is clearly only being nice because we have mutual friends. He told me flat out he never dates. That obviously includes me.

"I have a guest room and extra toothbrushes and stuff. I've had friends stay over before. It's no big deal."

To him, maybe. He was messing around in the club, helping keep that guy away from me. I damn near molested him in front of a huge crowd when I tried sticking my hand right down the front of his pants. He even told me I was playing a dangerous game. He's for sure not interested. My panties, however, are telling me I sure am.

"So where does Devon live?" I ask, trying to change my current thought pattern.

"He's in an apartment building not too far from my place. At least it's on the way, so if he's not there, we'll already be near my side of town."

"What about you? Where's your place?" I picture him living in some fancy penthouse overlooking the city. I already feel awkward and out of place. I am not a fancy person.

"I live in one of the older neighborhoods on the edge of town."

Oh. That's not so bad. I hope it's a normal house. Actually, what I really hope is that Devon is home and has my keys. That would be the best-case scenario. I have a sneaking suspicion that's not how this night is going to go, though. My luck is not that good lately. Just look at the way my law enforcement career turned out.

"So, what about you? What's your story? How long have you known Devon and Xena?"

"Seems like forever," I say. "Kaden was my first partner, and has been my only partner since I got out of the academy. He took me under his wing and I've had his back ever since."

"That's great. Doesn't really explain Xena and Devon, though."

"Oh, well..." I'm hesitant to tell him about my upbringing, but a little information can't hurt, right? "When Kaden found out I grew up in the foster system and didn't really have a family, he brought me home to his. His parents are awesome, and Xena is like a sister to me."

"Foster kid, hey? That's rough."

"Yeah, it wasn't always great. But it could have been a lot worse." They could have left me with my mom.

"Did you get good foster parents, at least?"

"Um, yeah, they were pretty good, I guess. I had food, clothes, and school supplies, anyway."

"Well, I'm glad to hear that. You hear some real horror stories."

I nod in the dark, not really wanting to answer or continue this conversation. Dwelling on the past has never gotten me anywhere. Nobody wants to remember being shuffled house to house with only a garbage bag to hold your belongings. Luckily, we're now pulling into a parking lot at an apartment building.

This must be Devon's place.

"Keep your eyes peeled for a black Escalade. That's what Devon drives."

We drive around the lot for five minutes, but Devon isn't here. Figures.

Aiden pulls out his phone and tries calling him again.

"Straight to voicemail. Again."

All I can do is laugh. "This day keeps getting better and better."

"It could be worse," Aiden says as he drives out of the lot. "What if you hadn't noticed your keys and phone were missing until I was gone? At least you have somewhere to sleep tonight, instead of the doorway of your building." There's a note of irritation in his voice, like maybe he would have preferred that to being forced to offer me a place to stay for the night.

I nod again and watch the city lights go by as we drive. I suppose things could be worse. I still haven't figured out what to do for work, but at least I have enough savings to get by for a little while. And I still have my apartment, which is reasonably priced. Other than no longer having my dream job, I'm doing alright.

City lights give way to residential street lights and soon we're pulling into what I assume is Aiden's driveway. I'm surprised when he noses up the garage door but doesn't open it, turning off the car and getting out in the driveway instead.

"Got a garage full of crap? How come you're not parking your sweet station wagon inside?"

"It's not really a garage. It's where the guys and I used to jam, and now it's my private rehearsal space. It's full of instruments and equipment." The irritation I thought I heard earlier is there for sure now.

"Sorry to put you out like this," I say. "I guess I need to have my own little fanny pack next time I go out with Xena so this doesn't happen again." A nervous chuckle escapes my lips, but I refuse to look at Aiden.

"Don't worry about it," he says, waving his hand dismissively. "I've got lots of room."

He walks up onto the porch and unlocks the door, throwing it open and standing back to let me go in first.

"Make yourself at home. Grab yourself some water from the fridge. I'll be right back." He doesn't wait for an answer before he storms upstairs. I wasn't wrong. He has been getting more upset the closer we got to his place. What a grouch.

Well, this should be a fun sleepover.

10

I Was Wrong, Mario is Sexy

Aiden

SHIT, WHAT THE HELL am I doing? How is this woman affecting me so much? I barely know her. It was hard enough when I was supposed to drive her home safely. I could even deal with driving around trying to track down Xena and find her keys. But having her sleep here, in my house, for the entire night? Not a good idea.

I dig around in my dresser, looking for something she can sleep in. She already has my t-shirt on, from when we traded in the club, but I grab her a clean one, anyway. All I need now is a pair of joggers. When I finally find some in the back of a bottom drawer, I grab them and jog back downstairs.

"So you can wear the shirt you've got on if you want, or this clean one, and here are some joggers for you. Bathroom's upstairs, first door on the right, and your room is across the hall from that. There's a new toothbrush in the medicine cabinet for you." I give her the joggers and step aside to let her up the stairs.

"Okay, yeah, thanks. Um, do you mind if I grab a shower? I hate to put you out any more, but the smell of tequila is oozing out of me and I can't stand it."

"Yeah, no problem. Towels are in the closet beside the bathroom door. Here, let me show you." *Aiden, you dumb motherfucker.* I chastise myself as I lead her up the stairs. It was bad enough when she was just sleeping here. *Now she's going to be naked, in your shower. Good luck keeping your mind off of that.*

She follows me up the stairs, and I grab her towels and wash-cloths from the closet.

"Here you go," I say, handing her the stack. She takes them from me and when her hand brushes mine, tingles shoot up my arm. I react like an electrical current runs through it, instead of merely tingles, and jump back out of her reach. When I look up, it's just in time to see the frown on her face before she turns to go into the bathroom. She says nothing before she closes the door in my face.

Fuck.

I know I can't get involved with her, but that doesn't mean I want to hurt her feelings.

I'm sure she'll be fine by morning, though. She's probably reacting to the effects of the tequila, rather than actually being attracted to me. She's way out of my league, anyway. If she's a ten, I'm a zero. Maybe even a negative five. Yeah, there's no way she's attracted to me. That would be crazy.

But I still can't seem to stop thinking about her in my shower.

I stand in the hallway, staring off into the distance, and imagine what it would feel like to be massaging my fingers through her thick, sandy hair right now. What f I were to join her in the shower and take over washing her hair, and her body, while she relaxes completely beneath my hands? My cock strains against the zipper of my jeans from imagining what her moans would sound like. From imagining the feel of sliding my hands over her skin.

I blink out of my daydream and go into the spare room to make sure it's ready for Rhea. As much as I enjoy dreaming about her, I know we can't actually do anything about it. It's better to get the bed ready for her to sleep in, alone, and then get myself away from here before she gets out of the shower.

I get her bedroom ready, pulling back the blankets, turning on the bedside lamp, and grabbing some water and painkillers in case she needs them. I don't know exactly how much tequila she drank, and I don't know her well enough to tell based on her actions tonight, but I'm sure she'll appreciate the water, regardless.

There's a pressing need in my chest to see her again before I go to bed. To make sure she's okay, or something, maybe? I don't know, but I sit on the couch in front of the TV and turn on a video game, anyway. I don't want her to think I'm sitting around waiting for her, even though that's exactly what I'm doing, so I keep myself occupied with some of the Mario Kart Devon and I were playing earlier.

Rhea showers faster than any woman I've ever known, and she's back downstairs in less than ten minutes.

The sight of her barefoot in my joggers and shirt, with her damp hair hanging loose down her back, has me shifting uncomfortably in my chair. It seems my dick didn't get the memo about not being attracted to Rhea. I might have to have words with him later. Or a fucking long, cold-ass shower.

"Thanks. I feel so much better now." Pointing to the screen, she asks, "What's this?"

Is she serious? "Really?" I look from the screen to her and back.

"Well, I can see it's a video game of some sort."

"It's Mario Kart. Do you want to play?" I really should go to bed and get away from her, but this can't possibly do any harm. It's Mario Kart. No offense to my man Mario, but he's got to be one of the least sexy video game characters.

"Um, yeah. Sure. Why not? I don't know how to do it though," she says as she settles in next to me on the couch. "Put me in, Coach." She laughs.

I laugh along with her while I grab her a controller and get her set up, showing which buttons she needs to push to get started. We're playing on the Super Nintendo so it's not too complicated; I'm sure she'll figure it out quickly.

"Okay, so, all the characters have their own strengths and weaknesses, but for now pick whichever one you like best and we'll take it from there."

I sit back on the couch beside her, and I notice too late I'm a little closer than I was before. It would be weirder if I moved away now, though, so I'd better stay put. I almost regret not sitting a little closer, since this is going to be my only chance to do so.

"I'm going to be this little green dragon guy," she says, picking Yoshi. "He looks like he's lucky."

"He's who I usually play with, so I have to agree with you. Of course, you won't beat me, no matter how lucky he is. I've played this game more than is healthy in the last thirty-odd years, so I'm pretty much a professional." I pretend like I'm bragging about myself seriously; hopefully she can tell it's a joke.

"Oh, is that right?" she asks, with a hint of a laugh in her voice. "We'll see about that. Me and my dragon guy are taking you down."

I shake my head and laugh. She can try to beat me, but I doubt it will happen. I haven't lost since I was a kid. I wasn't entirely kidding when I said I'm a pro. I've played far too many video games in my life. It's always been my escape, starting when my dad was alive. It was the only time I felt good in this house when he was around. I could lock myself in my room and play whatever cute game took me away from him. If he couldn't see me, I was usually safe. It wasn't often he would track me down to my room.

We play a few races before she hits her stride, and she's actually good. She's beating all the other racers, aside from me, in the highest class, and she's not all that far behind me when I win.

"So, did you not have any video games when you were a kid?" I ask, my curiosity finally getting the better of me. It's weird she didn't even know what Mario Kart was before tonight. "None of your friends had any?"

Her tongue pokes out of her mouth while she concentrates on racing. She sways side to side a little when she makes her turns and it's kind of adorable. Without taking her eyes off the screen, she answers.

"Well, we didn't have extra money for that kind of stuff when I was still with my mom. She had, uh, other stuff she'd rather spend money on. And then the foster homes I was in didn't have any either, because the good stuff always got destroyed. I was a big reader, anyway. I spent a lot of time at the public library. Not a lot of time left over for friends."

That comes as a surprise to me. A woman as gorgeous as she is would have been really popular in school. If I'd known her when I was a teenager, I'm sure I would have been crushing on her hard. I wouldn't have pegged her for much of a reader, either. Most cops I've had the displeasure of dealing with didn't seem smart enough for recreational reading. I can't really reconcile that love of reading with this woman deciding to become a cop.

"What made you become a cop?" I ask, unable to resist the urge to find out more about her.

"Um, well. My home life when I was a kid wasn't great. A female cop was the first person who took me seriously and got me out of my house. She's the reason I went into foster care, and she's the reason I became a cop. I wanted the chance to help kids the way she helped me, I guess."

I see her shrug from the corner of my eye, like it's not a big deal to tell me a cop rescued her. She seems well adjusted for someone who needed that kind of intervention. I see kids from tough backgrounds at the shelter all the time. Hopefully, they can become as settled as she seems to be.

It might be way too late for me now, but I still want the best for those kids.

"Haha! Suck it, loser!" She yells, as she jumps off the couch, dropping the controller beside me. "And you said my dragon wasn't lucky enough to beat you."

My eyes snap back to the screen where sure enough, her Yoshi is doing a victory lap, pumping his arms in the air. Meanwhile, the Donkey Kong I chose is ramming himself against a wall, facing the wrong direction. I guess I spent more time looking at Rhea than I thought.

I look up at her again, and she's doing a little victory dance, complete with more of her awkward looking hip thrusts and booty shakes. The shock of lust gets me like a punch right in the gut. It hits me so fast my dick is instantly hard.

I need to get out of here. I can't let her see me excited like this. She'd be so uncomfortable.

"Okay, that was fun. Goodnight." I force out while switching off the Nintendo and the TV. "I'll take you to get your keys in the morning."

I run up the stairs two at a time, ignoring how difficult my now raging hard-on makes it. Who knew my kink was being beaten at a video game?

It's probably good that Devon wasn't able to accomplish it earlier today, then. Of course, I doubt a hip-thrusting, booty-shaking victory dance from him would affect me quite the same way Rhea's has.

11

Video Games and Voyeurism

Rhea

WELL, THAT WAS FUCKING weird. Not to mention rude. I beat him in a race and he gets pissed off and runs away? Talk about acting like a child. It makes sense, I suppose, when I look around and see just how many video games he has around here. He may be as old as his old as fuck car, but he clearly has the mentality of a child.

He's still insanely attractive, though.

I put the controllers and video game machine back on the shelf, in the only empty space, assuming that's where they go. If not, then Aiden can fix it himself. If he wanted it done perfectly, he should have stayed and done it himself instead of running away like a baby. Honestly, a grown man being that upset over losing a game is ridiculous. I snicker, thinking about how silly he looked running up the stairs like that.

I turn off the lights as I make my way up the stairs and into the room Aiden said would be mine. I hadn't noticed when I got out of the shower, but at some point he must've come in here and brought me water and painkillers. He even left the lamp on and turned down the blankets for me. That was actually pretty thoughtful.

I wonder if he regrets it now that I've beaten him at his silly video game?

A yawn escapes me without warning, reminding me it's probably very late now. Without a phone or a watch, I can't tell what time it is, only that it's late. I slide under the covers into a bed that is more comfortable than I expected. I swallow the painkillers Aiden left for me and in no time I'm comfortably snuggled up in bed, my mind drifting off into a dreamless sleep.

* * *

Morning comes too soon, and along with it, a fierce headache and a stomach roiling with nausea. I'm not as hungover as I thought I would be, though, so I would say I successfully survived Xena's attempts at cheering me up. If I make it through the day without throwing up, I will consider this a resounding victory.

I sit up in bed, taking my time raising my head because it throbs when I move too quickly. Something on the nightstand catches my eye and I see two new bottles of water in addition to more painkillers.

Huh.

Aiden must've checked on me at some point and brought me more painkillers when he saw I'd taken the ones he left me last night. Yet another thoughtful gesture from a man who was such a sore loser he had to run away when I beat him at that video game. Such a strange contradiction.

Fuck. I hope I wasn't drooling or anything when he checked on me. That would be embarrassing.

I take the fresh painkillers and down both bottles of water before making my way to the bathroom across the hall. I take care of business and then use the toothbrush Aiden gave me last night to get the disgusting taste out of my mouth. Getting into the shower was my only concern last night, so I didn't notice the bathroom was actually really nice. Nothing at all like any of the bachelor's bathrooms I've ever been in before.

Didn't stop me from noticing the bottle of lube on the shower shelf, though.

Wait a minute. Maybe it's not a bachelor's bathroom. I don't know if Aiden is even single. Maybe he's married, or has a live-in girlfriend. Good thing I didn't act on my attraction last night when we got back here. Of course, I can't even be sure I'm even still attracted to him. Not when he ran away after losing the game. It's probably better if I'm not interested in a man who takes something like that so personally, after all.

Ugh, too bad it's not so easy turn off the attraction.

After I finish in the bathroom, I make my way downstairs, taking a better look around than I did last night. Aiden has a ton of family pictures on the wall, but they all look pretty old. I don't see any in which Aiden looks older than a teenager. There are several where he is pictured with a woman who is probably his mother, and a much younger girl, probably a sister if I had to guess. A closer look tells me the pictures originally had a fourth person in them, Aiden's dad if I had to guess, but someone has ripped or cut them out. I wonder if Aiden's dad caused his shitty home life like my mom caused mine? Not that I'm going to ask him. If he wanted me to know, he would have told me already.

The closer I get to the bottom of the staircase, the louder the music coming from somewhere in the house gets. Sounds like Aiden is awake already, too. That's good. The sooner he can take me to get my keys, the faster I can get away from his moody ass. Seriously, he did so much smiling, brooding, laughing, and running away last night I may have whiplash.

I turn the corner to the kitchen when I make it to the bottom of the stairs and I can see where the music is coming from. What I'm guessing is the door to the garage is open, and the music is coming from there. Detouring to get another bottle of water from the fridge, I make my way to the doorway and peek in. The entire room is painted black and there are guitars hanging on the opposite wall. A stack of something that looks like big speakers is just inside the doorway beside me and assorted cords are hanging neatly from the wall above them. It's not until I step in a little further that I see the most amazing sight.

It's Aiden. Sweaty and shirtless, with his hair flying as he plays a set of bright pink drums like a madman. All the while looking like the sexiest damn man in the history of men. This is the Aiden from the front of the shirt. Now I see the resemblance.

And Ho-ly shit.

I only got a glimpse of his body last night at the club, and I was pretty sure the tequila I drank messed with my mind a little. Apparently, though, Aiden is as built as I thought he was.

Standing in the doorway watching him play so aggressively, seeing the definition in every muscle, is giving me major lady boner. The facial expressions he makes as he plays are not helping with keeping the lust away, either. They're practically obscene, and I can imagine those expressions are a variation of what he looks like when he comes. I feel my pussy throb in response, and I swallow hard.

I guess he didn't drive away the attraction with his poor sportsmanship like I had hoped. Imagine that.

He hasn't noticed my presence in the doorway yet, so I take advantage of this opportunity to really look at him. He's wearing black shorts, and black and white Vans sneakers, and nothing else. He's moving so fast I can see the sweat flying off of him, but I'm sure once he stops, it will drip down his skin like he just got out of the shower. His hair is even wet, and it's flying around his head, sticking to his skin occasionally as he moves. I don't know how long I stand there watching him play, but it has to be at least a few minutes.

He leans over and turns the music off now, so I guess my chance to perv on him is over. Too bad, I was really getting into it. I'll definitely be keeping what I've seen stored away in the old spank bank for later, though. Can't let excellent material like this go to waste.

"Hey, how are you feeling this morning?" He asks, grabbing a towel and standing up. He wipes the sweat off of his body as he walks over to where I'm standing, stunned and staring at him. I was right before. Sweat is dripping down his body, tracing the lines of his muscles, drawing my eyes and making it so I can't look away.

Aiden reaches up and I follow his hand with my eyes, until he taps me under the chin with his knuckle, closing my mouth.

"You got a little something there," he says, as he wipes my lip with his thumb. "A little drool maybe?" A little smirk flickers on his mouth and he raises an eyebrow at me.

He turns sideways and passes me in the doorway, heading back into the house. While his back is turned, I quickly wipe my mouth. There's no drool. Jerk. Shit. What if he was talking about finding me drooling last night? Still, I feel like an idiot because he clearly caught me staring.

"I'll grab a quick shower and then we can go get your keys," he says, heading upstairs.

It's a good thing he doesn't appear to be expecting any answers from me this morning, because seeing him nearly naked and sweaty has left me seriously tongue-tied.

12

Taking Care of Business

Aiden

RHEA MUST'VE STOOD IN the doorway for ten minutes. Well, it was ten minutes after I noticed her standing there. Who knows how long she was there before I saw her.

And the way she watched me. It was like she wanted to lick me all over, claim me as hers. And fuck if that doesn't turn me on. Once again I find myself running up the stairs two at a time, trying to hide my hard-on before Rhea notices. Because there's no way she actually wants me.

Even if she did, there's no way I could actually have her.

I left the door to the house open this morning, hoping Rhea would come and find me when she woke up, and it looks like it worked. I wanted her to see me play, not come eye-fuck me within an inch of my life, leaving me with the hardest of all hard-ons. Even though I doubt that's what she was actually doing. I'm a more athletic drummer, with lots of moving around and getting my whole body into it. I'm sure she was surprised to see that much action. But hopefully after all she saw, she'll at least believe I am who I say I am. Usually I go out of my way to ensure people don't recognize me, but for some reason it feels important that Rhea acknowledge my accomplishments as a musician.

Stupid ego.

As soon as I get up the stairs, I duck into the bathroom, kick off my shoes, strip off my shorts, and jump into the shower, nearly pulling the glass door off its track and closing it too roughly. I'm in such a hurry I don't even bother warming the water up first. The cold water will be good for me, anyway. I don't need to be having these kinds of thoughts about Rhea. I'm sure she's not a one-and-done kind of girl, and that's all I can ever offer. And it's been a hell of a long time since I've gone that far.

But I can't stop my mind from wandering back to how she looked last night in those little shorts and her bra when she stripped her shirt off on the dance floor. Or how she felt when I had her ass held tight against me after I got rid of the idiot who was grinding on her.

And fuck, when she pushed her hand into my shirt and tucked her fingers into the top of my pants? I thought I would come right there in the club, while staring down some asshole who was getting into her space. It took everything I had in me to adjust myself without pulling her against me and grinding my hard-on into her hip, to show her how she was doing to me.

Which is the same thing the mere thought of her is doing to me right now. The cold water at the beginning of my shower did nothing to quell the stiffness of my traitorous dick. The damn thing's gotten harder, if anything.

I try to think unsexy thoughts while I wash and condition my hair. I picture the terrible trio, Gran, Gladys, and the latest addition to their Peaceful Pines gang, Lana, the way they looked last time I went to visit with Ryder. Apparently it was pudding wrestling day at the old folk's home, and all the geriatrics were in their speedos and bikinis. And covered in pudding. It was... interesting. But the residents all loved it, and they seemed to have a great time, so who am I to judge? When I'm old, I'm definitely moving to some place like Peaceful Pines. Those old people know how to party.

But, even though the terrible trio's lewd behavior is usually enough to make any dick soft, nothing is getting these thoughts of Rhea out of my mind. Even her weird hip-thrusting, ass-shaking victory dance last night was hot. And if I'm going to be driving her around to find her keys today, I need to take the edge off this attraction I'm feeling. Otherwise I might be tempted to act on it.

Considering I don't do relationships, and I don't do casual sex often, I'm quite familiar with 'taking things into my own hands'. Like eating well and working out, it's something I do to keep my body healthy. And that's all this needs to be this time, even though it will also serve the purpose of getting Rhea out of my head. I grab the bottle of lube I keep in the shower for this purpose.

Yes, I'm sure I could use soap, but lube feels better, and works better, too.

I squeeze a little into my hand and set the bottle down on the ledge in the shower. Leaning against the shower wall, I grab my dick and spread the lube with a couple of tentative strokes, running my palm up and over the head, ensuring I'm fully coated with the slick liquid. I almost feel bad for jerking off while Rhea waits for me, but if I don't do this now, I won't be able to keep my attraction at bay, and that's the last thing either of us needs to deal with. Particularly with her losing her job only yesterday.

Having me drive her around with an obvious erection likely wouldn't make an already difficult time any less difficult for her.

I close my eyes and feel hot water cascade down my body from the multiple shower heads placed at precise intervals around the stall. I grip the base of my hard cock, slowly stroking from root to tip, root to tip, and the orgasm is building already. I've had a near constant erection since I saw Rhea at the club last night, and my dick is so fucking sensitive it almost hurts. My mind runs replays of Rhea in those tiny shorts she was wearing before switching to thoughts of what it would feel like to be pushing my cock into her slick heat. I imagine she's bent over in front of me and instead of using my hand on myself, I'm driving my dick into her from behind.

I squeeze harder and increase my pace, thrusting into my hand as my fantasy changes. Dream Rhea is on her knees in front of me now, taking me into her mouth, while she stares up at me with her wide, hazel-green eyes. The thought of her soft lips on my stiff cock has me speeding up my strokes, propelling me closer to the edge. My balls tighten as I picture Rhea taking me to the back of her throat, moaning like she can't get enough.

My release rips through me, painting the dark tile of the shower as jet after jet of come rushes out of me. My abs tense as I pump through my orgasm, the sensitive tip of my dick sparking at every stroke making me moan. The last of my orgasm surges, my body shuddering as the aftershocks rush through me, and I stroke a couple more times before letting go of my dick and dropping my arm to my side.

"Fuck," I groan as I let the hot water flow over me while I recover.

Fuck. That was almost too intense.

I rest my head on my arm for another minute and then I wipe all evidence of my activities off the shower wall. After a quick wash and rinse of my body, I step out of the shower only to see I neglected to bring myself a towel.

Actually, I was in such a hurry to hide my ill-timed erection from Rhea that I also left the door wide open.

Shit.

I hope she didn't hear me.

13

Ohmygod, Your Penis!

Rhea

I FIGURE I MIGHT as well collect all my stuff while Aiden is in the shower, so I'm ready to go when he is. I'd hate to inconvenience him any more than I already have. It was really nice of him to let me stay here last night, even if he was a little weird about the video game thing.

Before I go upstairs, I look through the kitchen drawers until I find an empty grocery bag to throw my stuff in. I should probably leave Aiden his t-shirt and joggers, but I can't bring myself to put on my clothes from last night. I'm sure they still smell like tequila, not to mention they're not exactly daytime appropriate. At least not compared to what I normally wear. I can get his clothes back to him some other time, or maybe I can have Xena pass them along through Devon.

As I walk up the stairs, I can hear the shower, and it sounds kind of loud. When I get to the top of the stairs, it's easy to see why.

Aiden left the door open. Wide open.

Did he do it on purpose? Nah, not possible. He has a glass-encased shower stall, so I'm sure he wouldn't leave the door open when anyone could look in and see him.

And see I do. When I walk by, I can't help but notice him standing there, his arm against the wall. His ass looks even better naked than it did last night in his jeans. And I think it might really turn me into a biter because, once again, I really want to go in there and sink my teeth into it.

But his ass isn't even the most impressive thing I see right now. From this angle, I can see his cock. His very large, very erect cock.

While I stand outside the door, Aiden moves his arm, grabbing himself with his fist. With his large hand wrapped around his dick, he pumps slowly, and I can't fucking look away. He's jerking off in the shower, and I'm standing here, like a creep, watching. It's the most erotic thing I've ever seen and I can't look away.

Now I know what the lube I saw last night is all about.

The flowing water has plastered Aiden's long hair to his back. I can see the muscles in his ass and legs flexing as he grinds into his hand, his arm matching the speed in an equal, but opposite rhythm. Wetness floods my thighs with no panties to hold it in place, my desire instantaneous and extreme. I feel my core throb, my pulse matching Aiden's thrusts almost perfectly, the need to be filled by him threatening to make me reckless. My body is torn between wanting to strip and get into the shower with him, and wanting to shove my hands in my pants and take care of myself while I watch.

Obviously, I can't do either of those things, but I still can't seem to tear myself away. I watch as he pumps faster, his mouth opening with what I can only assume are satisfied groans. Water drips down his body, tracing the muscles in his back and legs, his pace quickening until finally, finally, he comes. It spurts impressively far up the wall, splashing on the slate gray tiles, over and over again. After several moments, and a few more pumps of his hand, Aiden releases his dick, leaning his head on his other arm.

I stay rooted in place until he lifts his head and begins washing his come off the shower wall. Before he can see me, I turn and run into the spare room to gather up my clothes as I originally planned to do when I came up here.

I need a minute to get myself together, though, so I sit on the bed and take some deep breaths. Forget what I said about his shirtless drumming. *This* is going in the spank bank for sure. Actually, both things will probably make it. I don't think one fantasy of Aiden is going to be enough for me. Not after what I saw.

Aiden's body is pretty much my idea of physical perfection. He's muscular but lean. He looks like an active person, instead of someone who gets all their muscles from the gym. Which I guess jibes with what he said about drumming being his workout. Despite not being full of huge muscles, his body is incredibly masculine. All edges and hard lines. He has a little chest hair, barely even noticeable really, and the only reason I saw it was because he passed so close to me earlier, on his way up here. And that ass. Seriously. It's *ah-mazing*. Round, firm, and those dimples? Pretty sure it's the most perfect ass I've ever seen. I can picture myself digging my nails into it, encouraging him as he drives into me with his equally amazing cock.

Phew. Is it getting hot in here? I fan myself with my hands to cool off a little.

God, what the hell am I going to do? This is no time for me to be thinking about anyone like this. Getting fired flipped my whole life upside down. I need to change my career, find a job, and figure out a new dream, not become infatuated with some man because of his ass. Even if it is a spectacular ass. I heave a sigh. And even if the man it's attached to also happens to have an amazing dick.

While I sit and try to get images of Aiden out of my head, I hear the shower turn off.

Shit, I need to get downstairs before he comes out of there and guesses I saw him.

I jump up, throw my clothes into the grocery bag, and jog into the hallway.

And slam face first into a soaking wet, stark naked Aiden.

"Ohmygod, your penis!" I yell, while some instinct that is definitely *not* self-preservation has me dropping my bag and awkwardly covering his dick with both hands.

And some instinct, probably modesty, has him attempting to do the same thing, but my reflexes are faster. Know what that means? Yeah, that's right. Instead of covering himself, he's firmly pressing my hands against his dick.

"Oh shit, I'm so sorry," I blurt, trying to pull my hands away. He has a bit of a death grip, so it takes a moment to slide my hands out from under his. But not before I feel some stiffening action. *Maybe I can slip my hands back underneath his and keep holding on? That would be fine, right?*

"Uh, I forgot to grab a towel. Fuck, I'm sorry. Can you just... Can you grab me one from the closet there, please?" He points with a tip of his chin at a small door beside the bathroom.

I fling open the closet door and grab the first thing I see, handing it to Aiden with a hand over my eyes.

"Um, I think maybe I'll need something a little larger?" He says with a snicker in his voice.

I risk a look and notice I've given him a hand towel. He's holding it by two corners on the short end, head down while he looks up at me through his eyelashes, a smirk on his face.

"Oh yeah. Sorry. Yeah. That is definitely not going to be big enough, is it? I mean, not that I saw much. Or anything. I mean, I saw nothing. At all." I'm rambling and laughing nervously and searching through the closet all at the same time. "Where are all the damn towels?" And why can't I shut my stupid mouth? "Definitely didn't see anything when I came upstairs. Nope. I went right into the guest room and gathered my clothes. What shower?"

I finally find a larger towel and hand it off. Aiden raises an eyebrow at me in question.

"Oh, yeah. I'll turn around." I spin so my back is facing him, and bend to grab my bag.

"I'll go get dressed and then we can head out," Aiden says before walking down the hall and disappearing into another doorway.

I let out a breath, scrunching up my face and resting my fist on my forehead.

What did I say when I ran into him? '*Ohmygod, your penis!*'? Ugh. What the hell is wrong with me?

14

Family Photos

Aiden

I TURN AWAY FROM Rhea and walk down the hallway to my bedroom, playing it cool and not breaking into a run. Did I really grab her hands and hold them to my dick? I can't believe I did that. My only consolation was that she seemed more embarrassed about the whole thing than I did. I mean, she yelled out, *Oh my god, your penis* and then tried to cover me up. With her hands. Directly. On. My. Dick.

God, I hope she didn't notice I was getting hard while she was pulling her hands away.

I have to admit; she is pretty adorable when she's embarrassed. It was especially cute how it seemed like she couldn't stop herself from talking while she was helping me find a towel.

Wait! Did she say she didn't see anything when she came upstairs? Fuck. That means she definitely saw something. She can't have seen much, though, can she? If she had just come up the stairs and gone into the room right before I came out, she would have only seen me soaping up and rinsing off.

Yeah, I'm sure that's all she saw.

I can't think about the possibility she saw me jerking off. My brain can't handle something like that right now. Besides, she would have had to come up a few minutes earlier for that to happen. Not only that, she'd have had to stand there and watch.

Despite the way she was looking at me while I was playing earlier, there's no way she'd do something like that. She's not actually interested in me, so I don't think I need to worry about it.

Still, the faster I get dressed, the faster we can get out of here and I can get back to normal without the temptation of Rhea in my house. Once I don't have to see her anymore, this won't be a problem for me. Out of sight, out of mind, right? I'm only attracted to her because she's clearly hot. It's not like I'm not in love with her or anything.

I pull on a pair of jeans and a long-sleeved, gray henley before throwing my hair up in a loose bun. After I put on socks and load up my pockets with my wallet and phone, I pick up Rhea's shirt from last night, and leave my room.

The door to the spare room is open when I walk by, and Rhea isn't there. She must be downstairs already, which makes sense. She already had her stuff when we collided in the hallway.

And then she held me so gently, my dick says, celebrating. Great, now my dick is weighing in on this situation. He's not exactly known for being a voice of reason.

I jog down the stairs and find her standing, looking at some photos on my walls. When I moved back in here, I packed up everything that reminded me of my father, but I couldn't get rid of the pictures of my mom and sister. Instead, I cut my dad out of the pictures. A crude solution, to be sure, but I really couldn't stand the thought of looking at photos of him for the rest of my life. Not after what he did.

"Hey, all set?"

Rhea jumps when she hears me.

"Shit, you scared me," she says, her hand over her heart. "I must already be losing those great cop instincts I thought I had if you could sneak up on me like that."

"I hate to say it, but I wasn't sneaking. The neighbors probably could have heard me running down the stairs." I tease. I was quiet, and the stairs are carpeted, which helps to muffle the sound, but I wasn't sneaking. She should have heard me coming.

"Yeah, yeah. Whatever you say." She smiles and walks to where I'm waiting. "Is that your family in the pictures?"

My body stiffens, but not in a good way. I hate when people ask about my family, but I should expect it when I keep all these pictures around. I so rarely have new people in the house that it's been a while since I've had to deal with the questions.

"Yeah, that's my mom and my sister. They died a long time ago." Short answers usually give the impression that a person doesn't want to talk about something. Rhea is a cop at heart though, and she's used to asking questions of people who don't want to talk. So she ignores me and keeps talking, of course.

"I notice your dad's not in any pictures."

"No, he's not." I turn to the door, shoving my feet into my worn out old Chucks. "You ready? Let's go."

I open the front door and stand out on the porch to wait for her, still holding her shirt from last night. She slips on her boots, grabs her bag, and joins me outside.

"I'm sorry. It's none of my business," she says, looking up at me and placing her hand on my arm. "I shouldn't have asked about your dad."

Before I can answer, she walks down the steps and around to the passenger side of the car. She dropped the subject fast, and I'm grateful. I hate talking about my dad, and I avoid it at all costs. But I still feel like an asshole for talking to her that way.

I meet her at the car, going around and opening her door for her. Once I'm settled in my seat, I turn and look at her.

"My dad wasn't a nice guy, and I don't talk about him. But I still shouldn't have been rude to you. I'm sorry."

She looks at me, a small smile on her face, almost like she understands. "It's okay. You don't need to be sorry. I really shouldn't have asked. There's obviously a reason he's not in the pictures, even though it's easy to see he was at one point. But whatever the reason is, it's none of my business." She reaches over and squeezes my hand. "I'm having a hard time hanging up my cop hat, I guess."

I nod to acknowledge what she's said, and start the car, leaving my house and all the pictures behind.

Before long, we're out of the suburbs and on our way back through the city. As we're about to turn on the street toward Bump & Grind, Rhea's stomach growls so loudly I almost think my car is making noises. That's the last thing I want to deal with today. Pretty sure I've already paid enough in repairs for this car that my mechanic can afford to retire, and he's only thirty. Feeding Rhea seems like a much more enjoyable, and much less expensive, way to spend my morning.

"Hungry?" I chuckle. "Want to grab breakfast before we track down your keys?"

"Oh no, I don't even have my wallet. I spent all my cash on tequila last night, too." She smiles and shakes her head. "Xena is a bad influence on me."

"It's my treat. I'm starving too, and there's a place up ahead Ryder and Denise have been talking about non-stop. Come check it out with me?" This is probably a terrible idea, but I couldn't stop myself before the words were out. I want to spend more time with her. And it's not like I can act on my attraction at breakfast. I wouldn't bang her on a table in front of the breakfast crowd. We'll have breakfast, then after, we'll get her keys and she'll be out of my life as I originally planned. "We both need to eat, right?"

She hesitates a moment, probably remembering how I was an asshole to her a few minutes ago. "Sure, okay. Why not? I can't exactly deny that I'm hungry. My stomach has seen to that."

I laugh. "Great, because we're already here." While she was thinking, I turned into the small lot at Maggie's Diner. Denise's main pregnancy craving has been their milkshakes, so she and Ryder have been coming here all the time. And apparently it's not only the milkshakes that are great.

Despite my initial reservations, I'm actually looking forward to hanging out with Rhea. Maybe this will be fun.

15

Go Titties!

Rhea

"But did they really fire you for that?"

Aiden doesn't want to believe the police commission would choose to let me go rather than upset the mayor. Sadly, it's the truth. Law enforcement is more of a political game as anything else, I realize now.

"Yeah," I say around a mouthful of the best pancakes I've ever tasted. "The guy is friends with the mayor and I was a low-ranking officer. His wife refused to press charges and my partner's word doesn't count for anything without a witness."

Aiden chews his egg white omelet without answering. Who orders an egg white omelet at a diner, anyway? Pancakes and waffles are the only acceptable breakfast foods in a diner. Everyone knows that.

"And you've already used your appeals, so there's really nothing you can do?"

"Nope, nothing left. I need to figure out what I'm going to do with the rest of my life, now that being a cop is no longer an option. I almost wonder if I'm better off this way? It always felt like they tied my hands with red tape when I really wanted to help someone."

I take a drink of my coffee and have a look around the diner. We're sitting in a booth in the front window at the back of the diner, and I'm facing the door. I never feel comfortable with my back to the door, and if I can manage it, I like to sit with my back against a wall instead of another table. The thought of someone having access to me from behind bothers me.

The door opens and three older ladies walk in, making a bee-line right to where I'm sitting with Aiden. Well, the diner is a long train car with booths on one side of the aisle, and a counter on the other, so it's not like they could walk in a different direction, but they seem to stride with a purpose. They're all wearing track suits in complementary, but not matching, shades of purple, and the one in the front is wearing a trucker's cap that reads 'fuck bitches, get money'. The other two haven't accessorized their track suits, aside from the matching white high-top sneakers all three of them wear.

"Well, would you look at who it is?" The first woman, the clear leader of this trio, says while sliding into the booth next to Aiden. "Are you going to introduce us to your lovely friend here?" She gestures over to me.

Aiden rolls his eyes and mouths, '*I'm so sorry,*' before beginning the introductions.

"Gran, you remember Officer Ryan, don't you? She was there the day Denise's ex tried to get one over on you and Gladys? Rhea, this is Ryder's Gran, Delores, and her friends Gladys and Lana."

One of the women, Lana, slides in next to me, and the other, Gladys, sits on a stool directly opposite our table.

"Yeah, you old fart. Don't you remember the jack-off whose ball hairs I singed off with my stun gun? And then you tied him up with your pink rope?" says Gladys from her seat at the counter.

I laugh, remembering the excellent work these two ladies did of restraining the man. By the time Kaden and I had shown up, they had him gagged and hogtied on the floor at their feet while they sat on the couch drinking whiskey out of teacups. I could barely contain my laughter. Kaden cried because he was laughing so hard.

"Hello ladies, it's nice to see you again." I take a drink of my water. "Please call me Rhea, though. I'm not actually an officer anymore."

"What?" the old lady crew gasps in unison.

"You're such a good cop, though. I could tell by the way you handled yourself that day. Very professional. Not like your partner, officer gigglepants," Ryder's gran Delores adds.

The woman sitting next to me speaks up. "What happened, sweetie?" she asks, putting a hand on my shoulder.

Normally I hate when people use terms like sweetie and honey with me because it's hard to maintain authority when a person is patronizing you, but this woman is so cute and so ridiculous in her purple tracksuit that I can't hold it against her.

"I, uh, arrested the wrong person, apparently. Someone who had a friend in power and he used that relationship to get me fired. They lied and said I used excessive force when I arrested him."

All three ladies gasp, then turn to glare at Aiden with raised eyebrows. Like a synchronized scolding from grannies, and I'm glad I'm not on the receiving end of it. A chill runs up my spine in sympathy for Aiden.

"And... Have you done anything yet, Aiden?" Delores asks.

"Oh, no, Delores," I say. "Aiden can't do anything. I've used up all of my appeals and I could never ask someone to lie in my defense."

The ladies all laugh.

"First, call me Gran. I insist." Delores—I mean Gran—points at me. "Second, I wasn't asking Aiden to do that. I was asking if he'd used some of the special tricks he normally uses on deserving scumbags. This guy who got you fired sounds like a prime example of someone who needs to be taken down a few notches."

Aiden looks at me and mouths, *'sorry'* again, although I'm not sure what he has to be sorry about. These ladies are hilarious.

"I thought about that as soon as I heard, Gran, but Devon told me not to do anything. They would blame anything I could do on Rhea, and she has enough to worry about right now."

"Well, that is stupid. I'm sure you could figure something out. Oh, I know! You could take her on a date and be her alibi, and we could do it." Gladys hops off her stool, spry for a woman who has to be approaching eighty years old.

"Um, what are we talking about here? I don't want anyone taking revenge on my behalf. The law will catch up to him, eventually."

"Pardon me, Rhea, but I'm sure I don't have to tell you the law doesn't always work in favor of the victims. Sometimes a person needs to take justice into their own hands."

"I have to disagree with you on that. That's vigilantism, and it does more harm than good. It's best to leave law enforcement to the professionals." I'm a little worked up. I may not be a cop anymore, but I was for years, and it has always bothered me when people think they should take the law into their own hands. It's dangerous, and it usually winds up with the wrong people getting hurt. "Is that really something you do, Aiden?"

He at least has the decency to look a little uncomfortable. "Well, in a manner of speaking, yes. I don't really see it as taking the law into my own hands, though. It's more like giving a victim a sense of justice, in instances where the law has already failed them. It's not like I'm running around under cover of darkness, doing the job of the police for them. I'm not like I'm trying to be Batman or anything."

Silence descends on the table, with none of us saying a word. This is a touchy subject, and I think we're all a little uncomfortable. I know I am.

"Well, that's enough of that. Aiden, did you know the girls and I have been taking some new burlesque classes? When are you coming by so we can show you our new moves?"

Aiden chokes out a laugh. "I don't know, Gran," he says. "I don't think I've quite recovered from the pudding wrestling from last time. I might need a little more time."

"Hmmm, well, make sure you come see us before you lock down this cutie," Gladys says, pointing at me. "I wouldn't want to be forced to give up my dick quest before I've accomplished it, like I had to when Ryder married Denise."

Aiden shakes his head. "I'm so sorry, Rhea. I didn't mean to subject you to these crazies. I promise. And Gladys, you should give up your quest right now. I'm not showing you my dick."

"Oh, you never mind," Lana reaches over and playfully slaps Aiden's arm. "We haven't even been that bad today, and you know it." She grins.

"I am so lost," I say, looking between the four of them. Gladys wants to see Aiden's dick? I mean, I don't blame her, it is a pretty nice dick. But she's got to be nearly eighty years old. What's she going to do with a much younger man's penis?

At the sight of my bewildered face, they all start laughing, and Lana grabs my hand.

"You'll get used to it, honey. The more time you spend with Aiden, the more you'll see us. And we are damn delightful." She looks at the other two ladies for confirmation. "Isn't that right, girls?"

All together the three of them yell, "Go Titties!" and punch their fists into the air and I can't hold it in anymore. I burst into laughter. Unfortunately, it's immediately after taking a drink, and I spit a mouthful of water all over Aiden.

Shit.

16

She Deserves Better

Aiden

"Gah! I'm sorry. I'm so sorry, Aiden," Rhea says, while she leans over the table and tries to dry my face with napkins. "I can't believe I did that."

The three ladies who caused this commotion are laughing away, like I didn't get showered with saliva laced water.

"You don't need to apologize. The blame lies with these three lunatics here." I point to the three ladies in question.

"Why on earth did you guys yell 'Go Titties'?" Rhea asks. She's given up trying to wipe me off. My face is pretty dry now, but my shirt has seen better days.

"It's their cheer," I tell her. "They're the terrible trio. The initials are T.T. which they've, of course, adapted to titties, so now they call themselves the titty club. And trust me, they are not delightful."

Gran leans in close and smooches me on the cheek. "It's been fun, Aiden, but the titty club needs to get on with our meeting. We'll leave you to your date." She turns to Rhea. "It was lovely to see you again, Rhea. Please come and join us for tea at Peaceful Pines one of these days. Make Aiden bring you. He doesn't visit nearly enough."

The terrible trio, or the titty club, as they call themselves, gets up in unison and goes to sit in a booth a little further away from us.

"That was interesting," Rhea leans over and whispers. "Those women are funny."

"You have no idea," I murmur back. "They are three of the most bizarre, inappropriate, and hilarious women I've ever met. Although Gladys's obsession with seeing my dick isn't really hilarious. I almost wish Ryder and Denise hadn't gotten married so she'd still be obsessed with him and his dick." And it's too bad I'll never get married, because now she's going to be obsessed with my dick forever.

"Why is she obsessed with your... you know?" She asks, while gesturing toward my lap. "Seems kind of weird for a lady her age to be thinking about that."

"These ladies are nothing like any ladies you've seen before. You remember the scene when Denise's ex tried to hurt Gran? These women are like no grannies I've heard of. I love them. I just wish they wouldn't worry so much about what's in my pants."

Rhea's face goes a little red. "Well, I could always let her know what I found during my little cover up maneuver in the upstairs hallway earlier today. Maybe that would hold them off for a bit?"

My mind goes back to earlier when we were standing in my hallway, both of us with our hands on my dick. Fuck, her hands felt good. I think my body tried to keep her hands on me even when she tried to pull away. That's the only explanation I can think of for why I held her hands on my dick for longer than necessary. Not that her hands on my dick were necessary at all. Fucking amazing, yes. Necessary, no. Hopefully, it felt like I was trying to keep myself covered rather than trying to hold her hands on me a moment longer.

I shake my head and laugh. "I doubt that very much. It probably would make her more persistent. She'd try to get me into the shower when I visit, hoping I'd come out naked so she could do the same thing."

"Damn." Rhea's eyes light up with a smile, her face still red. "I was hoping my embarrassment could at least serve a purpose. There's gotta be a reason we were standing there holding your dick awkwardly, together."

"Who says we need a reason to hold a dick together? There doesn't always need to be a reason for awkward dick holding between near strangers. I mean, the situation presented itself and we did what needed to be done. But now that it's happened, we're going to have to admit we're more friends than strangers."

Rhea's face brightens, her smile turning into a giggle, which then turns into a full on laugh. God, she's gorgeous. Ryder's usually the one being a funny guy and if this is how it feels, I can see why he's always trying to make Denise laugh. I could listen to Rhea laugh all day.

But that's exactly why I need to get away from her. She deserves love and happiness and that's not something I can give her. I need to stop this before it can get any further. There's no way I can be what she needs.

"So, are you ready to go find your keys now?"

"Oh, um, yeah sure."

The lightness in her eyes is gone now, replaced with a look of disappointment. Yeah, we were having fun, but I can't allow it to continue. I feel bad but it's better this way. I'm not fit to be a partner for anyone, that's why I don't do relationships.

"Alright, I'll pay the bill and I'll meet you outside then. Take the keys and let yourself in the car." I stand up and take the keys from my pocket.

She nods and takes the keys from my hand. I watch as she walks to the doors before leaving the booth myself.

"You dumbass," Gran says as I walk by her table. "What did you do to her in five minutes to put that frown on her face?"

"You two looked like you were starting something. What went wrong since we left you?" Lana adds.

"Nothing happened," I say, pulling cash out of my wallet. "She's obviously amazing. She's way too good for me."

"Well, now that's definitely the truth."

"Thanks, Gladys. I knew I could count on you to make me feel better," I deadpan. "I don't do relationships; I'm not made for them. Rhea deserves more than what I can ever give her, so it's easier for everyone if I shut it down before it begins. Plus, she's not even interested in me, anyway."

"Oh geez, and here I thought Ryder was the dumbest one out of all you boys. You're giving him a run for his money, kid." Gran shakes her head. "You are made for a relationship. You just need to find the right person. But you can't do that if you push away anyone you have a connection with. And if there's one thing I can tell, it's that you have a connection with Rhea."

"I'll keep that in mind, Gran. Gladys, Lana." I nod my head at the three of them. "You ladies have a nice day."

I drop the money on the counter for our breakfasts and head out to my car. Rhea is already in the passenger seat waiting for me. I strip off my wet shirt and throw it into the back seat. Good thing I brought her tank from last night. Looks like I'll have to bring it to her some other time since I need to wear it right now.

"I was going to give this back to you today," I say as I get into the vehicle, "but I need to borrow it for a bit if that's okay?"

"Well, it is your shirt, right?" She laughs, repeating what I said to her at the club last night.

"Yeah, yeah, funny. You know what I meant."

"I do now, yes. It's good you don't look like that when you're out walking around," she says, pointing at the picture of me on the shirt. "It would look a little silly if people could tell you're wearing a shirt with your own picture on it."

"Yeah, my ego isn't that big. Ryder might do something like that, though." I laugh. "Or even Johnny, if he weren't currently being neurotic about someone who's playing him the way he usually plays women. Getting a taste of his own medicine isn't sitting well with him. It works out for me though, because when he's upset, he bakes, and he brings a lot to me."

"Who's Johnny?" She asks.

"Oh, he's in the band with me. He plays guitar. If you've ever seen anything of ours, he's the one covered in tattoos pretty much head to toe. He's basically the last person you'd expect to be a stress baker."

She smiles. "I wish I had friends who brought me baked goods. At least I have Xena, though. I can always get coffee. She even tried to give me donuts yesterday when she found out I got fired, but then she freaked out and threw them through the window when Devon showed up and reminded her of the whole cops and donuts thing."

I snort out a laugh. I can picture Xena panicking and trying to get rid of the evidence by throwing donuts all over. "At least coffee is always a good thing."

She looks out the window, so I don't continue the conversation. I suppose I was a bit of a dick at the diner, so I can't blame her for not wanting to interact right now.

We drive in silence the rest of the way to Bump & Grind. I know I should do everything I can to stay away from her, but want to keep talking to her, because I'm enjoying her company. Maybe we can be friends? She seems like someone I could have a good time with. I'm not sure I could handle being just friends, though. I feel like I'd always be wishing for more.

"Any thoughts on the job search?" I ask as I parallel park in front of the coffee shop.

"Not really," she says, getting out of the car. "I had this vision of myself as a private investigator, like in an old film noir, you know? But I wouldn't want to do that, really. It's not as exciting as the movies make it seem. I'd spend my life staking out cheating spouses. I went into law enforcement to help people, not to take pictures of people trying to fuck."

I bark out a laugh, and she gives me a wry smile.

"I think taking pictures of people fucking is an entirely different profession."

"If I'd gotten into that business instead of police work, I'd probably be a lot closer to retirement. Maybe I should start an OnlyFans? I hear some of those people make a ton of money." She's laughing because she's joking, but my dick doesn't realize that. I have a semi just thinking of what sort of content she would make on OnlyFans.

Just herself?

Toys?

A partner?

Fuck that. Heat crawls up the back of my throat at the thought of her with someone else. '*Mine,*' my dick says. You know, if dicks could talk, anyway. And if I listened to mine, which I don't, because he clearly doesn't understand we will never have a '*mine*'. I swallow my discomfort and open the door to the shop, waiting for Rhea to go in first.

"Hey you! How was it after I left last night?" Xena greets Rhea and starts pouring us coffees.

"Oh, you know, besides you running off with my keys and phone, and us not being able to track you down? It was great."

"No," Xena's face drops in a mockery of shock. "I had no idea." She winks. "So, did you sleep over at Aiden's, then?"

"Why don't you tell us where you slept?" I ask her. "Since we tried your house, Devon's place, and Devon's phone, all with no luck."

Xena's face goes red. "Oh, yeah, I…"

"Never mind," Rhea laughs. "Can I have my keys, please? And my phone?"

"Here you go," Xena passes them over, and then slides two to-go cups over to us. "And here's coffee, on the house, for all the trouble."

Rhea turns to me. "Thanks so much for everything. I much preferred your place to sleeping on the street."

"No problem." *I mean, other than finding myself so ridiculously attracted to you, I had to jerk off in the shower while you were there.* "I need to get to the studio to meet the guys. I'll see you both later." I reach over and grab my coffee from the counter. "Thanks for the coffee, Xena."

At least hanging with the guys should help me get my mind off Rhea, and the way her hands felt on my dick.

17

Cobwebs and Coffee

Rhea

"Okay, so..."

"So what?" I stir a little cream and sugar into my coffee while Xena looks at me expectantly.

"You slept over at Aiden's? Did he bang all your worries away?"

"What? Is that why you took off with my keys? And my phone?"

Xena at least has the decency to look a little guilty. "Well, not at first. But you have to admit, it's not a bad idea. You looked super hot last night, and the way you two were looking at each other, I could tell you were both interested."

"Yeah, he's hot. But that doesn't excuse the fact you left me with a virtual stranger."

"Oh, come on. It's not that bad. Devon vouched for him. He's not a dangerous guy. He doesn't sleep around or even date, apparently. He's the perfect distraction for you. You can hook up with him for some no-strings, gland-to-gland combat. Blow off some steam and come at your job search relaxed and ready."

I choke on my coffee. "Gland to gland combat? What the hell are you even talking about?"

"Duh, sexy times, obviously. Your dry spell has lasted almost as long as I've known you. You need to get someone to clear out those cobwebs. Nothing better than a few orgasms to relieve the stress of losing your dream job."

Shaking my head, I take my coffee and go sit at a table. I don't really feel like standing at the counter while we discuss my cobweb-filled vagina. Not that I want to discuss it at all, but Xena seems to think it's a legitimate concern. So concerning, in fact, she follows and sits at the seat across from me.

"My vagina is just fine, thanks," I say after a sip of my coffee. "And even if it weren't, it's not the first thing on my mind right now. You said it yourself. I lost my dream job. Not just my dream job, the *only* job I've ever wanted. Every class I took in school, every extracurricular activity I took part in, it was all leading me to being a cop. So I need to figure out what I can do, now that I can't be a cop."

"Yeah, and what I'm telling you is, get someone to dick you down real good, get some of those good endorphins flowing, and you'll have a much clearer head for a task of that magnitude."

I huff out a breath. Xena means well, I'm sure, but I don't agree with her assessment of the situation. With this much stress, I doubt I can focus on anything until I get at least some of it sorted. And I think contacting someone about the job I saw at the local shelter is a good place to start.

"Listen," I say. "I know you're looking out for me, but I need to get some of my job stuff figured out before I can worry about my vagina."

"Gah, you're no fun," Xena crosses her arms over her chest and pouts. "Okay, so what is your plan for your job thing then? Is there anything I can do to help?"

"Not yet, I don't think. I'm going to go home after I finish this coffee to do what I was trying to do yesterday. I found a couple of interesting looking positions, so I'll contact them and take it from there."

We're interrupted when the bell over the door jingles and new customers walk in. Xena jumps up to serve them and I stay seated, watching people go by on the sidewalk outside the front window. Xena has a great location here. She's close to downtown and a lot of the people who work in offices nearby come and get their coffee from her.

That's one great thing about Westborough. Everyone here prefers a local place over a chain. We've had a few major coffee retailers try to open locations here, but other than the big one out of Seattle, none have gained any traction. Xena's raking it in though. Bump & Grind is almost always busy.

I wave at two of her employees as they walk in to start their shifts. Tanya and Dax have worked for Xena for years, and they are two of the most amazing people you could ever meet. Tanya sees me and comes over to say hello, while Dax goes straight to the back to help Xena.

"Hey, Rhea," she says, sitting opposite me. "Sorry about the police force thing. It sucks you're not a cop anymore."

Well, it looks like the secret's out now. I should have guessed someone here at the coffee shop would know, at least. Xena needed someone to cover for her yesterday, after all.

"Oh, yeah. Thanks," I say. "It's not so bad. Now I get to find out what to do with my life all over again. Yay. Who *wouldn't* want to do that in their mid-thirties?"

Tanya laughs. "I hear you. Why do you think I've been working here for so long? Once I dropped out of college, I couldn't muster up the energy to look for a *career* again. Plus, I really like it here. Xena is a great boss."

I know she's not saying that because Xena is my friend, either. Xena pays a great wage and even offers benefits. It's one reason she'll never be rich. She's not one to abuse her position over others to make money. She wants her staff to enjoy coming to work, and to afford to have a life when they're not working.

Huh. That sounds pretty good, actually. Maybe I *should* come work for her.

"I'm not sure if I'm ready to go that route yet. They only made it official yesterday, so I still have some time yet before I decide to go a completely different direction. But if I do, you can bet this place is the first place I'd come looking for a job."

Tanya stands. "Well, it was nice to see you. I gotta get to work before my bitch of a boss gets mad." She raises her voice so Xena can hear her and winks at me. "See you around," she says.

"I heard that," Xena yells over the heads of the customers in line. "You're lucky I love you, Tanya."

I shake my head and snicker at those two before taking another long drink of my coffee and standing up. It's time I get going. I need to work on the job hunt, plus I don't want to be taking up a table that paying customers could be using.

After I double check I have my wallet and keys, I walk out the door and onto the street. It's close to morning coffee break time for people and the sidewalks are filling up. I'm getting a few strange looks for my outfit of outrageously large joggers, t-shirt, and combat boots. I'm sure it's a good look, particularly since I've topped it off with a reusable grocery bag as an accessory. Never mind that my hair is probably a giant fuzzy disaster.

It's a good thing I'm not one to be too concerned about my appearance, or I'd be mortified at the thought of all these strangers seeing me like this. As it stands, I'm only mortified that Aiden saw me like this before he dropped me off. He's so hot it probably offended his sensibilities to see someone as thoroughly not hot as me this morning.

I shake my head. Aiden time is over. It's best I stop thinking about him now.

I finish my coffee and drop the cup in a recycling bin outside my building. With a quick wave to Mrs. Dickerson, the owner of the nightmare factory, I mean, vintage doll shop I live above, I let myself in the side door and head upstairs to my apartment.

As soon as I get inside, I strip out of my clothes and go straight into the bathroom, into the shower. I still smell tequila oozing from me and the stench is making me feel sick. First order of business is a shower, and then I'll be ready to attack the job hunt with a fresh outlook. Not to mention a much needed fresh smell.

It's too bad I can't do anything about the cobwebs Xena was so concerned about.

18

We're Barely Even Friends

Aiden

"I DON'T KNOW MAN, she was gone before I woke up this morning." Johnny left with Becca last night like I thought, but it doesn't sound like the night went as well as he'd hoped. "She is so hard to figure out."

The whole band is sitting around in Connor's studio space at his house. Before he reconnected with Alex and proposed to her, he bought this house and had it outfitted with a studio. He even had his walkout basement renovated with a small apartment with rooms for each of us guys to sleep in, if we ever need it. When we get into a really good rhythm musically, it's nice to have a space to sleep in your own bed. It's way better than back in the days when the guys would crash at my place, spread throughout the house, sleeping on any available surface. If I never see Ryder's bare ass on my kitchen counter again, it will be too soon.

"You know what this is? It's karma." Ryder gestures toward Johnny with the licorice he's eating. Denise has been craving it non-stop apparently, thanks to her pregnancy, and Ryder can't get enough of it now either. "You were a love 'em and leave 'em wanting more type for so long that this is karma getting back at you."

Leaving them wanting more is just a nice way of saying Johnny had a habit of ghosting women after a few weeks. He wouldn't go completely ghost though. He would tell them it wasn't working out first and then he'd block them and go on like it had never happened. Not exactly gentlemanly behavior, but at least he did them the courtesy of telling them they were through. He didn't disappear completely, with no warning at all. That might count for something when it comes to karma.

"Haha. Fuck off, Ryder." Johnny's facial expression doesn't match the joking tone of his voice. He's pretty broken up over Becca. "We can't all magically fall in love with someone who's already in love with us. Some of us need to work for it."

"If you have to work too hard, maybe it's not meant to be?" I ask. "There comes a point where you will need to leave her alone, you know."

"Yes, thank you, Aiden. I am aware of that. And if Alex hadn't confirmed Becca was actually interested, I wouldn't be pursuing her. But she's interested, so I will keep trying. At least as long as she wants me too, anyway."

"Good afternoon, gentlemen," Devon yells as he comes into the studio, carrying trays of coffee from Bump & Grind. Alex follows along behind him with pizza boxes from Tino's. Ever since Alex moved in, Connor has become a lot more relaxed about his studio space. He never used to allow food in here at all, and now coffee and pizza are no big deal. Love really does change people.

"Where'd you go last night?" I ask, narrowing my eyes at him. I'm not positive, but I think he has something going on with Xena. I'm not going to say anything, though. Devon is friends with her older brother, and I'm sure he wouldn't like it if Devon were panting after her. "Rhea didn't have her keys or her phone. She had to spend the night at my place."

"Oh, did she now?" Devon asks, waggling his eyebrows. "And how was that?"

"What do you mean, 'how was that?' How do you think it was? It was weird, and a little uncomfortable. We barely know each other and she was forced to sleep at my house, so she didn't have to sleep on the street."

"Oh, shit dude. Sorry." Devon's passing out coffees while we talk. "Xena said it looked like you two were hitting it off. She wanted Rhea to blow off some steam last night. And I know you haven't been with a chick in a long time. The way you were grinding all over her on the dance floor, it sure looked like you were interested in making something happen."

Fuck. I was sort of hoping he hadn't noticed. It was more terrible judgment on my part than it was an actual attempt to make something happen. That's why I tried to keep my distance from her last night and this morning. Something about her is making me overlook my usual rules for engaging with a woman. One of the main ones is don't hook up with someone who you will ever need to see again. If I never have to see them again, there's no chance I will get attached and want something more. Rhea, whether or not she knows it, is involved in our lives, thanks to whatever Xena and Devon are doing. And that's only one reason she's off limits.

"Well, next time the two of you attempt to push Rhea onto anyone, I'd suggest you ask her first. She showed no interest in me like that. Not that I was looking at her like that, either. The dancing was a way to get some sleazy looking fuckboy away from her. I had to do it again after you guys left, too. For a former cop, she wasn't taking a very assertive stance with those douchebags at the club." Although, what if she was looking to blow off some steam, and I kept stepping in and clam jamming her? Nah, she seemed relieved for the help. Didn't she? At least she did when she nearly stuck her hands down my pants.

"My bad," Devon says, a big smile on his face. "I guess I assumed when she was going on and on about how hot you are, she was showing her interest in you. My mistake."

"Okay, hold on a minute," Alex says. She stops passing out pizza and looks over at me. "Who is Rhea? Have I met her? Oh, I have the best idea. You should bring her for dinner tomorrow!"

"No!" I yell, causing everyone to turn their attention to me. Shit, this is turning into a bigger deal than I wanted. "I mean, that's not a good idea. She has job searching to do. She got fired, and she's trying to figure out what to do with her life now."

"Yeah, maybe it's not such a good idea," Devon says to Alex. "At least not this week. She recently lost her dream job as a cop and she's a little lost now as she tries to figure it all out."

"Um, that's the best time to invite someone to join our family dinner get together. Besides, what's she going to accomplish on a Sunday? Nothing. She'll be sitting around, depressed, and probably alone. What better way to take her mind off of it than joining this lot of random weirdos?"

Shit. Alex has a point. Rhea has no family aside from Kaden and Xena, and Xena is most likely going to be here. Xena is one of Denise's oldest friends and ever since Denise and Ryder got married, she's been here for every family dinner Sunday.

"Wait a minute." Ryder sounds like he's figured something out. "Is this the cop who was there that day at Gran's?"

"Yeah, that's her. She was Kaden's partner."

"Well then, it's settled. We have to invite her. She helped my Gran and Gladys when Denise's dickhead ex tried to hurt them. That means she's family. Plus, Gran will be here tomorrow. I'm sure she'd love to see her."

I don't mention that Gran saw Rhea this morning at breakfast. I have a feeling telling everyone I took her out for breakfast won't help me convince them I'm not interested in her.

"There. It's done," Devon says, sliding his phone into his pocket. "I messaged Xena and told her to bring Rhea tomorrow for dinner." He looks over at me with a smirk. "There's no turning back now."

Why do these guys always think they know me better than I know me? I'm not interested in Rhea. She's hot, sure. But I can keep my dick in my pants and act friendly without expecting more. I've had years of practice denying my sex drive, so no matter how attractive she is, Rhea's not going to wear me down.

Not that she wants to wear me down. We're barely even friends, and that's exactly how we're going to stay.

19

Ulterior Meal Motives

Rhea

"Thanks for having me over," I say to Alex as she shows me to the kitchen where several other women are sitting around the island and around the kitchen table. Xena went off somewhere to see the guys as soon as we walked in the door. She brought a recorder with her and was intent on assaulting their ears with some elementary school songs. "I was looking at a night of shitty takeout and reruns on Netflix tonight. This is a vast improvement."

"You are more than welcome," Alex says, while she hugs me. "We do this pretty much every Sunday. Come anytime you want. This is the only time I get to cook for a large group anymore. I have to say, it's way more fun cooking for people I like than it was cooking for my personal chef clients. Plus, the only one around here who tries to grab my ass is my fiance, and I like it when he does it." She laughs.

"There you are, girl. I've been waiting for you. Come sit beside me." Gran pats the chair next to her at the table. "Let's have a little chat about our mutual friend, Aiden." She wiggles her eyebrows at me as I sit down.

"Hey Gran, where's the rest of the titty club? I figured you all traveled in a pack."

"Oh, I like you. You're sassy. Too bad you can't join the titty club yet. Your tits need to hang at least this low"—she marks an imaginary line almost at her hips—"before you can join. You're too perky still, I'm afraid."

All the women in the kitchen burst into laughter, myself included. Gran is quickly becoming one of my favorite people, thanks to her *give no fucks* attitude and decidedly un-granny-like behavior.

"Okay, before we get into the details, let's at least make sure Rhea knows everyone here. I'm Denise," the woman across the table says, "in case you don't remember me from the pink-rope prisoner incident."

"Hi, Denise. I definitely remember you. That arrest was probably the highlight of my career, thanks to Gran and Gladys." I laugh at the memory of them and their teacups full of whiskey, their feet resting on the man they had tied up on the floor. "Plus Xena has told me a lot about you."

"Yeah, it was pretty funny. Especially since no one got hurt during the whole ordeal." Gran leans over and pats Denise's hand while she talks. "But anyway, that over there is Becca, Alex's bestie." Denise points to a heavily tattooed woman with chin length black hair and dark eye makeup standing at the counter near Alex. "And of course you already know Xena, and Gran too, apparently. Then there's Ivy, my assistant slash replacement slash knight in shining armor."

"I do the stuff Denise is too pregnant to deal with. There's nothing very heroic about it," Ivy smiles, brushing off the compliment. "I'm incredibly lucky Denise gave me a job instead of kicking my ass when I stupidly tried to give Ryder my phone number right in front of her. Truthfully, I deserved the ass kicking."

Denise laughs and rolls her eyes. "You're more bothered by that situation than I am. It worked out great for me. Look at the awesome assistant I got out of the deal."

"Great, introductions are out of the way. Now about Aiden." Alex comes over and sits at the table. "Are you guys together? Hooking up? What's the scoop?" She puts her elbows up on the table and rests her face in her hands. "I need some details."

"Aiden hasn't dated anyone in all the years I've known him. His official stance is he doesn't date," Denise explains to Alex, and to me too, I guess. "Even in the wild years back when the band first got popular, Aiden was always the quiet one, almost always going back to his hotel room alone."

"Oh, horseshit," Gran says with a laugh. "Just because he hasn't doesn't mean he won't. And the way he looks at this woman right here," she says while pointing at me, "tells me he's more interested than he wants to think."

Xena walks in as I'm about to protest this strange conversation, and interrupts with her take on the situation.

"Oh, are you guys talking about Aiden and Rhea? Don't you think they'll be so cute together? You should have seen them yesterday, when they were wearing each other's clothes." She clasps her hands together and holds them to her cheek, fluttering her eyelashes the whole time. "I think it's true love y'all."

"I thought that was his shirt you were wearing," Gran accuses. "And I guess those must've been his pants, too? They were way too big for you, dear. You should pack yourself a bag when you're having an adult freaky-deaky fun-time sleepover, you know."

At this point, I'm not sure if I should defend myself, laugh it off, or give up and run away so no one notices the embarrassment creeping up on my face. These women all seem invested in my love life, almost as though Xena has talked to them about my cobwebby vagina. Xena is the only female friend I've ever really had, so sitting in a room full of women who all have an opinion on who I let into my lady garden is a little overwhelming.

"Thank you, all of you, really, for your concern, but whatever you think is or is not happening between me and Aiden is really none of anyone's business. I'm a grown ass woman. I can handle my own love life, thank you very much." There. Firm, but friendly. That should get them off my back.

They all look properly stricken, heads down, avoiding eye contact, and I think I've managed to get them to back off when suddenly they all burst into laughter, all at once.

"Oh, honey," Becca, the one with all the tattoos and the generally dark vibe, says, "you're one of us now. Your love life is everyone's business, I'm afraid. It's probably even scheduled on Ivy's calendar to check in on you two sometime." Ivy nods in agreement, like she does, in fact, have it booked already.

Alex jumps in. "Just wait, as soon as we're done with you, we'll be talking to Becca about Johnny." She winks over at Becca while everyone laughs some more. Everyone except for Becca.

"That *is* on today's agenda, actually," Ivy jokes. "I've got you penciled in for six o'clock."

"Look, that really is none of your business. I'm serious." Becca points a warning finger at everyone around the table. "Stay out of it."

The laughter gets louder, and I remember something Aiden mentioned.

"Oh, so you're the baking muse Aiden was talking about? The reason Johnny has crazy baking marathons?" I ask Becca, ignoring the giggling band of crazies who are still laughing so hard they're struggling to breathe.

"What do you mean, 'baking marathons'? Johnny doesn't bake." Alex has calmed herself down enough to join in the conversation. "He's never baked for me." She sticks her lip out in a pout.

"Oh, I mean, that's what Aiden told me. Maybe I mis-heard?" I hope I didn't just spill this guy's secret. We've never even met, and I'm already dragging skeletons out of his closet.

"No, Rhea's right. He bakes when he's stressed. I keep telling him I don't want a relationship and he's upset about it. So he bakes and brings most of it to Aiden for the shelter."

For the shelter? Aiden didn't mention that.

"What do you mean, he brings it to Aiden for the shelter?"

"I volunteer at a local domestic violence shelter. I bring Johnny's baked goods for the moms and kids using the services there. A home-baked treat goes a long way when I'm making friends with kids who've had their whole life uprooted. I usually play with the kids while their moms talk to the director in private." Aiden walks into the kitchen, followed by what must be the rest of the guys in the band.

"And I do the baking." A man who I'm guessing is Johnny comes over and offers me his hand. "I'm Johnny. It's nice to meet you." He looks back at Aiden. "You're right man, she is hot." He turns back and winks at me, not in a creepy way, more in an 'I'm letting you in on the joke' way. Becca stares daggers into the back of his head. Hmm. Looks like there's more there than she wants to admit.

Another man steps up to me. This one I recognize is Ryder. "We've met before. I'm Ryder. You know Devon." He points back to where Devon stands. "The soulless ginger is Travis, and the ugly one over with Alex, is Connor."

"Fuck off, Ryder," Connor says, laughing.

"Um, hello? Wife? You're supposed to be protecting me when these assholes tell me to fuck off. Or did your vows mean nothing to you?" Ryder looks at Denise, palms up, eyes wide, questioning where his backup is.

"Yeah, I think I need to amend that vow," she says. "I will defend you if you don't deserve it when they say it. This time you deserved it."

Everyone around the table laughs while Ryder pouts his way over to Denise. He bends down to kiss her and then he's smiling again. I guess he wasn't upset after all.

After we all exchange pleasantries, Alex takes us into the dining room where, surprise surprise, I'm seated next to Aiden.

I lean over and whisper to him, "It seems like your friends had ulterior motives when they invited me to dinner."

He chuckles ruefully. "Yeah, sorry about that. I would have warned you, but after they informed me you were coming, I couldn't convince anyone to give me your number. Gee, it's almost like they didn't want me telling you their nefarious plans or something."

I snicker, which draws a look from Alex and Gran, both laced with a little bit of 'awww' and 'I told you so'.

These people are going to be the death of me. It would be easy enough for me to keep my mind off of Aiden if this were a normal dinner, but everyone here seems intent on throwing us together at every turn. If only they knew they didn't need to try this hard. They had already thrown us together rather effectively just yesterday. I can still feel his dick hardening under my hands, as a matter of fact.

My face heats remembering him in the shower yesterday, and I take a sip from my glass of water to calm myself.

Maybe if things were different, I could see myself falling for a guy like Aiden. He's definitely attractive. And despite our differences, I enjoyed spending time with him, even if he is a sore loser when it comes to video games. I don't have time to chase after a guy right now, though, so after tonight, it will be business as usual. I need to focus on the job search, not on a guy who isn't even interested.

20

Babies and More Babies

Aiden

"So then Aiden came around the corner and saw what was happening, and I swear the boy froze solid. It's like he'd never seen a pool party before or something."

"Gran, you and your friends were all in skimpy bikinis, including the men, and you were all covered in pudding!" Everyone is laughing while I'm having flashbacks to all that wrinkly, pudding-covered flesh on display. Assholes.

"Well, what else were we supposed to do after we accidentally dumped forty thousand pudding cups into ten kiddie pools? Let it go to waste? That's not very eco-conscious of you, Aiden."

Ryder pinches the bridge of his nose. "Gran. We've talked about this. There is nothing accidental about acquiring forty thousand pudding cups which you then scoop into ten kiddie pools. The only way something like that happens is intentionally."

Rhea is laughing so hard beside me she's resting her head on the table and banging her fist beside it. Even if she's sort of laughing at me, I love the sound of it.

"Okay, then what about the time Ryder and I came by to visit and you and Gladys had been sculpting giant dicks out of crispy rice cereal treats and covering them with fondant? You had dozens and dozens of enormous, outrageously decorated dicks on every surface in your house."

"Hey, yeah," Ryder agrees, suddenly no longer laughing. "That was some disturbing shit, Gran. You've definitely corrupted us."

"Oh, you big babies. Those little wieners were nothing. You should have seen the gigantic dicks we had stored at Gladys's house. They were as tall as me and so thick and veiny." Gran sighs as if remembering the good old days. "Such a great baby shower."

"THAT WAS FOR A BABY SHOWER?" Ryder's eyes widen in horror. "Who in the hell for?" He leans in and whispers, "Are they okay?"

Gran shakes her head like she can't believe we're so dumb she has to explain this to us.

"It was for one of the staff at Peaceful Pines. It was really more of a gender reveal than a baby shower. You know how much I hate those things. So I figured, why let a blue puff of smoke have all the attention when what you're really wanting people to know is what kind of equipment the baby's going to be working with?" Gran looks around at everyone at the table, all of us staring at her with our mouths hanging open. "What? It was a boy."

The table erupts into uncontrollable laughter again. How could we not? Gran is the only person I know who would think throwing a penis party instead of a gender reveal party is the more appropriate way to go, but I suppose it makes sense when you think about it. The only thing the gender scan really tells you is whether the baby has a penis or a vagina.

"Oh my god, Gran," Rhea forces out between breaths. "What would have happened if it had been a girl?"

Gran looks at Rhea like she's sprouted another head. "Well, obviously Gladys and I would have spent hours and hours crafting edible vaginas instead of penises. Actually, I have a plan in mind for a balloon vagina archway for next time someone I know has a baby girl. It will be glorious." She shoots a pointed look over to Alex and Denise, the two pregnant women in our little group. "I can't wait to find out what you girls are having."

"It's a surprise," Alex, Denise, Connor, and Ryder all blurt out at the same time. I don't think any of them want Gran planning their baby showers now that they know what she's capable of.

"Well, Gran," Rhea says, pulling Gran into a side hug. "If I ever have a baby, I would love it if you would make me a balloon vagina archway, regardless of whether the baby is a boy or a girl. It would be hilarious to watch all the guests arrive through a giant vag tunnel."

Suddenly I'm not laughing anymore.

No matter how much I thought I didn't want Rhea, I still enjoyed the thought of her being a possibility. But now it is definitely out of the question. She wants kids, and I am having none. What my dad did to me and to my family has made me promise myself I will never pass on his genes. And I will never give myself the opportunity to become the same kind of man he was. His genes live in me, and having kids will only make them manifest. No thank you.

The conversation continues on around me, with Gran and Rhea coming up with a plan for a penis tunnel entryway involving white streamers and forcing guests to run through it to join the party. It's ridiculous and hilarious, and if I weren't in such a sour mood from thinking about my asshole father, I might laugh like everyone else.

I'm not feeling very social anymore, so I get up and excuse myself to the bathroom. Instead of going there, though, I wander downstairs and find myself in the bedroom that Connor keeps for me here. It's a basic room. A queen-size bed against the far wall with nightstands on either side, a dresser with a mirror on one side, and a bookshelf on the other. I keep a small selection of clothes and books here even though I rarely spend the night.

My muscles are tense, and my stomach has a lead weight in it after hearing Rhea talk about kids. Knowing I need to relax, I walk all the way into the room and crawl up onto the bed, curling myself around a pillow.

Why is it the thought of Rhea wanting kids making me feel so shitty? I've been insisting I'm not interested in her like that, and I know I can't have a meaningful relationship with anyone, let alone with someone who has confirmed that they want kids. But she's funny, and sweet, and adorable, and fuck is she hot. Thinking of her when I was in the shower yesterday led to the most intense orgasm of my life.

My friends are all falling in love and making it look so good. They love each other so easily, and it seems so comfortable. Alex and Connor have settled into their new life, and they have twins on the way. Even Ryder is married to Denise, for fuck's sake. And whatever Devon has going on with Xena, even though he swears it's nothing, makes them both look so happy. I don't begrudge my friends their joy, but I am jealous about how easy it is for them to feel happiness.

I've felt nothing but on edge for my entire life. At first, it was because I was doing everything I could to not set my dad off. Then, as I got older, dad got worse and worse, and I was never sure when I'd need to fight back until I finally moved out. And ever since the accident that killed my entire family, I've spent all my time trying to avoid becoming the same man my father was. I would deny myself any pleasure to ensure that never happens. No matter what else I do in life, nothing matters more than ensuring I don't turn into that asshole.

I used to think I was fine with that. But then I met Rhea, and I can't get her out of my head. Not that I've had many opportunities to try yet. I've seen her every day this weekend, and it's hard to forget someone when you're constantly being thrown together.

Thankfully, I have a full schedule at the shelter this coming week. The director is interviewing for new staff, so I'll keep things running smoothly while she's in meetings. Playing with the kids and helping the moms track down resources will go a long way in helping me keep my mind off of Rhea.

I hope.

21

New Friends and a Moody Drummer

Rhea

"Found him." Connor yells out from somewhere in the house.

Alex and I have just come back in from checking to see if Aiden slipped out into the yard while she was giving me a tour of the pool house. I think the story of how she and Connor reunited after so many years, when she was hired as his chef, unbeknownst to both of them, is so romantic. Makes me wish I had a love story of my own, but I've been so focused on my career all these years I haven't made time for romance. It didn't really fit into my life before, and now, with having to refocus on a new career, I'm not sure it ever will.

"Where was he?" Alex yells back. "We've looked everywhere."

Connor comes around the corner and into the kitchen to where we are.

"He was sleeping in his room downstairs. I can't even remember the last time he was down there. He never stays over anymore."

"Oh, you didn't wake him, did you? I can call an Uber." Looking around, I realize when Alex was giving me the tour, everyone else left. I came with Xena and she took off, as did anyone else who could have given me a ride back to my place. Which makes me think they all planned this together in advance. "I don't want to be an inconvenience. Really. It's no problem."

"He wouldn't have stayed all night, anyway," Connor assures me. "He never does. It can be three in the morning and he'll still go home. He's a bit of a homebody, I guess."

"It's true. Aiden keeps to himself more than the other guys. He's the smart, quiet, responsible one of the bunch."

"It should offend me that my fiancee is saying that, but it's a fact. Aiden is more mature than the rest of us put together." Connor wraps his arms around Alex and her growing baby bump. She said she's about four months along, but since she's pregnant with twins, her belly is adorably huge.

"Well, I hope he's not too put out at being stuck with me again. Although, I suppose it's a little better this time. At least I have my keys, so I'll be able to get into my place. I'd hate to invade his home again."

"It would probably be good for him if you do," Connor says. "With all the terrible memories he has in that place, he should have sold it long ago. I don't know why he's insisted on living there all these years."

Alex walks over and loads the dishwasher. It looks like everyone was kind enough to bring everything back from the dining room before they made their hasty escape.

"What do you mean, terrible memories?" I know he didn't want to tell me about his dad, but was it really so bad the house would hold that many bad feelings?

"Are you ready to go, Rhea?" Aiden comes around the corner so suddenly I jump in surprise when he speaks. My heart races and a nervous laugh bubbles up. I feel like he caught us doing something naughty instead of talking about a house. I wish he'd waited another minute to come up, though, so I could have heard what Connor was trying to tell me.

"Oh, hi Aiden. Sure. Only if you're sure it's not a problem. I can call for a ride instead, if you prefer. You've done so much for me this weekend, already. I feel bad asking you for anything else." And I really do. Not only because I don't normally need to rely on anyone, particularly someone I hardly know; I'm also a little nervous about being alone with him again. I know he's not attracted to me like I am to him, and I don't need any reminders. Just let me go home with my fantasies to my battery operated boyfriend. Less chance of rejection that way.

"It's no problem at all," he says, looking over at Connor and Alex. "In fact, with the way everyone's been behaving today, I probably should have expected it and tried harder to stay awake."

Alex and Connor look at each other, small smiles on their faces and guilty looks in their eyes. They had something to do with this alright. It's not a coincidence the only people left in the house are the ones who live here and me and Aiden.

"That's true. At least it's on the way, right? I can't guarantee anything, but it's possible you can slow down in front of my building and I'll be able to tuck and roll myself onto the sidewalk. You don't even have to stop." I do my best to keep a straight face. If he wants to be ridiculous about giving me a ride, then I can be ridiculous about accepting it.

Aiden laughs, while Alex and Connor look shocked. "That's a mighty nice offer, and I might have taken you up on it, but I don't think it's wise of you to be pulling any stunts wearing that dress. Next time, wear jeans and a leather jacket and I'll consider it."

I wanted to look nice tonight, so I wore one of the three dresses I own. This one is the short, yellow sundress with big pockets. And yes, I bought it for the pockets. And so I didn't feel too girly, I paired it with the same combat boots I wore with my fishnets and shorts the other night. At least I'm consistent, right?

"Deal." I turn to Alex and Connor. "Thank you again for inviting me. I had a great time."

"The invitation stands, as I told you earlier. We do this every Sunday and you are welcome to join us whenever you can." Alex comes over and gives me a hug, her little baby bump pushing into my stomach. "It was great to meet you."

"It was great to meet you, too. And thank you for dinner. It was delicious." Alex went Southern with her cooking and we ate from a selection of fried chicken, hot and cold salads, Mexican street corn, and the best mac and cheese I've ever tasted. She said it wasn't a fancy meal, but for someone who grew up on packets of instant ramen and plain oatmeal, any meal that has flavor is fancy.

"Thanks, guys, I'll see you this week sometime. I'm doing some extra work for the director while she works on some other stuff, though, so I probably won't be around much." Aiden gives a little two-finger wave and then holds his arm out for me to go first.

"Thanks for driving me home. Again," I say once we've made it to the car and Aiden opens the door for me. "I promise I have my keys this time."

"It's fine," he says, not even looking at me before he shuts the door behind me. He closed it so abruptly, I barely managed to yank all my arms and legs inside the car first. That could have been quite painful if I hadn't been paying attention. Also, it was kind of a dick move.

What's his problem now? He offered to drive me home.

"Um, excuse you?"

"What?" He asks as he starts the car.

"You nearly amputated my limbs with the door. Did I do something? I told you I was fine calling an Uber."

"I said it's fine. Don't worry about it." His words are clipped, and he doesn't even look at me, despite the fact he's not driving yet.

"Well, you might try working on your 'it's fine' face before you need to use it again. Because right now your face says 'fuck off' not 'it's fine'." I cross my arms over my chest and huff out a breath as I lean back in my seat. "There are enough things for me to worry about already. I don't need to add moody drummer to the list."

22

Stupid. Fucking. Asshole.

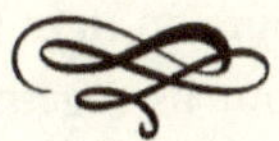

Aiden

"A MOODY DRUMMER? WHAT the hell are you talking about? What? Because I'm not hugging you like a hormonal pregnant woman and telling you how amazing it is to meet you, suddenly I'm moody?"

Her mouth drops open. I turn away and put the car in gear to start the drive to her place. I feel like I've stepped into an alternate reality and I need to get home and get to bed. How can she be sitting here calling me moody when all I'm doing is driving her home? I mean, I guess hearing Connor tell her my house has terrible memories has me on edge, but moody?

"No, idiot. I'm saying you're moody because you nearly closed my leg in the car door. And because you're acting all put out about giving me a ride, even though *I told you* I didn't mind getting an Uber. And because of the myriad other ways you've been acting moody toward me ever since we met. No one is forcing you to drive me home. You could have said no."

Did she just call me an idiot? I open and close my mouth a few times before I can get any words to come out.

"I'm only trying to drive you home. I don't know where you're getting all this other shit from," I say through gritted teeth.

She makes a noise that sounds like a combination of a grunt and a growl, and if she weren't so obviously mad at me, it would probably hit me right in the dick. Oh, who am I kidding? I'm getting hard just hearing it. This woman is way too far under my skin. I need to get away from her.

Maybe she's upset because my friends are trying to throw us together? She has a lot going on right now, and having all these nosy assholes trying to put us together is not something she needs to be dealing with. None of them know what it's like to lose the only job you've ever wanted, so of course they don't understand that she has more important things to think about.

"Look, I'm sorry if I closed the door too quickly. I'm distracted, and a little frustrated at my friends trying to push us together. They have no sense of boundaries. I was worried that they were making you feel uncomfortable, and I guess I was the one making you uncomfortable. So I'm sorry. I'll talk to them and get them to back off."

She responds to my apology with a nearly imperceptible nod and a slight raise of her eyebrows. If I hadn't glanced over at exactly the right moment, I would have missed it altogether. Whatever. I'm not apologizing any more than I already have for something she has to realize was an accident.

The rest of the ride to her place, neither of us says a word. I don't even have music on, so the only sound is the sound of the road passing beneath my car. Once we're back downtown, I pull up directly in front of Rhea's building. The creepy doll store is closed, as are most of the other stores on the street, so traffic, foot and vehicle, is minimal. It's much quieter than I would have expected a place downtown to be.

Once I'm parked, I turn off the car, and Rhea and I both sit staring out the windshield. Finally, she breaks the silence.

"You know, I don't get you. First, you chase me around trying to get me to go out with you, and now it's like you can't get away from me fast enough. It's not like I'm looking for a boyfriend or anything, but this going around in circles is making me dizzy." She unbuckles her seat belt and opens the door, leaning out of the car. Before she steps out, she turns her head and looks at me. "But thanks for the ride. I'll make sure it doesn't happen again." She gets out, closes the door behind her, and turns to her building.

Follow her around? When did I follow her around? Looking for a boyfriend?

I can't stop myself from chasing her. Before she even opens the door leading up to her apartment, I'm out of my car and beside her. She gets the door open and I follow her into the stairwell where I reach out and grab her hand, turning her to face me.

"Okay, let's get something straight. Maybe I have been trying to get away from you for the last few days. But that's only because I can't get you out of my fucking head. Ever since I saw you sitting on the sidewalk crying, you're all I can think about." I reach up and run both of my hands up into her hair, holding our foreheads together. My voice comes out in a growl. "And my dick has been at least half hard since I saw you at the club wearing that tank with me on it. And damn, your ass in those fucking tiny shorts was too perfect. All I've wanted to do since then is kiss you, taste you, and fuck you until you forget your name."

Her breath hitches, and my heart pounds in my chest. I can't bring myself to open my eyes, not wanting to see her face. If I see any amount of desire reflected at me, I don't know that I'll be able to control myself. As it is, my cock is hard as steel, trying to throb its way out of my pants to get to her.

"I saw you in the shower," she says in a rushed whisper. "When you left the door open. I stood and watched you touch yourself until you finished. It was the hottest thing I've ever seen."

My eyes fly open to see hers, lids low, pupils enormous. She slams her lips against mine, thrusting her tongue into my mouth, grabbing my shirt in her fists, and pulling me closer.

Holy fuck, she wants me too.

I return the kiss, meeting her enthusiasm with more of my own, and push her back against the wall. I run my hands over the soft skin of her shoulders and down her back, stopping to squeeze her ass before grabbing the backs of her thighs and lifting her legs up and around my waist.

"Fuck, Rhea. I want you so fucking bad," I whisper harshly against her mouth. "Tell me you want me too."

I shouldn't be fucking doing this, but I can't make myself stop. My need for her is burning a hole in my chest.

"I want you, Aiden. You're all I can think about."

She wants me too. Fuck, yes.

"Hands around my neck, Rhea," I whisper against her mouth. "We're going upstairs."

She slides her hands around my neck, moaning a noise that could be a 'yes' into our kiss. We kiss all the way up the stairs, where I'm pleased to find there's only one door. Rhea has the only apartment in this building. I'm going to make her scream my name tonight, so it's a good thing she doesn't have neighbors.

Rhea wiggles her way out of my arms, putting her legs on the floor without breaking our kiss. Her tongue massages mine while she fumbles around in her pockets.

"Got it!" She breaks away from me and spins around, shoving the key into the lock on her door. I wrap my arms around her waist and step into her from behind, placing kisses along the side of her neck, down past the strap of her dress and onto her shoulder.

Once she has the door open, I spin her around again, walking her backwards into her apartment and pressing my lips to hers. Her tongue comes out to lick the seam of my mouth, urging me to open for her. She reaches her hands up into my hair, slowly unwinding the hair tie's holding it up, before getting it loose and dropping it somewhere. Her fingers find their way back into my hair, running through it and shaking it loose, her nails scraping gently along my scalp and sending shivers down my spine.

I busy my hands undoing the buttons down the front of her dress, pushing it back off her shoulders and letting it fall to the floor.

"You smell so good," she says, nuzzling into my neck, and scraping her teeth along my collarbone. "Get this off. I need to see you." She's pulling up on my shirt in a hurry to get me undressed.

I step back, reaching back to pull it over my head. She growls when she sees me and the sound goes straight to my cock, forcing it to jump against my zipper.

Rhea is standing in only her bra and panties, having also lost her shoes somewhere along the way. If I had any thoughts about stopping this before it went any further, the sight of her nearly naked has driven them all out of my head. All I can think about is getting inside her.

A more beautiful woman has never walked the earth.

Rhea isn't built like the groupies and models who used to follow us guys in the band around, where I would pick my one-nighters from, back when I was experimenting with doing that. She's tall, even without shoes, and she's solid. Not too muscular, but I can see the strength in her thighs and the separation in the center of her abs. She's strong, and it shows, but she still has a softness about her that I can't resist.

I reach out, taking her by the hip and drawing her close to me again, using one hand to tilt her head while I bend down to kiss her. I take her soft lips in mine, slower than before, savoring the taste. My lips kiss a trail along her jawline. One hand in her hair tilts her head to expose her neck to me. I run my nose down the soft skin of her shoulder, inhaling her salty, fresh scent.

"God, you smell good," I tell her, as I trace kisses along her bra strap, following it down to the cup, which I pull down, exposing her breast. The prettiest little pink nipple pokes out from her areola, and I reach out and flick it with my tongue. "And you taste even better than I thought you would."

Rhea's hands tangle into my hair again while I continue to lavish attention on first one nipple and then the other. We've barely made it past the entryway of her apartment and I'm ready to come in my pants like a clumsy teenager. I slide my hand up from Rhea's hip and, with a flick of my fingers, undo her bra. She lowers her arms and helps me slip it off, leaving it to fall to the floor at our feet. I stand back and look at the gorgeous woman in front of me. Her soft skin has tan lines, making it obvious she spends a lot of time outdoors in shorts and tanks. I'm willing to bet she's not just tanning out there, though. Her body looks like it's made for being used, not for lying around.

"You are so fucking incredible," I say, palming her breasts, running my thumbs over her taut nipples.

"Bedroom," Rhea pants as she moves and tries to pull me along with her. I kick off my shoes and fist her hair, taking her mouth in another desperate kiss. I've never felt this out of control before. I know this shouldn't be happening, but I can't seem to stop myself. I need to feel her, to touch her everywhere. I need to be inside her.

I need it like I need air.

My hands roam Rhea's skin, seemingly of their own volition, and once again I'm lifting her by the thighs, encouraging her to wrap her legs and arms around me. I can't even pretend I have any control. The only thing going through my mind right now is making her scream my name.

Somehow she directs me to her bedroom without breaking the kiss or letting go, and once inside I kick the door closed and slam her against it with my body. I grind my cock against her, groaning as I thrust my tongue into her mouth, her answering whimpers and moans telling me it feels as good to her as it does to me. Slowly, she slides down my body, dragging her heat down the length of my dick, causing me to release a few more groans of my own.

Fuck. I don't think I'm going to survive this.

She reaches her hand down, working on my belt buckle, and soon she's pushing my jeans and boxers down to the floor as she drops to her knees.

"Fuck, Aiden," she groans before licking my dick from root to tip in one long, slow stroke. "I'm going to enjoy this."

She circles the head of my cock with her tongue and my head falls back as a moan leaves my mouth. I'm lost to the sensation as she pulls me to the back of her throat, surrounding my cock with the slick heat of her mouth. It feels even better than I imagined.

"As much as I would love to let you keep doing that," I say, finally gathering my wits enough to pull her to her feet, "a gentleman always makes sure the lady comes first." I kiss away her protests and lean her against the door.

Bending over slowly, I kiss a trail along her neck, down to her breasts again, pulling a nipple into my mouth briefly as I kick my pants away. I don't stop at her breasts, though; I continue kissing a trail down her stomach until I'm on my knees in front of her. It's the opposite of my shower fantasy, but the view is even more amazing.

She reaches down, trying to pull me up again, but I ignore her frantic hands and gently lick along the waistband of her panties.

"I don't think I could live another day if I don't get my mouth on this sweet pussy of yours, Rhea," I murmur against her skin. I pull down one side of her panties a little and graze my teeth against the skin of her hip. "Can I?"

I look up to meet her eyes, and she nods her assent.

"Yes. God, yes. I want that so much."

I take my time lowering her soaked panties, kissing and licking every inch of skin as I uncover it, feeling Rhea shake a little as she whimpers. I slide her panties all the way off and lift one of her legs, placing it over my shoulder. She's wet, glistening, and so ready. Teasing her, I place gentle kisses just above her clit, and down along the creases where her thighs meet her body. The smell of her arousal hits me suddenly and I can't stop the growl that starts deep in my throat. I need to consume her, devour her, mark her as mine.

"Fuck, Rhea, your pussy smells amazing. Do you know how crazy you're making me? I need to feel you come on my tongue. Can you do that for me, baby? Will you come on my tongue and let me taste you?"

I don't give her time to answer before I plunge my face into her pussy, licking her from entrance to clit in one long stroke. Her moan is the only answer I need. I lick, flick, and suck her clit, alternating with plunging my tongue inside her until I feel her tremble, and she grabs me roughly by my hair, fastening me in place, grinding her pussy against my face. My cock pulses as she grinds on me, fucking my face, and I reach down and fist myself in one hand, groaning at the tightness of my grip. I focus all my attention on Rhea's clit, sucking it into my mouth and using little side-to-side flicks with my tongue, until she freezes, pressing my face into her, mewling whimpers escaping her throat.

"Yes, Aiden, don't stop. Like that," she chokes out in a harsh whisper.

I continue to suck and lick her through her orgasm, each flick of my tongue causing a tremor to run through her, matched only by the throbbing in my cock, until she pulls me up her body by my hair. It should hurt, but instead, the sting of it feels amazing.

She slams her mouth into mine, thrusting her tongue in deep, and reaches down, taking over my grip on my cock. I still have her leg over one arm, and a moan escapes me as she squeezes my dick and pulls me closer with her other hand. She slides my cock along her slit, wetting the head with the evidence of her arousal, using it to rub her clit more, before lining me up with her entrance, and lowering herself slightly, taking me inside her a little.

"Fuck, you feel so fucking good," she says into my mouth. "I want to feel all of you."

In one motion, I pick up her other leg and thrust all the way into her, ramming her so hard against the door there's a slight cracking sound. She grabs my face in both hands, kissing me roughly, moaning against my mouth. I slam into her again. This time, the cracking sound is louder, making me stop to look into her eyes.

"Forget it," she says, pulling me into another rough kiss, tightening her thighs around me to slide up my dick.

"Bed," I grunt, hoping she gets my meaning as I'm pulling her off the door and turning around. I carry her to the bed with my cock still buried inside her, the motion of my footsteps causing me to pump into her slightly. If I don't get this under control, I'm going to come too soon. She feels fucking amazing. I want this to last as long as possible. And I definitely need to feel her come on my dick.

When we reach the side of the neatly made bed, I lower her down gently, following her body with my own, ensuring we don't come apart. I grip one leg, pulling her knee up to my shoulder and begin slowly pumping into her, rolling my hips to grind against her clit every time I bottom out.

"Ohmygod, Aiden," Rhea breathes. "Don't stop. I will kill you if you stop."

"Don't worry, baby. I will never stop." I chuckle at her threat. But I mean it. I could do this forever with her and die a cheerful man. This feels too fucking good.

She grabs my hair with one hand and my ass with the other, forcing me deeper while she bites and sucks on the sensitive spot where my neck and shoulder meet. She's marking me and I don't even fucking care.

"I knew your ass would feel amazing as you pumped into me," she groans against my shoulder, squeezing my ass for emphasis. "I thought about it when I watched you in the shower. You looked so fucking hot I couldn't look away."

I may not have a lot to compare to, but I'm pretty sure sex has never felt this good. If I'd ever felt anything like this in the past, then sex would have been a lot harder to stay away from. Whatever this is with Rhea, it's something different altogether.

"Rhea, you feel too fucking good, baby. Please tell me you're close." The tingling in the head of my dick tells me I won't last much longer, but I really want to feel her come once more before I do. My balls are tightening, pulling in close, readying for my release.

Her body freezes slightly, and her pussy pulses around me, and I recognize the beginnings of her orgasm. Finally, I can let myself come. My vision goes black and sparks shoot up my spine, my thrusts becoming erratic. I take her lips in a deep kiss, slamming into her one, two, three times, before I still, collapsing on top of her, spilling into her, filling her up, grinding against her while she spasms around me, her pulsing orgasm dragging mine from me as she milks me of every drop.

My heart skips a beat. My breath catches.

Every drop?

EVERY FUCKING DROP?

"FUCK!"

I jump up off of her, scrambling to my feet. My hands fly to my hair as I look frantically for my clothes. *How did you let this happen?*

"We forgot to use a fucking condom. I can't believe I did that! Why didn't you say anything?"

I'm scrambling around, throwing on my boxers and jeans, buckling my belt, and periodically running my hands frantically through my hair. Rhea lies naked on the bed and looks at me dumbfounded, probably wondering if I've lost it.

I *have* lost it.

I have never forgotten a condom, ever. And certainly not since my family's accident. I never want to risk passing on my genetic material and yet, shortly after meeting this woman, I throw caution to the wind.

"I can't believe I fucked you bareback. What the fuck was I thinking?"

I race out to the living room and gather up my shirt and shoes and let myself out of Rhea's apartment without so much as saying goodbye.

Fuck, I'm an asshole. A stupid. fucking. asshole.

23

Peanut Butter Cups Full of Sadness

Rhea

WELL.

That turned out a lot differently than I thought it would.

Of all the things I logically expect to happen when I sleep with someone, having them run away screaming immediately afterward is not anywhere near the top of the list, yet here we are.

I'm laying here, still naked, listening to Aiden run down the stairs to the main door of my apartment. He jumped off of me so fast when he came it's almost as though he shot himself out of me like a champagne cork. Except instead of bubbles, I'm stuck here with his come leaking out of me onto my duvet cover.

So that's fun.

I can't even begin to piece together his massive overreaction, so instead I get up and take myself to the shower to get cleaned up.

Once I'm in the shower, my mind takes a darker turn, wondering what the hell is wrong with me to cause him to run like that. Is this like the video game incident the other night? Did I beat him at sex and he had to run away in shame?

He seemed pretty concerned we forgot to use a condom, and it's not that I'm not concerned, but if he'd stuck around long enough, I could have at least told him I have an IUD. I've never forgotten to use a condom either, and I know for a fact I'm clean. I have a copy of the test results to prove it too, if he'd been interested in that. I can only hope he has a clean bill of health as well.

I wash on autopilot, still in shock from Aiden's hasty departure, and before I realize it, I'm turning off the shower and stepping out onto the bathmat. Wrapping myself up in a fluffy bathrobe, I walk out to the living room to find my phone. Xena's going to hear about this disaster. She's the one who wanted me to use him to bang my worries away, after all. It's only fair she deals with the aftermath. After a quick detour to my freezer to grab some chocolate peanut butter cups, I settle in on the couch and send Xena a text.

Rhea - Cobwebs are gone, but you owe me an explanation.

Xena - Yes! It worked. Wait until I tell Devon.

Rhea - Yeah. It worked until he ran away screaming as soon as he was done. Ask me how awesome I feel about that.

Xena - He did what?! Why the hell would he do something like that? What an asshole.

Xena - And you are awesome. Don't forget it.

Rhea - Uh, yeah.

Rhea - It was practically in-stantaneous, too. He came, and then he jumped up and started ranting and getting dressed. I don't think he even put his shirt on before he went out to his car.

Xena - What a dick. He's getting the sword treatment next time he comes into the shop.

Rhea - Tell me about it. And thanks. If anyone deserves the sword, it's him.

I unwrap a peanut butter cup and toss it into my mouth, throwing the wrapper onto the coffee table in front of me. These treats have been in my freezer for months and I haven't had a reason to get into them until now.

I initially bought them in case I needed a little pick-me-up while I was waiting to hear from the police commission, but I was too hopeful during that time to need them. I really didn't expect that I wouldn't be rejoining the force. I suppose my three months off could have been better spent looking for work, or thinking about future career choices, but instead, I spent a lot of time trail running and keeping up with my weightlifting routine at the gym. Because I wanted to stay in great shape for when I got my badge back. Looks like that wasn't necessary after all.

The three dots on the messaging app keep appearing and disappearing, telling me Xena is trying to type me a message. I'm not even sure it's worth talking about anymore, to be honest. We had sex and then he left. Granted, it was super hot, amazing sex, but he literally ran away from me the *second* it was over, so it was a fuck and chuck all the same. It's not like I was expecting him to stick around and hold me all night after or anything, but a little consideration would have been nice. Maybe a thank you, and a nice high five for a job well done, or even a hearty handshake?

My phone chimes, telling me Xena has finally figured out what she wants to say.

```
Xena - Okay, so from what I
hear, this is not Aiden's normal
behavior. But he apparently has
more than a normal fear of
getting someone pregnant, and
Devon thinks he hasn't actually
slept with anyone in ages. Maybe
even years.
```

Well, fuck. That makes a little more sense then. No wonder forgetting a condom freaked him out so much. He probably thinks I'm going to get pregnant and he'll be stuck with a kid he doesn't want.

Rhea - Shit.

Rhea - It was pretty spur of the moment and we forgot to use a condom.

Xena - You what?! What the hell, girl? You gotta wrap that shit up. No glove, no love. You know better.

Rhea - Yes, I do. I was so caught up I don't even know what happened. It's like he was the only thing that existed. I've never had anything like that happen before.

Xena - Well?

Xena - Was it good at least?

I don't think there are enough words to even explain how good it was. Good? Great? Amazing? Magnificent? Fucktacular?

The way he touched me, it was like he knew my body better than I did. And the things he said? Fuck. Just thinking about it is getting me all hot and bothered again. If that asshole has ruined sex for me, I'm going to be so pissed. You can't give someone the best orgasms they've ever had and then run away immediately. That's a dick move if there ever was one. But I can't deny that it was good. And my body does feel more relaxed than it did before. I feel sort of boneless, actually. And his ass felt more amazing than I imagined. My fingers flex involuntarily, wanting to squeeze it some more.

Not that I'm going to tell Xena all of this. Knowing her, this entire conversation is going to make its way to Aiden through Devon, probably before I even fall asleep tonight. I love her, but she has a big mouth.

Rhea - Yeah, it was pretty good.

Xena - See? I told you he would bang your worries away.

Rhea - I still don't have a job or even an idea of what I'm going to do, but for tonight that's okay. I'm going to kick back and read for a bit and then go to bed. I'll talk to you soon. You'll see me tomorrow sometime when I come in for coffee.

Xena- Sounds good. I'll expect more details when I see you. I need measurements, reenactments, and details. All the details.

I reach for another peanut butter cup while I pull up the Kindle app on my phone. I might as well finish the romance novel I've been reading. I may not get my own happy ending, but I can live vicariously through the characters in a book for a while. They'll help me forget my own shitty lack of a love life.

Sometimes I wonder if the men in these books could actually exist. Not the characters, but men like them. Strong, sexy, loving, and all the other good stuff I've never found all together in one actual human male. The older I get and the more men I meet, the less it seems possible.

I'm nearly at the end of the book, so it doesn't take all that long to finish reading it. I'm a little surprised at the enormous pile of peanut butter cup wrappers I've amassed on my coffee table. Thinking back, I can only clearly remember opening three of them, but there are at least a dozen wrappers staring back at me. I guess Aiden running away the way he did is affecting me more than I thought if I'm eating my feelings like this. Probably need to unpack that a little more tomorrow, but for now, I'm going to forget it and go to bed.

I replay everything with Aiden while I wash up and brush my teeth. It was such a brief encounter, but I'm feeling almost like I've broken up with a boyfriend. I'm a little hollow in the chest, and a lot sad, especially after the gorgeous, happy ending the couple in my book had.

It was a much better ending than the dude running away as soon as he nutted, anyway.

24

Revenge is Best Served Drunk

Aiden

FUCK, AIDEN. HOW COULD you be so stupid? You're nearly forty years old. You should know better than to forget a condom. What the fuck?!

To say I'm pissed at myself would be an understatement. I haven't even made it home yet, because I've been driving around berating myself for being stupid enough to forget a condom.

And, as if forgetting a condom wasn't stupid enough, I jumped off Rhea and ran out of there like my ass was on fire. She's pretty cool, and she definitely didn't deserve that. I'm going to have to apologize, but I can't bring myself to get near her again. Not when I can get that out of control. I'll need to get her number from Devon. It's better if we don't see each other in person anymore.

And, not that it's more important than any other consequence that will come from this, but I'm sure I won't be able to get coffee at Bump & Grind anymore. Not if I don't want to be on the receiving end of one of Xena's sword tantrums. I'm sure I deserve it, but even being subjected to a beating with a rubber sword probably isn't enough of a punishment.

I should have tried harder to stay away from Rhea. I knew something was going on with me. And now, I don't even know what could happen. I'm not worried about diseases or anything like that. I know for a fact I'm clean. I'm pretty sure she would have had regular physicals at least until recently and she doesn't seem like the type to purposely try to infect anyone with anything. But I am worried about the no condom thing, because even worse than a disease, would be the chances of having a baby with half my DNA. Because my DNA is poison.

Just like dear old dad.

This shitty self talk lasts about an hour, all while I drive around in a daze, until eventually I'm pulling into my driveway, parking next to Johnny. His door opens as soon as I get out of my car.

"What the hell are you doing here?" I have a lot of my own shit to deal with. I don't need Johnny crying over his love life right now. I don't have it in me to console him.

He holds up two bottles and sways a little. "Thought maybe you'd want to have a drink or seven with me? Gotta warn you, though. I got a head start." He lifts the bottle to his mouth and takes a few swallows, spilling some onto his shirt.

"Fuck, dude. You didn't drive here like that, did you?"

"No. No, no, nooo." He drags out the last word and then takes another drink. "I've been waiting here for a while. Tried to get Becca to talk to me when we were leaving Connor's place and she was going on another date. So I figured it's time for me to give up, and I came over here to get drunk with you. Travis has been too busy with whatever secret shit he's been up to lately, so I thought maybe you'd be a good surrogate brother."

Seems like Johnny forgot that I rarely drink, but he might be onto something for tonight. I wouldn't mind having a few drinks and forgetting what an asshole I was leaving Rhea the way I did. Fuck it, I might as well drink. I made a pretty huge mistake already today. And it's not like I'm going to run out and do something dumber than that.

"Come on in," I say, unlocking the door and motioning Johnny to head in. "I could use a drink or two."

Johnny goes in ahead of me and settles himself on the couch. I detour to the kitchen and grab myself a glass. Johnny may be fine drinking straight from the bottle, but I'm not planning on getting trashed tonight, so I'm going to need the glass.

I grab the unopened bottle of whiskey Johnny brought and pour myself two fingers. That's more than enough for my purposes right now.

"So tell me what's going on with Becca."

Johnny gives me the rundown. Seems he's been after her for a while now, and she's not looking for a relationship. She likes to date around, but thinks a relationship will take up too much of her time.

I refill my drink as he tells the story.

"So, like I said before, then? She's got her hands full with her business and doesn't have time. So what's your problem then? You've never wanted to settle down before, either."

Talking Johnny through the problems in his love life isn't nearly as good a distraction as I thought it would be. I pour myself another drink while he thinks over what I've just said.

Johnny looks down at his bottle, nearly half empty now, and lets out a breath. His shoulders slump and he leans forward with his elbows on his knees.

"You've got it all wrong, man. I've always wanted to settle down. I've been looking for the right woman. I thought Becca was the one," he says to his hands. "But I guess I was wrong." He sits up and takes another deep drink from his bottle before finally putting it down on the coffee table. "Maybe it was indigestion?"

He leans back against the couch and laces his hands behind his head, closing his eyes and putting his feet up on the table.

"This sucks, man," he says.

He's not wrong. It does suck. I throw back the rest of my drink and pour another.

"Wanna jam for a bit?" I ask, standing with my drink in one hand and the bottle in the other.

"Yeah, sure," Johnny says, standing and grabbing his bottle, too. "Back in the garage, for old time's sake."

I lead the way to the garage, flipping on the lights before heading over to my drum kit.

"Take your pick," I say, pointing at the guitars on the wall and the amps stacked up by the door. "I know they're not what you're used to, but I'm sure you'll find something you like."

I keep a small collection of instruments here, not that I'm an expert at playing them all. I'd say I'm proficient at playing bass, and adequate at guitar and piano. All the other instruments I have in here are percussion instruments and though I rarely use them, I can play them all.

"I have an acoustic up in my room too, if you prefer. Sometimes I play around with it if I can't sleep." I've been messing around with writing some of my own song for something to do. They're not really Sleeping Dogs style songs though, so I've never brought them to the studio to show the guys. I stick to the drums when I'm with them.

Johnny grabs a vintage Gretsch I bought at auction and had fully restored a few years ago. He gets himself all set up with the pedals he wants, connects the amp, and tunes the guitar.

I get on the throne behind my custom drum kit, my favorite of all my kits, because I could have it finished in a neon hot pink color. It was my little sister's favorite color before she died. Not to mention I selected everything myself, from wood type, to grain orientation, to drum head material and hardware colors.

"What do you want to play?" Johnny asks when he's finished tuning the Gretsch. "You start and I'll jump in."

I start us off with a blues shuffle and Johnny jumps in with a classic blues riff that gradually morphs into something a little more complicated. Seems like we're both on the same page with the style of music tonight. I haven't shared the issues I'm having because of my encounter with Rhea, but a little bluesy rock feels about right for where my mind is right now.

We play for a couple of hours, alternating between playing and drinking, until we're both sweaty and exhausted, laying on the floor of my rehearsal space, staring at the ceiling.

"So you're having a shit day too, huh?" Johnny asks, attempting to drink out of his now empty whiskey bottle. I pass him mine, even though it's nearly empty too.

"Yeah, you could say that."

He drinks from my bottle. I'm not sure how he's still conscious. Then again, I'm not sure how I am either. I never drink this much. I do stupid things when I drink this much.

"Is it because of that Rhea chick? You were looking at her with hearts in your eyes this afternoon."

"Shut up," I say, and reach out to punch him in the arm, missing entirely even though he's right next to me. "It's complicated."

Complicated is an understatement. I have possibly impregnated her with my demon DNA, and she recently got fired from her dream job. Her life was already fucked up, and I made it worse. Well, the asshole she arrested deserves some of the blame for fucking everything up in the first place. Someone should make him pay for that.

Shit! That's it.

"I have a great idea. Come on." I jump up, well, more like stumble up, from where I'm laying on the floor, and make my way back into the house. "We need to go somewhere."

I don't wait to see if Johnny follows me before I start rummaging around in the cleaning supplies closet. I grab a shopping bag and fill it with supplies before grabbing my phone and calling the one person who can help us right now. I only hope he answers. It is the middle of the night now, after all.

The phone rings three times before a sleepy Devon mumbles a greeting.

"Devon, I need a ride. Right now. And I need you to find out the name and address of the guy that got Rhea fired. It's time for my side business to be put to some use again."

"Oh, fuck. You know this is a stupid idea, don't you? You're going to get caught. And if you don't, she certainly will. She's the only person who has reason to retaliate against this guy."

I had thought that before myself, but if he's the kind of guy who'd push his wife down the stairs in front of a cop, then there have to be other people he's wronged along the way too. I'm pretty sure none of us will feel much if any, blowback from this.

"Devon, get your ass over to my place and pick us up. Johnny needs the distraction, and I need to do this. She didn't deserve what happened."

"Ugh, fine. I'll be there in twenty minutes. Don't leave without me." He hangs up before I can answer.

I called him for a ride. Why would we leave without him?

"What are you doing?" Johnny finally finds his way into the house. "What's in the bag?" He points at my shopping bag full of supplies. He seems to have left the rest of the whiskey in the garage, which is probably a good thing. Neither of us needs any more liquid courage for what I have planned. In fact, it's probably best if we sober up a little. I get the coffeemaker going while I grab us each a bottle of water from the fridge.

"Drink this," I say, tossing him the bottle, which he promptly drops on the floor. "We need to be sober-ish before Devon gets here to pick us up."

I reach into the cupboard above the coffeemaker and grab two travel mugs. We're going to need as much coffee as we can get.

"Oh sweet. Devon's coming? That's awesome, man. What are we going to do?"

"We'll decide for sure once we get there. I have a few ideas, though." I sit beside Johnny at the counter and explain my plan to avenge Rhea while we wait for the coffee and for Devon. If all goes well, this guy is going to have a lot of explaining to do to his neighbors tomorrow.

And I, for one, can't wait.

25

Attack of the Fifty Foot Yard Dick

Rhea

THE SOUND OF MY phone buzzing on my nightstand wakes me up and a look over at the clock tells me it's only two in the morning. I stretch and grab my phone, sitting up while I answer.

"Hello?"

"*Hey, get dressed. I'm coming to pick you up.*" Kaden barks into the phone. He sounds pissed off. "*Your boyfriend is doing something stupid.*"

"I'm sorry. My what?!" I sit up in bed and rub my eyes. Something strange is going on and I have a funny feeling I know exactly who is at the bottom of this. The dumbass.

"*Aiden called Devon for the address of the guy who got you fired. So Devon called me to get it, and to let me know to meet them there. He wants me make sure nothing gets too out of hand. I figured you'd want to deal with this yourself.*" I can hear him shuffling around in the background, keys rattling and doors closing, before he starts his car.

"Oh, for crying out loud. He's not my boyfriend. But he *is* a dumbass." I roll my eyes, but I get out of bed and pull on my joggers, anyway. "I'll meet you downstairs."

"*See you shortly,*" Kaden says, and hangs up.

That fucking idiot, Aiden. What the hell is he thinking? Doesn't he realize that I'll get blamed for anything he does to this guy? Plus, getting into it with Franklin Martin is only going to get him an assault charge. I don't think the rest of the guys in his band would be too happy with that, considering they're all settling down and starting families now. The last thing they want is bad press because one of them doled out some vigilante justice for someone he hardly even knows.

I grab a hoodie from my closet and walk out to the living room while pulling it over my head. The peanut butter cup wrappers are still on the coffee table where I left them, so I clean those up and drink a glass of water in the kitchen. I wish I had a coffee but Kaden will be here right away and I don't have time to make one. I'll get him to drive through somewhere after we stop whatever idiocy Aiden is getting himself into.

Making sure I have my keys and my phone, I leave my apartment and go downstairs to wait for Kaden in the entryway. He lives nearby, so it's not long before he pulls up in front of the building in his beat up old pickup truck. He says it's red, but the only color I've ever been able to pick out is rust brown. It's so rusty, I can almost see through it.

"Oh, good," I say, climbing into the passenger side. "You brought a nice, reliable vehicle."

"Haha, very funny, Ryan," he says, glaring at me with tired, red eyes. "This thing is going to last until the end of time. Nothing can stop this beast."

"Yeah, it's like a cockroach that way." I smile at him and he shoots me a dirty look.

Kaden loves this truck because his grandfather gave it to him years ago, and he won't get rid of it until it's impossible to fix. He hasn't said as much, but when that happens, I'm pretty sure he's going to use it as a lawn ornament or turn it into a fountain or something. To be fair, all the rust on it is the same rust that was there when he was given the truck. He takes care of this thing like it's a three hundred thousand dollar Bentley instead of the rusty bucket of bolts it is.

"So what's going on, anyway?" I ask. He didn't really explain what that asshole Aiden was up to, only that we needed to stop him.

"I'm not totally sure," he says, navigating his beast of a truck away from the curb. "Devon just told me to meet them there. I don't think he knows what Aiden and Johnny are thinking."

"Johnny is there too? These guys are a lot dumber than I thought."

"Maybe not. Sounds like they want some justice for what this guy did to you. Maybe their methods aren't sound, but it is kind of nice. If I weren't a cop, I might have been tempted to do the same thing. You know it's not right the way they fired you. That was a clean arrest. I'm pissed off my word means nothing in your defense." He's been ranting about this off and on in text messages and phone calls ever since the police commission denied my first appeal.

"Well, if the precinct would have been on top of things and gotten body cams into the budget a long time ago, like they promised they would, then this wouldn't be an issue. We would have had the whole incident on film and his story wouldn't have meant shit." Not that I'm too upset at his denial of the facts. That's to be expected from abusive dickheads like him. I'm more disappoint his wife wouldn't press charges against him. "I only hope his wife is okay. He won't stop until someone stops him, or until she gets away." *Or worse*, I think to myself. *I really hope it doesn't come to that.*

"Thank god they don't have any kids. When she leaves, she can make a clean break and she'll never have to see him again."

Kaden knows about my mom, and he feels strongly about getting children out of abusive situations. I'm lucky I was young when I got away from her, and I'm even luckier that my foster families weren't as bad as some of the horror stories you hear about. Aiden was relieved about that too, if I remember correctly.

The asshole's house is on the same side of town as Connor and Alex's place, but in a slightly less exclusive neighborhood. Alex's place has a large parcel of land, and it seems like it isn't even in the city anymore with how private it is. This guy's neighborhood is expensive, but you can tell the builder wanted the biggest houses on the smallest lots possible, to maximize sales. It's one of those places where all the houses look like matching out-of-place monstrosities. And you just know that you can see into the neighbor's bathroom.

I'd rather my tiny apartment downtown any day. For as close as it is to everything, it's actually very private. That's what happens when you live upstairs from a nightmare factory slash creepy doll store.

"Here we are," Kaden says, pulling up behind a black Escalade a few houses down from where I made that fateful arrest. "Let's go see if we made it in time to stop them."

We both slide out of the truck, closing the doors quietly. A truck like this might draw too much attention in a nicer neighborhood, but it looks like Kaden put a decoy lawnmower and some gardening tools in the box. If necessary, we can say we're the landscaping crew, I guess. We both pull our hoods up, instinctively hiding our faces, just in case.

"Nice cover," I say, pointing to the lawnmower. "Very clever."

"Oh, haha, yeah," he says, running his hand over the stubble on his chin. "I was actually helping a friend with their yard work earlier today. But yeah, it is a good cover story. I bet the people in this neighborhood would love it if their landscapers would work in the middle of the night. That way, they'd never have to see them."

Walking up to the house, we see Devon standing with his hands in his pockets, eyes focused on the nicely manicured, if somewhat small, front lawn. It looks like he's had the same idea as us, and covered up with a hat and a hood.

And then I see two idiots running around, dumping something from containers, while giggling uncontrollably and periodically hissing out a loud 'shhhh' at each other. Looks like we're too late to stop whatever idiotic plan they've hatched. But at least they're also not easily identifiable.

Aiden and Johnny are in fine form, from the looks of it. Neither of them is staying on their feet for long, and neither of them is being what I'd consider quiet. I'd say this couple either sleeps like the dead or they're out of town. There's no way they wouldn't be able to hear these two idiots if they were home.

"Hey, man," Kaden greets Devon with a wave. "What do we have here?"

"Hey, Kade. Rhea. Sorry to get you up. Aiden got it in his head that he needed to avenge your firing and I thought maybe you'd like to see it, or stop it, or something. I'm not sure why. I figured you'd want to be involved."

I give him a nod of thanks and edge closer to where Aiden and Johnny are working their magic. It would have probably been better if I hadn't come, but I'm actually really curious about what it is Aiden is planning here. He looks to be dumping stuff on the lawn and running around in a big circle.

"You guys been here long?" I whisper back to Devon, loud enough for him to hear me over the giggle twins.

"Not too long," he says back. "Just long enough to realize no one is home and they don't have security cameras. So these two morons should be safe."

"Hey, baby," Aiden stumbles over to me, having finally noticed I was here. "What are you doing out so late, in a place like here? A woman in your condition should be resting." He smiles and exhales straight whiskey. I blink rapidly, fanning at my eyes, trying to lessen the burning sensation caused by his breath hitting my eyeballs. Thank god there are no open flames around here or he'd be getting a hurried introduction to the fine art of breathing fire. "You're so pretty," he says, booping me on the nose.

"Um, yeah, okay." I chuckle. He's definitely drunk. And what the hell does he mean by 'a woman in my condition?' "I got a call you were doing something I might want to see. What are you up to?"

He giggles and waves his arm. "I have a giant penis for you. Come, let me show you."

"Jesus, don't say it like that, you idiot," Devon yells from where he stands with Kaden. "She'll think you want to show her *your* dick, not the giant salt dick you made on this guy's lawn."

"Oh." Aiden leans over and says in what I'm sure he thinks is a whisper, "I already showed you that, though. Right, baby?"

I widen my eyes and give him the universal 'shut your fucking mouth' glare, and hope he's not too drunk to get the hint. He's fucking adorable right now, but the last thing I want is to talk about him showing me his penis earlier. With him, or with anyone else.

"Okay, I think that's enough talking for now," I say while leading Aiden away from a very surprised-looking Kaden, and a not at all surprised-looking Devon. "Show me this penis and then we can all go home before someone calls the cops."

I still haven't decided if I'm going to be the one calling the cops. I probably should, considering how long my only purpose in life was upholding the law, but I can't help feeling a little joy at the idea of getting revenge on the guy who got me fired.

Everyone else has talked about how unfair it is that I got fired. Talked, expressed concern, yelled, complained, and all manner of other verbal commiserations. Aiden is the *only* one who has actually done something about it. It's an incredibly stupid something, but it's nice to know someone cares enough to say fuck the consequences and take action. Drawing an enormous dick on a lawn isn't exactly chivalrous in the traditional sense, but it's the closest I've ever come to someone avenging my honor.

It's sort of sweet.

"Oh, yeah. Okay, yeah," he says, stumbling to keep up with me. "I did the balls and Johnny did the shaft. See?" He points to where Johnny is pushing a little one-handled bucket on wheels, leaving a trail of white beside him.

"Is that... is that what they use to make the lines on fields for sports?"

"Yup," Aiden says, puffing up his chest. "It's full of salt. This is part of my side business. I take meaningless, petty revenge on people. Rarely, I will also punch them in the face. But usually, I do something like ruin their lawn by burning giant dicks into them, as I did here."

What the hell?

"What? People pay you to do this?"

"What? Oh no, I call it a side business but I do it for free. It makes me feel good to ruin an abusive asshole's day. I suppose I could call it a hobby, but that sounds so childish."

"Oh, yes, definitely. Calling it a hobby is what would make this childish," I deadpan, gesturing to the giant salty dick in the yard in front of us. "It certainly couldn't be the dick drawing."

I shake my head and walk to the nearest salt line, part of one of the set of giant testicles. This dick has to be four or five car lengths, at least, and I could lie down and stretch out inside each testicle without touching the outlines. There is no way to describe this other than to say it is a giant dick and balls. It takes up the entirety of the Martins' front yard.

"I have a friend flying a drone over tomorrow when it's light out so we can see how it looks in its entirety. The trouble with dicks of this magnitude is it's hard to picture them as a complete unit."

I snort back a laugh. I must be delirious because this shit is hilarious. Aiden is standing beside me with the goofiest grin on his face. He looks so adorably proud of himself that I *almost* forget I'm still pissed at him for the whole popping-out-of-my-vag-like-a-champagne-cork-and-running-away-screaming routine he pulled earlier.

Almost. But not quite.

Yeah, never mind. That shit still stings. A lot.

"That's nice. I think it's time we all get moving along, though. I know how you like to finish and run. Try not to scream like a child this time." I storm back to Kaden, my anger at Aiden burning hotter with every step. "Let's go."

I leave them all standing there. When I get to the truck and look back, I see Aiden staring after me with his mouth hanging open. Good.

I'm tired of feeling this back and forth with him. I hope he feels bad for a long time.

Because the giant dick on the lawn? Yeah, that's not the only giant dick around here.

26

Hangover Cures

Aiden

"WHAT EXACTLY DID YOU mean when you said you showed her your dick?" Kaden asks, but I'm too busy watching Rhea walk away to answer. "When the hell did you do that?"

"Huh? Oh. I didn't." Rhea already told me Kaden is like the brother she never had. I'm sure he wouldn't want to know what we got up to earlier today. And he really wouldn't want to know the circumstances of how I left her place in such a hurry. Because I left like a giant dick.

Kind of like the masterpiece Johnny and I created on this dude's lawn tonight.

The guys have always thought of me as the responsible one in the group, partly because I'm the oldest, and partly because I've always presented a more serious side of myself to them. My family died when I was eighteen, but even before that, I had to take care of myself. It always translated into me working harder, and taking on more than the other guys. But when we started making money with our music, I used some of it to dole out my own personal brand of justice. What I've been calling my side business is really just my way of being immature and petty, but you know, for a good cause.

Right now, though, it feels like I need to do something like this to myself because of how I treated Rhea today. This asshole with the shiny new dick burned into his lawn may have gotten her fired, but I treated her like garbage because of my own hang-ups. I pretty much kicked her when she was down. I wonder if there's a store open right now where I could buy a giant inflatable penis to set up on my roof? I'm sure I deserve it.

Kaden shakes his head and walks toward his truck, where Rhea is waiting for him in the passenger seat. I wonder if he knows she thinks of him like a brother, or if he wishes there were more. Maybe now that they're not partners and working together, he'll make his move.

Mine! Some insane part of me screams out at the thought of Rhea with Kaden. A part of me that seems to have forgotten I no one can ever be mine. Because it's not safe.

No, dumbass. She's not mine. I thought we already went over this.

Of course, then I slept with her anyway, like an asshole.

I watch until the lights from Kaden's truck turn the corner and I can't see them anymore. I'm not sure what Rhea thought of the giant dick I made in her honor, but I hope she doesn't report me for it. Fucking Devon, calling them and getting them here. Having cops in my side business isn't a good thing. It may only be petty vandalism and destruction of property, but it's still not something I want to go down for. If I'd taken the time to plan this out like I usually do, I wouldn't have had to worry about getting caught.

I wonder what kind of time a guy would do for as much vandalism as I've done over the years? I've never signed it or anything, but it would be pretty easy to track down if a person were so inclined. How many giant salt dicks and various other penis-themed graffiti do you have to see before you start thinking maybe the same person is responsible?

"Are you all done there, Johnny?" I yell out. "It's time to get going." All the whiskey we drank is catching up to me. The water and coffee we had at my place must not have sobered me up as much as I'd hoped. My thoughts were fuzzy before, but the world is spinning on me now, and I would hate it if Devon had to carry me home. Would serve the fucker right, though, for calling Rhea and Kaden.

Somehow I find my way back to the Escalade, even though Devon moved it a few blocks further away while we were doing the salt outlining. Either that or I am much drunker than I thought. I pull myself up into the back seat and spread myself all the way across, barely getting my head down before all that's left is blackness.

* * *

"Good morning, my beautiful darlings!"

Someone is screaming in my ear while using a saw on my skull, but I can't seem to force my eyes open against the blinding light surrounding me. *Where am I?*

"Drink this and then get your asses up. We've got work to do."

I peel one eyelid open with my fingers and look around. At first, all I can see are industrial light fixtures hanging above me. *So that's where the blinding light is coming from.* I look over to my left and Johnny is lying there looking as rough as I feel. I'm not positive, but it looks like he might have both eyes open. He's lying on the ground, staring straight up, though, so it's hard to tell. I roll to my stomach and push my hands under me, against what feels like rubber of some sort. I force both eyes open wide, and I see black rubber flooring, like in a gym. Pushing myself to a sitting position, I take another look at my surroundings. There's an octagonal ring in one corner, treadmills, rowing machines, and stationary bikes on one wall, and a section with weights and machines on another wall.

So we *are* in a gym.

"I don't have all day, sunshine," a gruff-sounding voice says from somewhere above me. "Get off your ass, drink this shit, and get ready to work the rest of the liquor out of you. Ryder, go get a couple of buckets from the janitor's closet. I have a feeling these two shitheads are going to need them."

My stomach gurgles roughly at the sight of the slimy-looking green concoction sitting in a plastic cup on the floor beside me. I think I'd better wait for that bucket before I attempt to drink it.

My tongue is thick and sticky in my mouth. "Can I get some water?" I ask the room in general because I can't even tell who's here. "And maybe all of the painkillers? I'm pretty sure I'm dying."

"You and me both," Johnny groans from his position on the floor. He hasn't even sat up yet, so I'm doing alright. "What the hell did we do last night?"

"You drank a LOT of whiskey, and committed some crimes." Devon laughs as he explains our shenanigans. I can sort of remember playing music with Johnny in my garage and calling Devon for a ride. But after that, it's pretty fuzzy. If I committed crimes, though, it must involve a giant dick drawing or sculpture on some deserving asshole's property. That's about the only type of crime I would commit. I would hardly even call it a crime. It's more like a prank really, because the damage isn't really permanent. I mean, even when I do the salted lawn thing, the person would only need to dig up the damaged soil and lay new sod. But I only do that to the worst offenders, or the ones I dislike the most, so I don't feel bad about that at all.

"Great," I say, accepting the bottle of water and Advil that someone hands me. "So why are we at a gym, then?"

"Well, by the time I got you guys out of there, it was almost morning. So I figured why not get Ryder to come and let us into the gym? You guys could sleep a bit, I could work out, and then we could put you through the paces to get you sobered up," Devon explains. "So drink up, water and smoothie, and then we'll get started. Alex's Pops says he has a special workout for you, guaranteed to make you sweat out all the alcohol."

"I said puke it out," Pops yells from the back of the gym. "I guarantee you will puke before we're through." He laughs a maniacal old man laugh. "It's been a while since I've made anyone puke. This is going to be fun."

I force myself to stand up, even though my head pounds when I lift it. The green slime drink is in my hand, and I start sucking it back. It's fucking disgusting. I gag trying to swallow it, but when I try to tip my cup down, Devon is right there, tipping it back up to my lips.

"Drink up. Pops says this helps."

Plugging my nose with my hand, like a kid with medicine, I choke the rest of the slippery concoction down, coughing a little as I swallow. It tastes like a mixture of lawn clippings, vomit, and kitty litter. I can't see how this is supposed to help. I want to throw up more now than I did before I drank it.

"Buckets," Ryder calls out, running back with the buckets just in time. The green shit is working its way back up as I lunge for a bucket. I hug it to my chest and proceed to forcefully vomit up the entire green drink plus water, Advil, and something that smells suspiciously like a distillery. So much for puking during the workout. I don't think there's anything left to come out now.

"Alright, let's get this shit show going," Pops yells at me and Johnny. "First things first: jumping rope. Grab 'em off the hooks over there, start jumping, and don't stop until I tell ya."

Pops leads us through a lengthy workout, and I'm sad to say that I do indeed puke again. Johnny and I both throw up what looks to be way more than we drank last night. Unless, of course, we drank a lot more after we called Devon, but somehow I doubt that's the case.

We're just *that* hungover.

Even after we have nothing left to puke up, we continue to dry heave. Pops seems to think that's when things are getting good though, because he pushes us even harder after that.

The workout lasts about an hour and a half. After our jump rope warm up, Pops leads us through a series of strength and endurance exercises and then has us finish with a series of so many burpees that I'm inspired to come back later and burn this gym to the ground. I would never do that, of course, but I might be tempted to come and draw a giant dick on the front of the building in chalk. You know, enough to be hilarious and get the message across, but still easily washable.

"That was a fucking nightmare," Johnny huffs out, dropping to the ground as he finishes his last burpee. I'm still a few behind him, but when I finish, I join him on the floor.

"I'm never drinking again," I promise, like I'm a teenager with his first hangover, instead of a fully grown man who should already know better.

"Yeah, I'm regretting drinking that much last night, too." Johnny rolls onto his stomach. "Oh, that feels nice," he says, spreading his arms and legs on the rubber floor, letting it cool him.

"How're the hangovers, boys?" Pops asks, leaning over us where we lie. "I got some whiskey in my desk. Who wants a drink?"

"No fucking way," and "Get that shit away from me," Johnny and I blurt over top of each other, laughing.

Surprisingly, I don't think there's much space left in my agony-filled body for a hangover to reside. Aside from being tired and worn out from the workout, I feel pretty good. In fact, I could really go for some breakfast now.

"Hey, Dev, can you bring me home so I can shower and change? I want to go out for some breakfast, but I smell like a sweaty stool in a dirty dive bar."

"Ugh, fine. But you're sitting in the back, and we're keeping all the windows open. Sweaty stool in a dirty dive bar doesn't even come close to describing your stench. Johnny, I'll drive you too." Devon turns to the door. "Thanks for the help, Pops. Much obliged."

"Anytime, boys. You come see me for a workout whenever you like. Any friend of Alex is a friend of mine. Oh, before you boys leave," he says, pointing to me and Johnny, "you go wash out your own buckets. I don't pay anyone enough to do that for you. And even if I did, I'd still make you do it yourself." He laughs as he turns to climb the stairs to his office, which is really just a platform surrounded by a chain-link fence, since this place doesn't have a second story, despite the high ceilings.

Johnny and I take care of our mess, and then we head out with Devon. Ryder is sticking around at the gym to talk to Pops about the Jiu Jitsu classes he teaches in his off time. He's really become a responsible, community minded guy since he married Denise. Being an actual adult looks good on him.

Right now I'm hoping a shower and some breakfast will help me recover some of my memories from last night. I'm not sure exactly what I did, but I'm pretty sure it was stupid.

Worse than that, I'm pretty sure it involved Rhea somehow. After the way I bolted when we slept together, I hope I didn't give her any more reason to be mad. I fucked up badly enough as it is. The last thing I need is to hear that I said or did something stupid to her while I was blackout drunk. If I'm going to be supporting her through a pregnancy, it would be a lot easier if she didn't completely hate me at the same time.

27

Running from Problems

Rhea

"Want to tell me what he meant when he said he already showed you his dick?" Kaden demands as soon as he gets in the truck. "Why the hell would he be showing you his dick?"

"Drop it," I mutter. "Not up for discussion."

"Okay," he drawls. "Sorry I asked."

Kaden drives me back to my place. We spend the entire ride in silence until we pull up in front of my building.

"Thanks for picking me up," I say.

"Hey, listen. I'm sorry I tried to ask about Aiden. It's none of my business whose dick you look at."

I snicker a little, a smile creeping up on my face.

"You know I think of you as a sister. I don't want some idiot in a band to think he can get away with mistreating you because he's a little famous. You deserve the world. Not some guy who shows you his penis sometimes." He winks and laughs.

"Yeah, yeah. Thanks, Kaden. It's nice to know you're looking out for me." I get out of the truck. "But it's still not up for discussion," I say before closing the door. I give him a wave through the passenger window before turning to let myself into my building.

Only once I'm inside with the door safely closed behind me does Kaden pull away from the curb. It is nice having someone look out for me, but damn is it ever a pain in the ass sometimes. As if I want to talk to my almost-brother about whose penises I've been looking at. Yeah, I'll pass, thanks.

I drag my ass up the stairs to my apartment, locking the door behind me. It's nearly four in the morning now and I never got that coffee I was hoping for. I can probably get a few more hours of sleep, though, so I bypass the kitchen and head straight to my bedroom, kicking off my shoes before I climb under my covers and close my eyes.

I toss and turn for far too long. The sheets tangle around my legs, the blanket is too hot, and I can't get comfortable.

Not to mention I can't get the thought of Aiden out of my head. I know he was drunk, but why on earth would he mention showing me his dick? He can't possibly have forgotten running out of here like his ass was on fire? Does he really think that is normal behavior for an adult who has just had sex with someone?

Ugh, and now I can't stop thinking about the sex. How he took the time to make me come first with his mouth and still gave me another orgasm after that? Fuck. It was the best sex I've ever had, and now I won't get it again. That stupid asshole. Why'd he have to do such a great job fucking me if he was going to jump up and run away?

I look over at the clock and see it's already almost six in the morning.

"Fuck this," I mumble, untangling myself from the sheets and standing up. I may as well hit a trail if I can't sleep.

I drag my feet over to my closet and pull out my running gear, stripping off articles of clothing and replacing them as I go. Within fifteen minutes, I'm out on the sidewalk, my hydration bag on my back and my running shoes laced up. I do a few stretches and then I take off on my run.

There's a park with an extensive running trail throughout the city, and it's only paved in parts. It's the spot I go when I need to run, but don't want to drive out of town to get to the more advanced trails. If I go around the complete system of trails, it should take me around an hour and a half to finish. That should be enough time to run Aiden out of my system.

Hopefully.

I pop in my earbuds, turn on a running playlist, and take off at a moderate pace. I love the feel of the air on my face as I run. The air is crisp at this time of the day, and it's wonderful for keeping me cool.

I pass a few other runners and a couple of bikers on the trails, but not too many people are up this early today. That suits me fine. I like the solitude. Kaden and Xena always try to get me to run closer to town, or to take one of them with me, but they both talk so much that I end up more irritated than anything else. My runs are my time to think through my life. I can see them any other time to have conversations.

Maybe one day I will have a running partner who knows how to shut the hell up. It's not a bad idea to have someone with me when I run, for safety's sake, anyway, but I need someone who can run in companionable silence. So for now I run alone, music down low, and I pay attention to my surroundings.

I run in near silence and enjoy the scenery. The trail system takes me through most areas of the city, and I can say that Westborough does a great job keeping up its parks system. There's a small man-made lake on one side of town, and the trail loops all the way around it. It's one of my favorite places to run because on the side of the lake there's a tiny island with a fountain that cascades over the trail, making it feel as though you're running under a small waterfall. I come across the island near the end of my run today, so I stop for a moment and let the spray cool my sweaty body.

Not once during my run have I thought about Aiden. Until now, that is. I can't decide what to do about him. Why does it all have to be so complicated? If he hadn't run off the way he did, I think maybe I could like him. That shit he did with the giant dick on Frank Martin's lawn is hilarious. Illegal, but still hilarious. And it's kind of cute how he took it upon himself to avenge me.

I blow out my breath in a long, calming stream before starting to run again. I think I'll stop at Bump & Grind before I head home, grab a coffee, and maybe see if Xena has some time to talk. And then it's back home to continue the job search. Hopefully, I hear from one of the places I already contacted. Those jobs seemed like the best fit for me.

Or I could give in and work for Xena.

28

Coffee and Apologies

Aiden

"I'm telling you, you said you'd already shown her your dick and Kaden got kind of pissed off. She's like a sister to him. He didn't take too kindly to the idea that you'd whipped out your dick and showed it to her."

Devon and I are sitting at Bump & Grind having coffee. After we went for breakfast this morning, I convinced him to meet me here for coffee, under the guise of helping with my hangover. My hangover is non-existent, but I'm not ready to admit to Devon that I'm hoping to see Rhea here, so I needed an excuse. I don't know where else she would go that I could accidentally bump into her, and it would be too weird if I showed up outside her place. Plan B, if this doesn't work, is to go check out the creepy doll store below her apartment and hope I spot her going in or out of her place.

"That doesn't really seem like something I would say," I tell him, hoping he doesn't notice I'm not making eye contact. I mean, I did show her my dick, but I'm not one to talk about sexual exploits in front of the guys. It feels wrong to talk about Rhea like that, anyway. I'm keeping that memory for myself.

"You were beyond drunk last night, man. I've never seen you like that. Ever. I wouldn't have been surprised if you'd dropped your pants and pulled your dick out right there." Devon laughs.

"Oh, come on. I can't have been that bad. You're saying I was so drunk I nearly turned into Ryder?" Before Ryder married Denise, he had a penchant for showing us his dick all the time, because he thought it was hilarious. "I think I would still have some shame, no matter how drunk I am. At least around a woman I hardly know, and a cop."

"Eh, not too sure about that. You've been different lately. Not as serious or something. Who could say how that will turn out? Maybe you'll be taking over Ryder's dick flapping showcase now that he's a married man? Someone is going to need to make the groupies think they have a chance. Why not you?"

I actually shudder when Devon says that. I have less than zero interest in playing the part of the promiscuous, indiscriminate rock star. I do everything in my power, short of wearing an actual disguise, to keep from being recognized. There's no way I want to spend time hanging with a bunch of vapid women who only want to sleep with me because I'm famous. Even if I didn't sleep with them, I can't imagine the conversations would be very stimulating. 'So you're in the band? Do you like it? Wanna fuck?' Fuck that.

"Pass. I have standards. I love our fans, but I don't want to spend time with groupies. Not my scene." I take a gulp of my coffee. "Maybe Travis can take that on? Connor and Ryder have Alex and Denise. Johnny is obsessed with Becca, and I'm out, so that leaves Travis."

"I have a feeling Travis wouldn't be too interested, either. He's pretty busy these days. Even Johnny doesn't see him much, and they're brothers. And they live together." Devon looks behind the counter to where Xena is talking to a customer. From the looks of it, I don't think I'm the only one who's going to be on Kaden's brotherly radar. It's going to be so much worse for Devon, though, because Xena is Kaden's actual sister. And Devon is Kaden's best friend.

Oh yeah. I can't wait to see how that all goes down.

The bell above the door jingles, and in walks my own problem.

Rhea takes a few steps in before turning her head toward me. She's wearing head to toe spandex, and her curves and toned body are on full display. She has her hair tied up, but she looks flushed and sweaty, like she's been working out. Maybe she just came from the gym?

"Hey Rhea," Devon calls out to her, "come join us."

"Dude, what are you doing?" I whisper to him. I'm not ready for her to come over here yet. "Stop trying to make trouble for me."

He smiles at me and gives me a little wink. Fucker. It's too late to do anything about it now though, since she's already on her way over here.

"Hi Rhea, good to see you. Get any sleep last night?" Devon asks. "I know I didn't. Between dragging this drunk asshole around and sobering him up this morning, I might need to see if Xena can hook me up to a coffee IV or something."

Rhea chuckles. "Yeah, I could use one of those, too. Or maybe something stronger than coffee, but less than cocaine?"

"Did you just come from the gym? You look sporty today." Devon points at me. "We forced Aiden and Johnny to work out until they puked this morning to help sober them up."

"Between throwing up and drinking a shit ton of water, we sobered up and got rid of the growing hangovers we had. Well, it was those things or the greasy diner breakfast we had at Maggie's." I may as well join in on this conversation before Devon tells her everything and makes it sound like a scandalous secret. "I've never been much of a drinker and after last night, I'm positive I never will be. I don't even remember most of it."

"Oh? Well, you nearly burned my corneas with your whiskey breath, so I'm not surprised you don't remember." Rhea sits down, joining us at the table. "From what I could see, though, you and Johnny made quite the impression on some asshole's grass."

"Ah shit," I run my hand down my face. "I thought that's what the guys meant when they said I was committing crimes. Was it the guy who got you fired? Is that why you were there?" The only reason I can think that Rhea would be at the scene of one of my revenge plans is that I was getting petty revenge for her. She's been on my mind non-stop, and that she got fired for arresting some asshole who's abusing his wife? Yeah, that doesn't sit right with me at all.

"Yes, and yes. You got the address from Kaden through Devon, and then Kaden picked me up to bring me there. He's pissed off at the guy too, so you don't need to worry about him bringing you in. It helps that you chose vandalism rather than violence as your tactic, too."

I release a rough breath. A lot more planning normally goes into these revenge plots, and I'm usually not so drunk. I don't even know if the guy was home, what kind of security the neighborhood has, or any of the information I usually gather well before I go onto a property to make a giant dick. Hell, the guy could have had guard dogs there to rip me to pieces for all I know. It was pretty stupid of me to do that job in the state I was in last night.

"Thank you," I tell her. "I'm so relieved to hear you say that. I don't remember being there last night, and I don't remember what I told you about... that side of what I do, but I'm glad you won't have me arrested for it."

"I'll go grab you a coffee, Rhea," Devon says, as he stands. "You guys can keep talking."

"Oh sure, thanks. Xena knows what I like."

Devon heads to the counter, leaving me alone at the table with Rhea. I'm not too stupid to realize he's giving me a chance to apologize in private. And I won't waste this opportunity.

"I hear I owe you an apology," I begin. "I'm sorry for what I said."

"For what you said?" Her face scrunches up, a confused look on her face.

"Yeah, for what I said. Devon tells me I announced to everyone that I'd shown you my dick, and Kaden was a little pissed off. So I'm sorry for saying that."

"And that's all?"

"Um, yeah? I don't remember what I said or did last night, and that's the only thing Devon told me about. Did I say something else?" I'm so confused. I thought she was only there for a few minutes. What else could I have said in that short amount of time to make her mad?

She huffs out a breath. "No, you said nothing. It's fine. I'll see you around." She gets up and joins Devon at the counter, leaving me sitting at the table, alone and so confused.

29

Not a Date

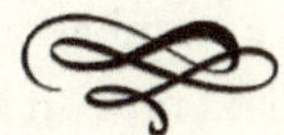

Rhea

"Hey, I'm going to take that to go," I tell Xena, prompting her to pour my coffee into a paper cup. "Aiden apologized for saying he showed me his dick. So there's no reason for me to stick around longer."

"*That's* what he apologized for? What an ass." Xena blurts. She's angry on my behalf, and probably a little upset she'd tried to orchestrate the whole scenario to begin with. She *is* the one who thought Aiden should help me break my dry spell, after all. She puts my coffee cup on the counter and I grab it.

"Wait a minute. What else should he be apologizing for?" Devon looks back and forth between the two of us with a confused look on his face.

That's surprising. I thought Xena would have told him I slept with Aiden. Or that Aiden would have said something.

"You didn't tell him?"

"I only told him the basics, not the ending."

"Oh, is this because you guys slept together? Was it bad? I could see how it would be. Aiden is pretty out of practice with the ladies. He never dates so..."

Out of the corner of my eye, I notice Aiden is getting up from his seat, probably about to come over here.

"I'm going to get going. I'll talk to you later. Nice to see you again, Devon." I give them both a wave and walk to the door. I don't wave at Aiden because I'm feeling petty.

Why would he apologize for possibly announcing that he showed me his dick, rather than apologizing for running away screaming after he fucked me? It doesn't make any sense. Unless he really is a dumbass.

All the calm I gathered on my run around the city is rapidly leaving my body, and I'm feeling frustrated and pissed off. Aiden is complicating my already complicated life.

At dinner yesterday he was friendly, joking with me about his friends trying to push us together, but then when he was driving me home he seemed upset. Which apparently is because he's attracted to me, but that's no excuse. And it's not a good reason to leave the way he did after we slept together.

No matter how much I think about this, I can't sort it out. But it doesn't matter now. Aiden had the chance to apologize, and he did, but he was sorry for the wrong thing. Even if I thought I was starting to like him, there's no way I could entertain the idea of being with someone who didn't realize that sort of behavior was something to apologize for. I won't put up with that.

I'm so busy ranting in my mind that I'm letting myself into my building before I realize. I must've been on autopilot the entire way home. Pulling my phone from my pocket as I walk up the stairs, I notice I missed a call. I connect to my voicemail while I unlock my door, walk into my apartment, and kick my shoes off.

It's a message from the shelter I applied to. She wants me to come in for an interview this week sometime.

"Gah," I squeal, pumping my fist in the air. "Yes!" At least something is going right.

This is the job I was hoping for. I don't want to get ahead of myself, but if it works out, this could wind up being even more to my liking than being a cop was. After taking a few deep breaths, and okay, squealing a few more times, I've calmed down enough to call her back.

The director's name is Winnifred, but she insists I call her Winnie. She's got me booked in for a morning meeting the day after tomorrow. She seems even more excited than I am at the thought of me working there. She says they've been relying heavily on volunteers, but the volunteers aren't always available. And with my background in law enforcement, she thinks I will have a unique ability to help. I can't wait to meet her.

This day is turning out to be okay, after all. I think I'll take a day off from job hunting to celebrate. It's a good thing, too. A look around the apartment tells me I will be better off if I spend my day cleaning, anyway.

I busy myself with taking a shower, and getting dressed, and then get to work cleaning the apartment. I'm about an hour into cleaning when I check my phone and see that I've missed some text messages. From Aiden.

> **Unknown -** *Hey, this is Aiden. I got your number from Xena. I need to talk to you. Can we meet somewhere?*

Ugh, Xena. Why would she give him my number? She knows he was an asshole to me. Why would she think I want to talk to him? Regardless, I program him in as a contact.

Not that I want to contact him.

Because I don't.

At all.

Aiden- It's important.

Aiden- I know you don't want to talk to me, but it's really important. Please message me back.

Aiden- Are you avoiding me? I deserve that, but please, just meet me this one time, and then we won't have to talk again.

Geez, four messages in an hour? This guy is desperate.

Rhea- What is it? I have things to do. Can't you tell me in a text?

Aiden- No, it's too important. It has to be face to face.

Rhea- Fine. When do you want to meet?

Aiden- I'm volunteering until
6. How about we meet for dinner?

It's a good plan on his part. I can't yell at him much if we're meeting in a public place like a restaurant. But I am going to yell at him. Because he deserves it. And I don't give a fuck if we're in public.

Aiden- Meet me at Marcus at 7?
Does that work for you?

I've actually been wanting to try Marcus for quite a while, but I never seem to find the time. That and I have no one to go with me. It's kind of a date place, but if Aiden wants to go there, I'm going to take him up on the offer. Just so I can finally try it, that's all.

Rhea- K. I'll see you at 7.

Oh, shit.

Now I need to figure out what to wear. Life was a lot easier when I spent most of it in uniform. I'm not one for dressing up, or looking fashionable, and I always have a hard time choosing appropriate outfits. Looks like I need to enlist Xena's help for this. As long as she doesn't dress me in super short shorts again, we should be fine.

Rhea- I need you to come over
when you're done with work. Help

me find something to wear to go
to dinner at Marcus tonight.

Xena- ooooh. Dinner at Marcus?
That sounds fancy.

Rhea- Shut up. Will you help me
or not?

I'm going to get enough shit from her when she gets here. I
don't need any of it right now.

Xena- Yup, I'll be over around
2. Plenty of time to find you
something to wear before your
big date. We can even go shopping if we have to.

Rhea- It's not a date.

Xena- Yeah, okay. Because everyone just goes to Marcus when
it's 'not a date'.

Rhea- I'm serious. It's not a
date.

I wait a few minutes and she still doesn't text me back.

Rhea- Not a date. See you later.

Or is it a date?

No, that can't be.

Can it?

Aiden wouldn't ask me on a date merely to tell me something. Would he? I mean, it's not like I know him that well. He could be asking me to dinner to tell me he wants to date. Or maybe it's just to apologize.

That's probably it. Xena and Devon must have told him why I was still mad, and he realized it will take more than saying sorry to make up for it. A nice dinner would be a good start. But only if it comes with an explanation.

Because more than anything, I want to know why he came and then immediately ran like he did. I don't think I've ever felt as shitty as I did when he jumped out of bed and ran.

But I still can't get him out of my head.

30

She Stabbed Me With a Sword

Aiden

SHIT, SHE LEFT BEFORE I got over here. I would have followed and talked to her outside, but Xena and Devon were already calling me over, apparently to give me shit.

"That was a bullshit apology." Xena reaches under the counter and pulls out her foam rubber sword, pointing it in my face. "How are you going to fix this?"

"I don't even know what I'm supposed to be fixing. I can barely remember anything from last night."

"I told you everything that happened after I picked you up. I don't know what you guys got up to before that, though."

Before that?

Oh SHIT!

I didn't even apologize for running off on her when we had sex. I can't believe I forgot to say anything about that. Fuck. I am such an idiot.

"The look on his face tells me he just remembered," Xena says with a smirk. She stabs me in the chest with her sword before placing it back under the counter.

"Ouch, that fucking hurt," I whine, rubbing the spot where she stabbed me. "But yes, I remembered. What should I do?"

"I don't know. All I can say is, you can't just apologize now. If you really want her to forgive you, you're going to need to make a solid effort."

Devon has been listening quietly this whole time, but now he speaks up. "I still don't know what the hell you're apologizing for. What did you even do?"

"I don't want to talk about it," I say. "It wouldn't be polite to Rhea."

"Oh, I see," he drawls. "It's like that then, is it? I know what you're saying."

"Shut up, Devon," Xena tells him. "Let's help him figure out what to do."

Together we plan an apology, with dinner, and lots of begging for forgiveness on my part. I'm not confident it will work, and even if it does, it doesn't take away the reason I freaked out. We didn't use a condom. To me, there could be nothing worse than fathering a child.

I get Rhea's phone number from Xena before I leave the coffee shop, and I send her a text before I drive home. Then I send a text to Alex to beg for the favor of getting me a table at her friend's restaurant. By the time I pull into my driveway, Alex lets me know I have a table for seven and Rhea still hasn't gotten back to me.

Finally, after I send a bunch of texts, Rhea sends me a message. I was worried she was going to ignore me completely, but I can't say I would have blamed her if she did. I can't even imagine how it would feel if someone did the same thing to me. Fucked me and immediately left. Not just left, but freaked out and ran away. She must have felt like shit, like she disgusted me or something. And nothing could be further from the truth. Just thinking about her standing naked in front of me has me hard again.

The way she tasted will be ingrained in my brain for the rest of my life. And the sounds she made as I licked and sucked her to orgasm? Fucking perfection. The feel of her clenching around me as she came was like nothing I'd ever felt before. So warm and tight, urging me to come right along with her. Which I did. Harder than I ever have before.

And of course, that's when I realized I forgot a condom and then fucked everything up completely. Rhea is someone who I could almost see myself trusting enough to have a relationship with, someone who I could trust with birth control. But I'll be lucky now if she even forgives me, never mind letting me near her naked again.

Tonight's not about that, anyway. The more I think about her, the more I want to know her. From what she told me a little about her childhood, I think we might have similar backgrounds. I have a feeling if anyone could understand my need to end my family line with me, it would be Rhea.

Is it possible I could have someone in my life after all this time thinking I would die alone? Rhea makes me want to find out.

Sitting here ruminating over the situation isn't helping any, so I do what I always do when I need to take my mind off of something; I turn to video games. I have a couple of hours before I need to be at the shelter, so I have some time to kill.

Video games have always been an escape for me, particularly cartoony, fantastical ones, with silly-looking enemies, and weird storylines. As a kid, it was a way for me to escape my fears and to imagine, for a little while, that I wasn't going to be on the receiving end of my dad's angry outbursts at any moment. When you're helping Mario save the princess, it's easy to believe that good guys can win. It doesn't work like that in real life, but at least I'm still here.

My front door opens while I'm still trying to decide on a game to play, and Johnny walks in balancing a stack of five bakery boxes.

"Hey man, I made some cookies and stuff for you to bring to the shelter today."

"When did you have time to do that? It's only been a few hours since I saw you." And when I saw him at breakfast, he didn't seem stressed out enough to need to do this much baking.

"I went home right after breakfast and started right away. I thought maybe today I could come with you if that's okay? I need something to distract me from the whole Becca situation. Something that isn't alcohol-related, because I don't want a repeat of this morning's hangover workout ever again."

"Yeah, that should be alright. Let me text the director and make sure it's okay."

Johnny busies himself by making a pot of coffee and I send off a quick text. The director answers almost immediately, and like that, she clears Johnny to come with me.

I'm glad he's coming, but I laugh a little on the inside. The poor guy has no idea what he's gotten himself into. The kids are going to eat him alive.

31

Shopping with the Ladies

Rhea

"What about this?" I hold up a floor length dress in a pale blue color and Xena makes a face.

"No. That's like an ugly bridesmaid's dress. Here," she says and passes me an armload of dresses. "Try these on. One of them is going to be the one."

I pass the stack of dresses to the saleswoman who's been hovering nearby, waiting to start a fitting room for me, and follow her to the back of the small dress shop. I've only been in a store like this once before, and that was to pick up the strange flamenco-style bridesmaid dress I wore for an old college friend's wedding.

It's not a coincidence that we lost touch after she made me wear that thing. Out of six bridesmaids, I was the only one looking like a flamenco dancer, and I didn't even know it until the ceremony. I guess it was her way of getting back at me for a crush that I wasn't even aware her fiance had on me at some point in the distant past.

That's beside the point, anyway. I'm uncomfortable in this store. My clothing choices tend toward sporty and casual. Now that I'm not wearing a uniform every day, it's even more casual. This store is way out of my comfort zone. Good thing I brought Xena. She seems to know what she's doing here.

The sales lady hangs up the dresses that Xena picked out and directs me into the fitting room. She tells me to call her if I need a different size and then leaves me to my own devices.

They made the first dress for a much shorter woman. It barely covers my ass and even though I am looking for something that Aiden will find irresistible, having my flaps hang lower than the hem on my dress isn't a look that I'm going for. The second and third dresses are better, but I don't like them enough to even leave the fitting room in them, let alone wear them out on a date. The fourth dress is the one.

It's a little shorter than knee-length with a slightly flared skirt, but not as indecent as the first dress, and it's black. The cap sleeves and high neckline look modest, but the back is open to my lower back with only a small ribbon up at the neck to tie it.

"Xena, where are you? I think this is the one." I step out of the dressing room to look in the three-way mirror just outside the door, to find not only Xena but also Alex, Denise, Becca, Ivy, and the Titty Club, all waiting to see me. "Oh shit. It's an ambush."

"Surprise!" Gran and her titty club friends yell. They're all in matching tracksuits with different shades of teal as the theme. They still have the white sneakers, and Gran is still wearing her *fuck bitches, get money* hat. "We found out you were going on a little date and decided you needed our help to choose an appropriate outfit. And I don't think that dress is it."

"What? First, how did you 'find out'? And second, what's wrong with this dress? I think it's perfect."

"Devon told us," Becca says. "He got the inside scoop from Xena and filled us in."

"And that dress is so boring," Gladys says. "Even I wear more revealing dresses than that and I'm so old I'm practically mummified."

"It is pretty plain," Gran adds. "Nothing much special to it."

These guys are nuts. This is more risque than any dress I've ever worn.

"Did you see the back?" I ask, turning to show them the complete lack of fabric. "I think that makes this dress special."

They make noises of approval. I guess the back really does it for them. Or, the lack of a back, that is.

"Well, why didn't you say so?" Gladys chuckles. "If I'd noticed that, I wouldn't have said anything." She looks at me and taps a finger on her lip. "Except I really do have more revealing dresses, you know. You need to have a really, *really* low neckline if you want any cleavage when your boobs hang down to your belt."

Gran and Lana laugh and nod in agreement. I guess they too have more revealing clothes. Seems funny that I've only ever seen them in tracksuits. Even when Gran was by herself at dinner the other day, she was wearing a tracksuit. I wonder if it's a club uniform or something?

"Okay, that's the dress." Xena claps her hands together, then says, "Now go get changed so we can pay for it and move on to shoes."

"Oh, I know just the place to go," Denise says excitedly. "I get all my shoes there." She points down at her feet, which are sporting electric blue stiletto booties, despite her pregnant belly. I can barely keep my balance on heels as it is. I doubt I'd be able to pull off wearing them while pregnant. That seems a little unsafe for me. She looks amazing, though, so I guess it's working for her. She clearly has good balance.

I turn back into the dressing room, closing the door on the conversation. I get changed while all the women argue about what shoes will look best with this dress. If it were up to me, I'd probably wind up wearing my old combat boots, so it's probably a good thing I have this team of women helping me out. I can't deny that the few times I've seen Denise, I've loved the shoes she's wearing. Maybe this store we're going to has something a little flatter for me though. I'm already pretty tall. Do I really need to add to that with a super high heel?

After I pay for my dress, we all pile into separate vehicles and make our way to the store that Denise recommended. It's a few blocks from Xena's coffee shop, in the opposite direction of my place, but still within the section of the city that houses all the trendiest specialty shops. Yes, that means that the creepy doll store under my apartment is a trendy shop. It's weird, I know.

Xena and I are the last to arrive at the shoe shop, the not-very originally-named Sole Mates, and by the time I walk in, the other women already have a pile of shoes they want me to try on. I didn't even tell them my shoe size. One of them must be a magical shoe wizard. My money is on Denise.

"Okay, these are all the options that will work with your dress, that they have in your size. Sit down, and let's start trying on shoes." Denise can barely contain her excitement. Her love for shoes is contagious. She's almost got me convinced I actually *want* to try all these shoes on. Almost.

"How did you know my size? Tell me the truth. Are you some sort of shoe wizard?" I ask her, squinting and giving her a once over.

"I'm pretty sure shoe wizards are actually called leprechauns. And last I checked, I was not a leprechaun. I am good at guessing shoe sizes, though. It probably comes from back when I worked part-time in a shoe store in high school. I'm sure you can guess that I loved it there."

I'm already trying to struggle into the first pair of shoes, a strappy pair of heeled sandals, when Denise sits on the bench beside me.

"I can imagine you've had quite the shoe collection ever since you worked there," I grunt while I pull off the strappy sandal.

Too hard to get on. It's definitely not the pair for me. "How big is your shoe closet?"

Denise laughs. "Since we moved out to the lake house Gran gave us when we got married, Ryder has given me an entire room to house my shoes. He had a closet designer come in and build floor-to-ceiling shelves with a library-style ladder I can climb to get to the shoes at the top. It's pretty impressive."

My jaw drops, and I look at her. "Seriously?"

"No, not seriously." She laughs. "I *wish* I had a room like that. But we did have special shelving put in the walk-in closet in the master suite. It's not quite enough room, but it does the job I need it to. For now." She winks.

"Don't let her fool you," Becca yells from in front of a wall of platform boots. "Her walk-in closet is bigger than my whole two-bedroom apartment. She has way too many pairs of shoes."

"You never mind," Denise says to Becca. "There's no such thing as too many pairs of shoes. Right, Rhea?"

"Uh, yeah, sure," I mumble, nervous at having been put on the spot.

I focus my attention on the next pair of shoes, a strappy bootie with a peep toe, and a high heel. I actually like these. They have a zipper on the back and the many buckled straps are thick and cross over each other so much that they're more like a solid boot than a sandal. I like them so much that I'm not going to bother trying on any others.

"These are the ones," I say, walking around the shop and looking at myself in the various mirrors they have placed around the space. "They're cute. I can walk in them, and they're a little edgy. I might even wear these again someday."

"Yes!" Becca yells. "I win. Pay up, ladies." She holds her hand out and the other women walk over and start placing five-dollar bills in her hand. "I knew you would pick those," she explains to me. "We all bet five bucks on our picks and I won. So thanks for helping me buy these boots." She points to a pair of black lace-up boots with a high platform. Becca has dark hair with short bangs and tons of tattoos and the boots match her vibe perfectly.

"Happy to help," I say with a laugh. "What's next on the agenda?" I'm having a good time with these women and with hours to go still before my date that's not a date, I wouldn't mind spending more time with them.

"We've got to head back to Peaceful Pines," Gladys says. "It's one of the other women's birthdays, and I've ordered a few young strippers to entertain us after bingo. I want to be there before those boys get down to their banana hammocks, so I can see what they're packing in the pee-pee department."

"Gladys is obsessed with finding out men's dick sizes," Denise says to me. "She was very concerned with Ryder's dick before we got married and hasn't quite gotten over the fact that she's never seen his penis, and now she never will."

"Oh yeah, she mentioned that when Aiden and I were at breakfast the other day. Something about not wanting to give up her dick quest like she had to with Ryder. "

"Never mind that, dear," Gran says to me. "Lock that boy down as soon as you can. Gladys needs to learn she can't see any dick she pleases. Certainly not those of handsome young men who are practically related to me. She can get her jollies from somewhere else."

"Oh poop," Gladys pouts. "You're no fun. I'll wait in the car. Come on Lana."

"Bye dear," Lana says, leaving the shop. "Good luck on your date."

Gran waves and walks out of the shop to join the other two, giving me a little wink before she's out the door.

This is shaping up to be the weirdest day ever.

"So," Ivy says, with her face buried in her phone. "We're booked for mani-pedis and massages in an hour and a half."

"Great," Alex says, rubbing her baby belly. "I'm starving. Let's get lunch before we go."

We agree to all meet at Maggie's after Denise insists her baby needs a milkshake and only Maggie's will do.

The rest of the women go on ahead while Becca and I hang back to pay for our shoes with a promise to meet them there.

32

Give Me Shelter

Aiden

"I can't believe you threw him to the wolves like that," Winnie says, joining me at the side of the playground to watch Johnny be mobbed by kids.

When they heard I brought someone new for them to terrorize today, the kids jumped straight into action and dragged Johnny out to play. He's been playing tag, pushing kids on swings, climbing the monkey bars, and singing songs for hours now. I've been off to the side hosting story time for any kids who weren't ready to warm up to a new person yet.

"He's doing surprisingly well. I didn't know he had it in him, to tell you the truth. I figured he'd have tapped out by now."

Johnny and Travis come from the most stable family out of all the guys in the band and I guess I never considered that it had to mean they had an extended family involved in their lives as well. Their cousins and nieces and nephews must be around a lot for Johnny to be this comfortable with kids. If it weren't for all his tattoos, and the obvious height difference, you could almost mistake Johnny for one of the kids he's been playing with this afternoon.

"Well, he's welcome to come play any time. And if you're telling the truth, and he's the one who does all this fabulous baking, he's more than welcome to drop some of that off any time, too." She smiles as she takes a big bite out of a cookie. "He's quite a talented baker."

"It's his stress relief," I tell her. "He's having girl problems." So am I, not that I'm going to let her in on that secret. Plus, if tonight goes well, maybe I won't have those problems anymore.

"Girl problems?" Winnie's eyebrows shoot up. "Is the poor girl blind? Has she seen him? I'm going to have to remind myself of how married I am every time he comes in here. Not that you're not also a good-looking guy," she stutters when she catches me staring. "But you're not really my type. Too hippie granola for me."

"Hippie granola?" I laugh. I can honestly say that's the first time anyone has called me that.

"Yeah, you know." She gestures to me, taking in my whole body. "The long hair, man-bun, scruffy face, worn jeans, old sneakers thing you've got going on. I can picture you in little yoga shorts wearing prayer beads while you meditate."

Hmmm, maybe it's time to rethink my whole look if that's what she gets from what I wear. I've always been attached to my ability to get around unnoticed, but the people in Westborough are pretty respectful of the other guys in the band, even Connor and Ryder, who are the most recognizable of all of us. I bet I'd have less trouble from fans than I thought.

"Huh, I don't even know what to say to that. If I have short hair next time you see me, though, you know why." I laugh when her mouth drops and her eyes widen.

"I'm so sorry. I meant nothing by it. You're fine the way you are."

"Don't worry about it. You're not the first person, nor will you be the last, to have an opinion on how I look. I've had more than one stylist tell me I should change my image. You're the first person to call me hippie granola." I put my hand on her shoulder. "Now, let's talk about your interviews this week.

Anything specific you want me to do while you're talking to people in your office?"

"Nope, business as usual. One of the part-timers is going to be here with you, so between the two of you, everything will be fine. I don't know what I'm going to do when you leave, Aiden. Having you volunteer so much when you're home is the only reason any of us can take vacations. And the money you donate helps us pay salaries, and keep this place up and running. I wouldn't feel like it was a lie to say that you're personally responsible for allowing us to get so many families to safety these last few years. You're the best thing that ever happened to this place."

Winnie is always trying to get me to accept awards, or at least let her publicly recognize me for what I do here at the shelter, but I refuse. That's not the reason I do it, plus it makes me uncomfortable to be rewarded for something that I only do because of my personal history. But every once in a while she can't hold back and has to thank me personally to let me know how much she appreciates it. This place needs money to survive and I give as much as I can to the cause. It's not as big a deal as she likes to make it out to be.

"Yeah, yeah. Thanks, Win. You're just trying to butter me up, so I make sure Johnny brings more cookies." I give her a little wink.

"Who needs more cookies?" Johnny asks, running to hide behind us during yet another game of tag. "These kids are taking it out of me. I'm not sure I'll ever have enough energy to bake again."

Two kids sneak around us, catching Johnny from both sides, leaving him with no escape. He tags me, making me it, forcing me to join the game. Winnie heads back into the building to check on the moms and leaves us to entertain the kids for the last hour of the day. After that, the kids will go back inside to their respective moms, and to helping with dinner, doing homework, and settling in for the night.

Even though this place is a temporary shelter, it is a home for a time for these kids, and we try to make it as nice as possible. Each family has their own space here, but there is a communal kitchen where everyone pitches in to make dinner, like a big supportive extended family.

When it's six o'clock, Winnie comes out and calls the kids to come in.

"Thanks again for coming in today," she tells me. "And thank you for bringing the cookies and the baker. I can't remember the last time the kids had this much fun out here. Johnny, you must have endless energy. You played tag for so long, I think I'm going to need a nap now."

"Thanks for letting me join Aiden today," he says. "I had a lot of fun. The kids were great."

"Well, come back whenever you want. Their moms are going to be so happy with how well those kids sleep tonight, thanks to you. I'm sure every one of them will appreciate that more than you know."

Johnny and I follow Winnie back through the building and out to the front door. She waves goodbye and goes back to her office after locking the door behind us.

"Thanks for that," Johnny says. "Kids are so good at making you forget all your problems. It's hard to be sad about a girl when a bunch of kids are chasing you around trying to tag you."

"True," I say, unlocking the doors of my car. "But you're going to have to figure that Becca situation out eventually."

"I'm thinking maybe it's time to let it go." He sighs and changes the subject. "What about you? What's up with Rhea?"

"Actually, I'm meeting her for dinner tonight. I need to get home so I can shower and change before I go meet her. I'm kind of freaking out."

"Aww, that's so cute," Johnny clasps his hands up by his cheek and flutters his eyelashes at me. "You're nervous."

"Shut up." I laugh.

"I've never seen you date anyone, man. This chick must be pretty special."

I don't really want to talk about this with Johnny, so I nod my head. He gets the hint and drops the subject, and we ride the rest of the way to my place in silence.

"Well, good luck tonight," Johnny says, opening the door on his car. "See you around."

I wave as he pulls out of the driveway, then turn and head into the house. I don't have a lot of time to get ready, so I need to be quick. Hopefully, I'm able to clean myself up enough that she feels like forgiving me for being such an asshole the other day. If not, worrying about whether it's even possible for me to have a relationship with someone doesn't even matter.

Because if it's not her, it will be no one.

33

The Boys Have My Back

Rhea

IT'S FIVE MINUTES TO seven when I storm into Marcus in a bit of a panic, the little buckles on my new booties making the slightest jingling noise, making me feel like an elf. I hate being late, and to me, being only five minutes early is being late. It took me forever to get my hair and makeup sorted and then I had a hard time finding parking when I got here, finally finding street parking a couple of blocks over. I can only hope that Aiden isn't here yet, so he doesn't witness me rushing around like this. I need to maintain some semblance of control. After all, he's the one who ran out on me right after sex, not the other way around. I'm not the one who should be worried here.

I check in with the hostess and she confirms Aiden hasn't arrived yet, then leads me to a table. We're tucked away in a private corner, which makes me wonder if Aiden requested this, and if he did, was it only so he doesn't get recognized or because he wants private time with me? I kind of hope it's the latter.

What the hell, Rhea? You're supposed to be mad at him.

I reach out and bring my ice water to my lips, my mouth suddenly dry. Despite what the other girls were thinking when we were shopping, I'm here to make sure he apologizes and feels bad for what he did. Not to attempt another hook-up. I will not leave myself open to that kind of hurt again. Even if it was the best sex I've ever had.

"Hello, darling," a large, cheerful looking man says as he slips into the seat across from me. "I'm Alex's friend, Marcus. She called me earlier to arrange this table for you and your gentleman friend and I thought I'd introduce myself to you privately, since I see you're here early and alone."

Holy shit! I'm meeting *the* Marcus, of the restaurant Marcus, and I'm more star-struck than I was when I found out Aiden is the drummer for Sleeping Dogs. I don't care what anyone says, chefs are the real celebrities. Plus, I'd barely even heard of Sleeping Dogs before. Marcus has been famous in Westborough for ages.

"Oh my gosh, it's so amazing to meet you, Marcus. I'm a huge fan. I've been wanting to come here since you opened, but I haven't had a reason to come, not that I would have even been able to get a table if I had one, but that's beside the point. I'm Rhea. I guess I'm Alex's friend too, even though we just met." I'm rambling and I'm sure I sound like an idiot, but I really can't believe I'm actually meeting *the* Marcus. I'm fan-girling hard.

"Well, any friend of Alex is a friend of mine. Next time you want to come in, you call me personally and I'll make sure you get a table," he says, and hands me a card he's pulled from his shirt pocket and I feel my eyes go wide. "But for tonight I just wanted you to know that if your gentleman friend is anything less than a gentleman, you be sure to holler for me and I will take care of it. Or my husband Domenic will. He's hanging out in my office tonight, and he used to be Special Forces, so... you know." He gives me a little wink and stands.

"I appreciate that. If it comes down to it, though, I was a cop until recently, and I should be able to handle it on my own." Holy shit. *The* Marcus is offering his help if I should need it. This is the best non-date ever.

"Of course, darling. But like I said, any friend of Alex is a friend of mine. And here at Marcus, I take care of my friends." He bends and kisses me on the cheek before turning to walk away. "Oh, and I'm personally preparing your meals tonight, so don't bother with the menus. I'll send your server over to get drink orders shortly."

Wow. It pays to be friends with some people. It's interesting though, that I'm getting special treatment for being friends with Alex, rather than because I'm here with Aiden. I thought people would be falling all over someone who is in such a famous band, but if it came down to it, I think Marcus would love the opportunity to throw Aiden out on his ass. I laugh to myself as I take another sip of my iced water.

"What's so funny?" Aiden says as the hostess directs him to his seat. "I think I missed something."

"Oh, it's nothing. I just met Marcus, and he said something funny, that's all."

My eyes widen as I take him in. It's clear Aiden has taken some pains to dress up a little tonight. He's wearing leg-skimming jeans, a dark gray t-shirt, and a medium-gray sport coat over it. He's also traded in his worn-out sneakers for shiny, dark brown, dress boots. He still has his hair tied up in a bun on top of his head, though, and his face is the perfect amount of scruffy. The overall effect is one of casual, sexy elegance and it has me flooding with heat unprompted.

Stay focused, Rhea. You're here for an apology, not a repeat performance.

"Anything I want to know about?" he asks, a smirk on his gorgeous lips.

"No, I don't think so," I say with another laugh. "Just know that if you don't behave like a gentleman, Marcus is going to have something to say about it."

"Somehow, that doesn't surprise me. Connor told me when he first met Marcus that he made it clear he would take Alex's side in any argument or confrontation. Alex says Marcus is very protective of women, especially those he's acquainted with."

"He seems like a nice guy. He said his husband is here tonight too, in case I needed extra backup." I chuckle a little.

"Domenic? Yeah, I guess he used to be Special Forces? I met him at Alex and Connor's engagement party, and from what I could tell, he's a really nice guy, too." Aiden takes a drink of his water, his eyes drinking me in. "I don't think you'll need their help tonight, though. I'm here to apologize. And I'm sure if I got out of hand you'd be more than able to take care of it, being a former police officer and all."

This is why I dressed up tonight. I want him to see what he's missing out on because of his rude behavior when he ran out on me. An apology won't make me feel a hundred percent better, but it's a start.

I just wish he didn't have to look so good doing it. That will make it harder for me to stick to my guns and stay away, even after an apology. I mean, if the apology is fantastic though...

34

Apology Not Accepted

Aiden

"I KIND OF WISH I hadn't picked such a public place for this apology. It doesn't seem like something I should broadcast across a busy restaurant."

"We're tucked away in the corner here. I think it will be okay." Rhea takes a dainty sip of the whiskey sour she ordered. "Plus, bringing me here almost makes me think you actually feel sorry for pulling such a dick move."

I wince. It was a dick move.

"I really am sorry. I panicked. I don't, uh, do *that* a lot, or ever really, and we forgot a condom, and I can't ever allow myself to have kids, and I've never forgotten before, and I couldn't believe how dumb—"

"Whoa, whoa. Slow down." Rhea interrupts my rambling monologue. "First off, I have an IUD. I was also recently checked, so I'm clean and disease free. You'd know that already if you hadn't run off screaming."

"That's great, but even IUDs can fail. Like if they slip out of position? I read a book once where part of the IUD poked the guy in the dick and pierced the condom and the woman got pregnant." I'm relieved that she's clean, I guess, but honestly, the only thing I've been worried about is the threat of pregnancy. That and the fact I really think I could like this woman. For real. That is what's most dangerous for me.

"I shouldn't even be bothering to console you, given how you made me feel, but I saw my gyno recently and my IUD is still where it should be. We're fine. You can relax. I won't be chasing you down for child support or anything like that." She chugs the rest of her drink and leans back in her chair with her arms crossed over her chest.

"Well, um... Thank you for telling me. That helps."

The server comes by before either of us can say anything else, delivering the first course of our specially prepared meal. We didn't even have to order. Marcus took it upon himself to prepare a special meal for us.

"Is that all you have to say?" Rhea asks when the server leaves again.

"No," I whisper back. "I was waiting until she left again, so we could continue our conversation privately." I take a deep breath. "I'm truly sorry for leaving so quickly after we had sex. And I'm sorry for ranting like a complete asshole the entire time I was leaving."

Rhea's face rapidly turns red, and her mouth takes on a sneer.

"You're sorry for 'leaving quickly'?" She makes air quotes. "You blew your load and shot off me like a cork out of a bottle, and you're *sorry for leaving quickly*?" She huffs an angry laugh, drawing the attention of other diners. "I can't believe you."

"What more do you want me to say?" I whisper, trying to get this conversation under control before we attract too much attention. "I am sorry. I wish it hadn't happened like that. I've never lost control before. My entire life I've been entirely focused on not passing on my genes, and one stupid mistake with you—"

"Stupid mistake?" She hisses, standing up abruptly, banging her lap against the table and causing our drink glasses to slosh.

"That's all I was, hey? A stupid mistake? Jesus, I should have known better than to expect an actual apology from you." She grabs her drink glass, and throws the contents at me, a couple of half melted ice cubes tumbling into my lap. "Of course it's fucking empty," she complains, rolling her eyes to the ceiling before grabbing my drink and dumping it over my head. "There. That's what I think of your apology."

She grabs a napkin and wipes her hands while I stare with my mouth hanging open. This isn't how I expected this to go. Probably should have chosen a less public place.

I turn to watch her storm away. Even as angry as she is, I can't help but notice how strong her back looks in the open back of her dress. Or how incredible her legs look in those heels.

My dick notices too, choosing this moment to get hard, just as Marcus strolls out of the kitchen and over to where I'm sitting.

"Well, well, well," Marcus smiles and tosses me a towel. "Looks like that went real well."

"It was a complete disaster," I say. "I don't even know what more I can do. I said sorry." I do my best to dry my face and hair, letting the liquid soak into my clothes rather than bother with it.

I give Marcus a quick rundown on the situation and when I get to the part where I apologized and Rhea got mad, he laughs. Like a big, booming, belly laugh, that has him doubling over and holding his stomach, begging me to stop.

"You pulled the ultimate fuck and chuck, and thought you could buy dinner and say sorry? And that would make it all okay?" He wipes tears from his eyes and gets his laughter under control. "Who the hell told you that would work?"

"Two friends of ours helped me come up with the plan," I say lamely. Thinking it over now, it really doesn't seem like something that would have worked. I should have asked Alex and Denise maybe, or even Gran. Scratch that, not Gran. Last time she helped Ryder apologize to Denise, she convinced him to propose. Who knows what kind of stunt she'd have come up with in this situation?

"Well, either your friends are stupid, or they weren't aware of the severity of the situation." Marcus sits across from me in Rhea's vacant chair. "So, what are you going to do about it?"

I lean back in my chair. "I don't even know," I say. "Is it even possible to make up for that?"

"I mean, I won't say you'll definitely be able to make it work. But if you really want her to forgive you, then you're going to have to at least try something really big."

Maybe it would be better if she didn't forgive me? Then I wouldn't have to worry about this attraction I'm feeling for her. It wouldn't matter all how I feel since she's so mad at me, the way I feel won't make a difference. It should be easy enough to avoid her for a little while, too. If I skip Sunday dinners for a few weeks, and I avoid the coffee shop, I'll have almost a month to forget about her. There's nothing saying that just because I'm thinking about having a relationship for the first time, I actually need to make it happen. I should stick to my original plan of staying alone, never passing on my genes, and working to help mothers and kids out of situations like I was in before it's too late for them.

"Thanks, Marcus. I'll think about that. Let me settle up and I'll get out of here, give you back your table."

Marcus waves the server over for me before heading back to the kitchen and I pass her my credit card. I leave her a nice tip even though we didn't end up staying for the full meal. No sense in the server missing out because I'm an idiot. After I sign the bill, I stuff my hands in my pockets and head out the door.

My mind is filled with thoughts of Rhea, and I'm in a daze until I'm pulling into my driveway. The sooner I get her out of my head, the better. I've been nothing but distracted since I saw her on the sidewalk that day. I don't even remember getting into my car and driving home tonight. That can't be good.

It's early still, so I strip off my jacket, settle into my recliner, and start up a video game. And that's where I sit, zoned out, for the next hour until I drag my sorry ass to bed.

Too bad I can't relax enough to sleep. Instead, I go over Rhea's angry outburst in my head, and allow myself to bathe in the shame of making her feel that way. I really am sorry, and I really do care that I hurt her.

But it's better for both of us if I let her stay angry so we can both move on. She deserves someone who will be with her one hundred percent, not someone who's too afraid of his nature to give himself fully to her.

35

Return of the Fifty Foot Yard Dick

Rhea

THAT IDIOT. I CAN'T believe he thought *that* would be enough of an apology for what he did. And how could he call what he did 'leaving quickly'? That is the understatement of the century.

I'm stomping down the street in my dress, its open back letting in the frosty evening air, so besides being tense with rage, I'm shivering in the cold. I must have a crazy look on my face or something because every other pedestrian is giving me a wide berth, giving the illusion I have my own private sidewalk. Thank god for that, because I absolutely do not have the patience to be battling slow walkers tonight.

How could he even consider what he did as an apology? He didn't even realize what he really did wrong. Leaving quickly? Leaving quickly my ass. He sped out of there like he was on fast-forward. If I'd blinked, I would have missed it.

And yet, for some reason, I still did what I could to reassure him there would be no baby to worry about. What did he even mean when he said he can't allow himself to have kids? I could understand not wanting kids, or not liking kids, but not allowing yourself to have them? That's some weird shit. He said he doesn't want to pass on his genes. Maybe he has some genetic condition that's hereditary? Like hemophilia? Or something like that?

Gah! If he has a legitimate medical reason, then I might feel a tiny bit sorry for him. But he still shouldn't have been a dick to me.

Of course, he tried to do something nice for me when he burned a giant penis into Franklin Martin's lawn. That was actually pretty cool. He's lucky he didn't get caught for that.

I wonder whatever happened with the drone footage his friend was supposed to send him. I would have liked to have seen it before I erased Aiden from my life forever. Not that it's going to be hard to stay away from him. If I don't go back to Alex's for Sunday dinner, and if I avoid Xena's coffee shop, then I should be fine.

It was nice having so many girlfriends today, though. I've never had such a fun experience shopping as I did today. They're all so friendly and nice, and fun to hang out with. And I can't forget Gran and the rest of the Titty Club. I want to be like them when I grow up. All tracksuits and not giving any fucks. Maybe she'll waive the droopy boobs requirement this once and let me join?

Luckily, my rage keeps me warm as I storm the entire ten blocks from Marcus to my apartment. And thankfully I remembered my tiny purse with my phone and keys, or I'd be stuck outside again, with nowhere to go, and no Aiden to rescue me this time. Not that I needed rescuing, but it was nice to not sleep on the street that night.

It's only when I'm unlocking the door to my apartment that I remember a critical piece of information: I drove to the damn restaurant.

I rage-stomped all the way home, in ridiculously high heels—ridiculously high for me, anyway— in the cold, when I could have driven in comfort. And now I'm going to have to walk my ass back there to pick up my car. I wonder if I can wait until morning for that? Probably not a good idea, considering

I parked on the street. It would be my luck to get towed and have to pick up at the police compound, just to increase my embarrassment.

Fine. I'll go pick the damn car up now. I'm not walking there wearing this stupid dress or these stupid shoes, though. I strip out of both until I'm standing in my underwear, digging around in my closet for something more comfortable. Finally, clad in comfy tie dye joggers with a matching hoodie, I put on socks, lace up my sneakers, grab my keys and phone, and head out on my way to retrace my steps along the same ten blocks I just walked.

It takes much less time to walk back to my car than it did to walk from the restaurant to my apartment. Thank god for small miracles. I guess my rage stomping wasn't as effective a method of transportation as I thought. Of course, sneakers are much easier to walk in than heels, which probably contributed to my increase in speed.

I don't waste any time getting home and parking in my spot behind the building. It's nice not needing to park on the street here, but having to walk around to the front of the building to get to my apartment is kind of a pain in the ass. I'm imagining what it would take to get a window that I can unlock from the outside so I could use the fire escape, so I don't notice the person standing near the entrance until I run right into him.

"Oh, sorry about that," I say automatically, without looking up.

"Hello, Officer Ryan. Oops, I guess I mean Miss Ryan. Because you're not an officer anymore, are you?" My head snaps up at being addressed by name. The asshole who got me arrested is standing in front of me with a sneer on his face.

"What are you doing here, Mr. Martin?" I'm not afraid, necessarily, but I can't say I feel good about having this guy hanging around my building after dark. "I thought our business concluded when you got me fired."

"See, that's what I thought, too. But imagine my surprise when I got home from a nice long weekend away, to see someone had vandalized my lawn. I wonder who could have done that? Any ideas?" He stands a little too close to me. Not enough that someone driving by would notice, but enough that it's making me uncomfortable.

This guy is crazy if he thinks I would tell him who did this. And he's even crazier if he thinks I did it. He has a strange gleam in his eye that tells me I should tread carefully.

"Oh dear," I feign concern with my hand to my chest. "Did you report it to the police? I'm sure they'd be able to help track down the culprit. Or maybe the mayor can step in to help you? You guys are close friends, right?"

Whoops. Guess I'm not so good at heeding warnings emitted from the eyes of crazy assholes who got me fired. That's probably a character flaw on my part.

"You know," he says, a smarmy look coming over his face. "That's a good idea, Offic—I mean, Miss Ryan. Calling on a friend, that is. You see, I have many good friends in Westborough. The mayor is but one of them. Are you aware that I also know many property owners? Why, I believe this building here actually belongs to a friend of mine. Isn't that interesting?"

This son of a bitch is threatening my home? I can't let him get away with this, can I? I groan internally. But what can *I* do about it? Franklin Martin already got me fired from my job. It's not a big stretch to believe he could get me kicked out of my apartment.

"Well, Mr. Martin. I didn't know that. You're right, it is interesting. If you don't mind, I'm going to be on my way now. I hope you get your lawn problem sorted out."

Rather than go into my building and risk having Martin follow me, I speed walk down the street a few blocks until I get to the first business open at this time in the evening, which just so happens to be Bump & Grind. It's not her night to close, but Xena is here anyway, and a uniformed Kaden appears to be keeping her company.

"Whoa, tiger. What's the big rush?" Kaden asks, when I continue running until I bang right into the counter. "What if I'd been standing there?"

I bend over, hands on my knees, and force my breathing to slow.

"Frank Martin was hanging around my building just now. He thinks I vandalized his lawn and basically threatened to get me kicked out of my apartment."

"He what?" Xena yells. "Are you okay?"

Kaden bursts into action, running out the door before I can stop him. He's on duty tonight, so he has his gun if anything terrible happens. If he finds Martin hanging around my apartment, he could probably bring him in for harassment or something. While it would be a weight off my shoulders tonight, it would probably increase the chances of him making me homeless soon.

Xena made her way around the counter while I was watching Kaden run out the door and now she's patting me down, making me feel like I'm acting the part of the victim in a first aid training class.

"I'm fine," I say, brushing her off. "He didn't do anything, only talked to me." And scared me a little, but I'm not telling her that. Not that I need to, really. She saw me run in here at full speed, so I'm sure she's aware. She leads me to the nearest chair and pushes me into it.

"He's gone," Kaden says, as soon as he pushes the door open. "I couldn't see where he went."

Kaden's radio squawks from its place on his belt and he steps into the back hallway to answer it.

I put my head down on the table in front of me. "What am I going to do? I don't want to move." I can't even afford it now, anyway. Plus, I don't even have a job. Not too many places want to rent to the unemployed.

"Well, you could turn Aiden in," Xena says, making it sound more like a question than a suggestion. "He's the one who did it, after all. Not you."

"No," I say, without hesitation. "There has to be another way." He may be shit at apologies, but I can't turn him in for this. It's not like he hurt anyone, really. Plus, he was trying to get revenge for me in a non-violent way. As ridiculous as it is, it's kind of sweet.

Not that I think *he's* sweet. I'm still mad at him.

Super mad.

Right?

My phone buzzes from the pocket of my hoodie. I pull it out to look and I notice it's from Aiden. Speak of the devil. And of the incident in question. He's sent me the drone video his friend took of the lawn dick.

And another apology.

And a joke.

"I think I have an idea," I say with a laugh to a confused-looking Xena. "Kaden," I yell so he can hear me from the back, "can you take me back to my place so I can get my car? I have something I need to do."

I just hope it's not as stupid as it sounds in my head.

36

Wooing. Wooing. Wooing? What the hell does that even mean?

Aiden

I'VE ONLY BEEN IN bed for about half an hour before an incoming text disturbs me. It's drone footage from my friend Nathan. I guess I made him promise to take some for me during daylight hours today, and I completely forgot.

```
Nathan - Here's the footage. I
got caught up in something after
I shot it. Sorry it's so late.
```

```
Aiden - Thanks, man. I owe you.
```

```
Nathan - No problem.
```

I open up the attached video and check out my handiwork, snickering like a twelve-year-old kid the whole time. That is one enormous dick we made. It's a good thing Nathan could help me out with the drone footage or I'd never have been able to see the whole dick in one pic. It would have been more like a dick pic puzzle than a dick pic.

Before I can talk myself out of it, I pull up Rhea's contact information and forward the video to her.

Aiden - That's footage of the lawn dick if you're interested.

Aiden - I'm really sorry about everything.

Aiden - Except that dick pic I just sent you :D I worked hard on that.

Aiden - Okay, I'll leave you alone now. Again, I'm really sorry. I never meant to hurt you. Also, I'm a stupid, fucked up asshole.

There. She's not going to magically forgive me now that I've made a pathetic dick pic joke, but since I've already decided it's probably better if she doesn't forgive me, it doesn't matter if she likes the dumb joke or not.

What if she could forgive me, though? What if I could let go of my hang-ups about being like my asshole dad? Could I have a life with someone? Like with Rhea?

All I know is my heart and brain don't seem to like the plan of letting her stay mad at me. Which must be why I'm sitting here, picturing her laughing at my stupid joke, and sending me back her own message, asking for a real pic. And then I'd send her a picture of someone named Richard, because no way I'm sending a pic of my dick for real. But then she'd laugh some more and come over and see my dick in person.

Well, would you look at that? My dick is a big fan of this little daydream, apparently. He's even having his own little camp out to celebrate it. I'm debating whether I should join my dick's camp out (aka jerk off) when the doorbell rings.

All the guys have keys, and it's not exactly early right now. So who could be at my door?

It's her! My dick yells with excitement. Okay, my dick doesn't really talk, but the thought that it's Rhea at the door crosses *my* mind. I was just imagining a very similar scenario, after all. But my dick and I are both going to need to get used to the fact that we won't be seeing Rhea anymore. No sense in hoping for something that won't happen. Eventually, we'll both stop thinking about her constantly. At least I hope we will.

The doorbell rings again. Whoever it is, they're impatient.

It's her, it's her, she's here to see me. My dick's getting excited now. I hate to ruin his party by telling him it's probably Johnny. I bet he got too drunk and forgot he has a key. And now he's ringing the doorbell. Again.

Fuck.

Groaning with the effort, I roll out of bed and pull on a pair of jeans without bothering to do them up. I tuck my hard on away a little better, but that's as good as it's going to get. Whoever is at the door is just going to have to deal with seeing me shirtless, with my pants undone. That's what you get for ringing my doorbell this late in the evening. At least it's late enough to know for sure there won't be any little kids out trying to sell me cookies or something.

I'm halfway down the stairs when the doorbell rings again.

"I'm coming," I yell out. "Calm down."

Without a thought for my safety, I rush to the door and throw it open. "What the hell do you wa…" I trail off, my jaw dropping to the floor.

It's Rhea.

Hold on. My dick was right?

Fuck yeah, I was, he says. *Now get her in here and strip her clothes off so I can get down to business.*

"Hey."

Told you, my dick says. I don't appreciate his smug tone, so I tell him to shut up.

"Hi. Uh, hey," I say, when I finally manage to pick my jaw up off the floor. "Did you get the video?"

"Yeah, that's why I'm here. Can I come in?" She shakes her head a little and finally looks up into my face. I guess going shirtless was the right choice after all. It appears she likes what she sees, anyway.

I step out of the way and motion for her to join me inside. She kicks her shoes off into the house and walks past me. It's not exactly like my daydream, but it's close enough that my already hard dick somehow gets even harder. I'm extra thankful I didn't do up my jeans because this hard-on pressing against my zipper would have hurt and it's already painful enough as it is.

"So, first things first. Yes, you are a stupid asshole. You made me feel like shit when you ran away. Not *left quickly*. You jumped off me and bolted, and it was a really shitty thing to do." She fixes me with a glare that would be enough to convince a convict to clean up his act, making me shudder and wince at the same time. "That's not the only reason I'm here, though. I'm here because Franklin Martin caught up with me outside my apartment tonight," Rhea says, sitting on the couch and wrapping her arms around herself. "And because your text came through at the perfect time to cheer me up."

"The asshole who got you fired?" I see red and it takes everything in me to calmly walk over and sit near her on the couch instead of racing out of here to track that bastard down. "How does he know where you live? And why was he there? Did he hurt you? Did you call Kaden?" I blurt the questions one on top of the other, too panicked to wait for her answers. My breath comes faster and a white-hot rage is filling my belly. Adrenaline courses through my body and I suddenly have too much energy to sit still. I jump up out of my seat and start pacing when I realize something. "Holy shit. This is my fault, isn't it?"

"He came because of the yard dick," she admits. "But he doesn't have any proof of who did it, and I'm not turning you in or anything. I'm only somewhat concerned because he said he knows the man who owns my building. He was making it sound like he could get me kicked out of my apartment."

"Well, fuck that. You can move in here." I shake my head. That's a terrible idea. "No, that won't work. Connor were right about this place being full of horrible memories and sadness. You can't be subjected to that long-term." I'm still pacing, mentally kicking myself for getting drunk and getting her into this mess. This is exactly why I normally spend so much time in the planning stage of my revenge missions. I can take precautions so things like this don't happen. Getting drunk and going off half-cocked causes nothing but problems. "I'll buy us a new apartment to move into. I'm sure there are units available in Devon's building. No, wait. You don't want to live with me. You don't even like me. And I can't blame you for that. Hell, *I* don't even like me."

"Whoa, slow down there, champ. You're getting a little carried away, don't you think?" She gets up and comes over to me, grabbing my hand and pulling me back to the couch to sit.

"You can't go home tonight," I say, releasing a huge sigh. "It's not safe."

"I know that." She looks up at me. "I was hoping maybe I could use your guest room again?"

"Anytime." I pull her into a hug. "Forever. Well, not forever," I say, releasing the hug but holding onto her arms. "This place isn't made for someone as good as you."

"What do you mean? As good as me? You're good. You're the only person who even tried to do anything other than talking to help me feel better about getting fired. You let me stay here the night I forgot my keys, even though you barely know me. I could have been a crazy stalker. I was wearing your picture on my shirt, remember?"

I laugh, remembering that interaction at the club. It's still funny to me how she pulled her shirt off and held it up to my face to determine if I was telling the truth.

"You acted so disgusted with me that I knew immediately you weren't a fan. Plus, the whole being a cop thing. And being friends with Devon and Xena. I had a feeling I'd be okay. And if you murdered me in my sleep?" I shrug. "At least I got to spend my last night alive in the company of a beautiful, smart, hilarious, and caring woman."

"That's the sweetest thing anyone has ever said to me," Rhea says, her eyes shining. "I mean, besides the whole murdering you in your sleep part."

I bark out a laugh. "Yeah, I probably could have left that part out. I'm not exactly practiced in the art of wooing women."

"Is that what you're doing? You're wooing me?" She chuckles. "I can't say that anyone has ever mentioned murder during that act of wooing me before. So... points for originality?"

We both lean back against the couch, side by side, shoulders touching. And it's the most comfortable I've felt in this house since... well, probably ever.

"I never thought I'd be wooing a woman at all, let alone wooing one wearing head-to-toe tie-dye." I glance over at her swirls of pink, blue, and yellow. "Also, I think I've heard 'wooing' more times in the last few minutes than I have ever heard it in my entire life. It doesn't even make sense anymore. Wooing, wooing, wooing. Nope. That's not a word. It's clearly nonsense."

She laughs. "This outfit is your fault, I'll have you know." She turns to look at me, one leg coming up onto the couch cushions, knee bent and pushing into my thigh. "I was so mad at you when I left the restaurant that I forgot I drove. I stormed home in just my dress and heels. I didn't even realize what I'd done until I was unlocking the door to my apartment."

I burst into laughter. "Oh fuck, I'm so sorry. I shouldn't be laughing. You must have been freezing." I slide a little further away from her on the couch and pull her feet into my lap. "And your poor feet. Those heels were something else, but I can't imagine they were the most comfortable to walk in. At least not for that distance." She looked fucking sexy in that dress and those heels, but I don't like thinking of her walking all the way home in them. Particularly since it's only because I'm such a fucking idiot that she felt she had to do it at all.

I grab one foot and start rubbing, pressing into her arch, sliding my thumbs front to back, side to side, and rotating my hands around, getting everything nice and loose. Rhea closes her eyes and leans back, resting her head on the arm of the couch.

"That's why I changed before I went back to get my car. I almost left it overnight, but I didn't want to risk it getting towed. It was a much warmer, and much more comfortable walk back." She snuggles further down into the couch, eyes still closed. "This is some quality wooing right here. Tell me why you never thought you'd be wooing anyone. And you're right. The word *wooing* now makes no sense."

Something about Rhea makes me want to tell her everything about me. Even though I know she's going to be scared of me when I'm done telling her, I can't help but hope she'll want to stick around despite her fear.

I let out a heavy sigh, preparing myself to tell another person about my father, and why I've never tried to be in a relationship before, for the first time in my life.

Here goes nothing.

37

Cautionary Tales of the Occult

Rhea

"I HAD A BIT of a rough start in life." Aiden says.

He's still massaging my foot, which feels absolutely amazing. Maybe I should walk all over town in heels more often if this is what will happen at the end of the day.

"My dad hated me from day one. I don't know why, or what I ever did to deserve it, but for as long as I can remember, he would take his frustrations out on me."

I open my eyes and look at him. He's looking down, watching his hands where he's rubbing my foot, and I'm not sure he even notices what they are doing anymore. I think he's using it to distract himself from what he's saying.

"It started out with insults and gradually got worse, until I was going to school with bruises, and making regular trips to the hospital." He releases a shuddering breath, still holding my foot, but no longer rubbing. "Social workers questioned me, school guidance counselors, teachers even, but nothing ever came of it. Somehow, they never removed me from my parents. My dad was never held accountable, and I didn't get away until I moved out the day I turned eighteen. I tried leaving when I was younger, but he always found me and had me brought home."

"I don't even know what to say, Aiden. I'm so sorry." I sit up and pull him into a hug, burying my face in his neck. "But you're going to have to tell me where he's buried, because I have this burning need to dig him up and kill him again for what he did to you."

Aiden snickers a little in my grip, wrapping his arms around me and pulling me in tight.

"Me too, baby. Me too," he says into my hair. He loosens his grip a little, but doesn't let me go entirely. We're sitting together on the couch, arms wrapped around each other, when he continues. "When my family died, I inherited this house and some money from a life insurance policy my mom had. I moved back in, bought my first set of drums, and used the rest of the money to pay tuition at an online university, where I got my degree in Social Work."

He goes quiet and I rest my head against his chest, my arms wrapped around him, and listen to his breathing. I suspected something like this when he told me he had a shitty childhood, but I didn't think it had lasted until he was an adult. I thought maybe he'd been in foster care like I had. I can't even imagine what it must have been like for him growing up.

"I need to tell you something I've never told anyone before," Aiden says after a long silence. "It's the main reason I behaved the way I did after we... well, you know, after we had sex. I'm not making an excuse, though. No matter the reason I did it, you deserved better."

I unwind my arms from around him and sit up. Aiden lets out a heavy sigh and takes my hands in his.

"I'm sure you know some of this, but when I was eighteen, my entire family died in a car accident. It was a single vehicle accident with no witnesses." He takes another deep breath and looks into my eyes. "I've always thought my father did it on purpose."

I take a minute to digest what he's saying. He thinks his father was responsible for the accident that killed his family? And he's been living with this, alone, for the last twenty-something years? My heart stops.

"Oh my god, Aiden. That's horrible. I'm so sorry you lost your mom and your sister. Did you tell the police about your suspicions when the accident happened? Did they investigate?"

"Yes, but there was no evidence to make them think it was a possibility. He didn't leave a note or anything. It's just a feeling I've always had." He sighs and looks down at his lap. "I know it doesn't make any sense. It happened so soon after I could finally move out. I guess I've always thought that without me around to vent his anger on, he just lost it and took it out on my mom and my little sister. That means it's my fault that they died." He clears his throat. "So I stayed away from relationships and avoided sex almost entirely because I don't want to pass on whatever fucked up genes caused my father to be such a monster. And the idea of me having a child and then turning into a monster like he was, scares me to death. That's why I lost it when I realized we forgot to use a condom. It wasn't anything to do with you; you were perfect. I'm just a messed up asshole."

I pull him into my arms and guide his head down onto my shoulder, rubbing his back and rocking him like I would a child who's been hurt. This poor man has lived the last twenty years believing that escaping his abuser is the reason his family died. That if he'd stayed, and let his father keep hurting him, his family would still be here. My heart is in my stomach and tears spill down my cheeks while Aiden releases a shuddering breath.

There is one thing from what he said that strikes me as odd, though, causing a full body shudder to roll through me. And it's nagging me so much that I need to ask him about it. I grab him by the shoulders and push him up so I can look him in the eyes.

"Aiden, are you telling me that this was your parents' house?"

He raises an eyebrow at me and then has a look around. "Uh, yeah?"

So *that's* what Connor was trying to say about Aiden's house having so many terrible memories attached to it. This is the house that Aiden lived in with his family. With his abusive father.

And Connor doesn't even know the worst of it. How Aiden can stand living here is beyond me. Knowing what I know now, five minutes after he told me about it, has me wanting to run out of here screaming because this place is giving me the creeps. I'm not normally one to put much stock into the vibe or feeling of a place, but I think in this instance I'm going to follow my gut.

I stand up abruptly, grabbing Aiden's hand as I do. "Get up," I say, already dragging him toward the stairs. "We need to pack you a bag. We're going to stay at my place. This place feels all wrong now."

"I... what?" Aiden drags his feet, forcing me to stop just shy of the stairs. "What do you mean? I can't just leave."

"Of course you can." I start dragging him again. "Frankly, I can't believe you've lived in this house as long as you have. I may not be entirely sure how I feel about you, but I know I can't get you out of my head. It might be nothing or it might be everything, but whatever it is I feel, I can't sit here imagining how your asshole of a father hurt you here. It's too much. So we need to go."

He stumbles along behind me as I drag him to his room. "What about Martin? What if he comes back to your place?"

"Come on. I'm sure you're not afraid of him. I'm not even afraid of him, really. He surprised me outside my building more than he scared me. I'm worried that he could get me kicked out of my apartment. But I can deal with that tomorrow. Tonight, we're getting out of this house.

"I'm not saying it's the next Amityville or anything, but I'm not sitting around waiting for green slime to come down the walls to find out for sure. And I'm really not interested in seeing a red-eyed pig man watching us through the windows."

"You realize they didn't actually die in this house, right? It's not like this place is haunted or something." He's chuckling a little. At least my irrational fear is good for something.

"For such a smart guy, I find it odd that you can't feel the weird juju, or mojo, or vibes, or whatever this place has. Why have you stayed here? I would have sold this place as soon as my name was on the papers. I bet if you tried to dig a pool you'd discover a secret cemetery under your property." I'm throwing clothes at him from his drawers, mostly jeans and t-shirts, letting him grab his own boxers. I don't need any more reminders of what he's got going on under his pants. We're in the middle of an evacuation here, we don't have time for that.

"Are you saying my house has a poltergeist?" He snickers.

"No, I'm not saying that, not exactly. I'm saying this house is giving me a bad feeling and I want to leave. And I want you to come with me. So let's get moving, buster. Time is money."

Time is money? What am I even saying? This place must really creep me out if I'm busting out weird stuff like that.

"Nah, I'm pretty sure you've been likening my house to haunted houses in horror movies. What's next? You going to worry about possessed dolls coming to life and running around here?" He laughs, a deep belly laugh.

"Don't be ridiculous," I tell him, stuffing clothes into a suitcase that I dragged from the closet. "Something like that is much more likely to happen at my place, considering I'm the one who lives directly above a creepy doll store."

Aiden shakes his head and laughs, but at least he also goes into the bathroom to gather up some toiletries. Good. Looks like he's won't put up too much of a fight about this little sleepover arrangement.

"You're going to thank me for this when neither of us winds up spewing pea soup vomit with our heads rotating all the way around," I yell toward the hallway. "I hear that stuff is a bitch to get out of the carpet."

"You know," he says, coming back into the bedroom and throwing a Dopp kit into the open suitcase, "something tells me you may watch too many horror movies. Just a thought."

"Horror movies?" I look at him and ask, putting what I hope is a puzzled look on my face. "Oh, you mean the educational cautionary tales of the occult that I like to watch late at night, in the dark, by myself?"

Aiden barks out a laugh and bends to zip up his suitcase. "Yeah right. Next you're going to tell me you sleep with a creepy doll from the store below your apartment."

"Oh no." I shake my head. "Uh Uh. No way. I know better. Remember what you said about possessed dolls coming to life? You think I'd invite something like that into my bed? Yeah. I'll pass thanks."

He chuckles while shaking his head at me. "Come on, scaredy cat," he says, picking up his suitcase in one hand and lacing his fingers through mine with the other. "You can tell me the rest of what you've learned from your *educational tales* when we get to your place."

Taking Aiden to my place is probably not the best idea I've ever had, but I can't bring myself to care. He's taken up residence in my head, maybe even in my heart, and I want to see where this goes.

38

Don't be a Stupid Fucking Asshole

Aiden

"SEE? ISN'T THAT NICE? Now, aren't you glad we took my car instead of yours?" Rhea asks, a smug look on her face. I almost don't want to answer. I'm too busy sinking into the plush, heated leather seats of her Jeep, letting the warmth soak into my back and soothe aches I didn't even know I had.

Pushing forty takes a toll on the body, that's for sure.

"Yeah, yeah. Smartass," I drawl. "You were right. Happy?"

"Very," she says with a laugh. "Being right is good for the soul. You should try it sometime."

I give her a one-eyed glare, which she, of course, laughs at. "How about you drive around for a bit and let me enjoy these heated seats some more and then I'll forgive you for that one," I joke before nestling down further into the seat and shutting my eyes tight. "Now hush. I need a nap before I take on all the crazy, possessed dolls at your place."

I hear her snicker and then feel a light smack on my arm. Neither of us says anything further. Instead, I cross my arms over my chest and relish the feeling of the warm seat against my back while Rhea drives to her place. I don't know how long this will last, but being with Rhea feels right. When she's not mad at me, anyway.

Turns out Rhea didn't drive directly to her place. She drove around for an hour and let me sleep.

"I'm sorry, I couldn't wait any longer," she says, rushing to undo her seat belt and get out of the car. "I have to pee so bad I'm about to burst." She dances in place outside the car, motioning for me to go faster, but I'm still a little out of it. "Screw it. I'll leave the doors unlocked for you. Just go around the building to the front."

She sprints off as I finally get myself out of the car and grab my suitcase from the back. Looking around the back parking lot, I can't say that I'm too happy Rhea has to park here. It is lit, but the lights seem dim, and there are lots of shadows where a person could hide if they were inclined to jump out and surprise her. And after that Martin guy surprised her tonight, I don't like the idea of her being alone here either. I guess it's a good thing that she insisted I stay here.

My suitcase isn't very heavy, despite all the clothes I saw Rhea pack. I wonder if she realizes she packed me enough to stay here for a couple of weeks? That can't possibly be her intention, can it? Does she really feel that strongly about the *vibe* at my house? I never would have pegged her as a superstitious person, but she sure didn't like my house after I told her about my dad.

I can hardly even believe I told her my suspicions. I told her my darkest secret, and she didn't look disgusted or anything. Well, she looked a little freaked out about the house, but not about me. How can she even stand to look at me, let alone invite me into her home now that she knows I have the potential to turn into such a terrible person? This secret has plagued me for so long because I was positive that everyone I love would leave when they found out.

Wait a minute. I wonder if it's because she was a cop. She's used to dealing with the dregs of society, so the thought that I could be a bad person doesn't affect her as much as it would someone who wasn't in law enforcement. That's got to be it. It would scare any normal person to death to be around the son of a probable killer. So I wasn't wrong; she's just numb to it because she's used to dealing with criminals in her everyday life.

But still... Just because she's used to it doesn't mean she'd want to be with a guy like me. I can't read too much into this, even if I find myself liking her more and more as the days go by.

"Are you going to stand there and stare at the streetlights all night, or are you coming in?" Rhea's voice snaps me out of my thoughts and I realize I've been standing out here with my suitcase at my feet, staring off into the distance. "It's been almost twenty minutes. I came to check on you to make sure nothing bad happened."

I pick up my bag and make my way over to where she stands at the back corner of the building. It's darker where she's standing and I'm a little angry at how unsafe it is for her to have to do this every time she gets home at night.

"This parking lot is too dark. Can't you park on the street instead?"

She gives me a funny look before turning to lead me to the front door. "I could if I wanted my car towed. Street parking isn't allowed overnight downtown. That's why I walked all the way back to Marcus earlier. I didn't want to deal with guys at the impound lot giving me shit over getting fired."

I reach out and pull open the door before Rhea has the chance, motioning her to go ahead. Once we're both inside, she stops to lock the door behind us and leads me up the stairs. The last time we were here, we were moments away from ripping each other's clothes off and it's hard not to dwell on the memory.

"Why would they give you shit?" I ask. "They have to be aware of the circumstances, don't they? It's not like it was really your fault."

"I'm sure they're aware, but I've always been a stickler for the rules. People must think it's funny that I'm the one to get fired for something like this. Everyone knows I would never use excessive force or do anything out of line. So they'd be teasing more than anything, but I'm still not ready to deal with it."

I open her apartment door at the top of the stairs and she enters ahead of me.

"So..." I say, after closing and locking the door behind me. "What now?"

"I didn't really plan this out," she says with a chuckle, walking into the kitchen. "I'm grabbing water. Want something to drink?"

"No thanks, I'm good."

I drop my suitcase by the door and look around her apartment. We were a little preoccupied, so I didn't notice much last time I was here. It's not a huge apartment, but it is a decent size. Big enough for a full-size couch at least, and that's where I plant myself now, hands clasped behind my head and feet stretched out to the coffee table.

"Are we going to watch one of your educational films? You know, to prepare me for when I go back to my house?" It was adorable how she jumped into high gear and started packing up clothes for me, but this clearly is not a very well-thought-out plan. I'm not sure what I'm even doing here, other than it seemed to make Rhea happy to have me go along with her. I really enjoy making her happy.

"Oh sure, *now* you want to benefit from the wisdom of the occult films, but at your place, you were laughing and telling me

I watch too many horror movies." She sits on the couch near me, but not beside me, and it takes everything I have to stop myself from sliding closer. "What makes you think I want to prepare you to return home, anyway? Maybe getting you here tonight is part of my evil plan to keep you locked up in my basement to use as I see fit?"

Yes! That's what I'm talking about. Use me! Shut up, dick. She's not talking about that. She probably wants someone around to help rearrange furniture and open jars and shit. There's no way she's talking about keeping me as a prisoner for sex. *But what if she is? Don't ruin this for me, asshole.* I shake my head to clear the imaginary voice of my dick. It can't be normal to hear the voice of an appendage as often as I do. Maybe I should see someone about that?

"Hey, you okay? You got lost there for a second." Rhea moves closer, still not touching me, but now within my reach. "Don't be scared. I wouldn't actually keep you locked up in my basement." She takes a drink of her water and adds with a wink, "I don't even have a basement."

I laugh. "Not scared, exactly. I am a little curious about what you would use me for, though. It could be a decent job if I decide I want to retire from the band. You know, something to keep me busy."

"I don't know if you could handle it, actually. It would be pretty physically demanding. You're not getting any younger. Your body is bound to give out on you eventually."

I'm at a loss for words. I still can't tell if Rhea is talking about sex or not. My body clearly wants her to be, though, and I'm trying to discreetly change my position to avoid her noticing my raging erection. *Don't you try to stifle me,* my dick says. *I'll have you know many men would be proud to have me so eager to perform at a moment's notice with no little blue pill required.* Oh my god, dick, shut up. I shift so my pelvis is twisted slightly away from Rhea, hoping that does the trick. *You're suffocating me,* my dick complains again.

"Oh, my... I'm so sorry, Aiden. I must be making you so uncomfortable. After everything you told me tonight, I can't believe I would sit here and flirt with you. I'm sorry. We can keep this strictly platonic." Her hand feels hot when she puts it on my leg. "You don't have to turn away from me. Just friends from now on, okay?"

Is she serious right now? Does she think I'm uncomfortable with the flirting? My brain couldn't even figure out that it *was* flirting. *But I figured it out,* my dick says in the back of my mind. Women like Rhea don't come along every day, and I figured I fucked up any real chance I had with her first when I ran away after sleeping with her, and second when I made a mockery of my apology earlier. This feels like a chance she's giving me and I'll be damned if I fuck this up, too.

Slowly, I turn my body back toward Rhea. "I'm not uncomfortable because of that, Rhea. I'm uncomfortable because of how badly I fucking want you. The amount of care you showed for me tonight is something I'm not used to."

39

He Talks to You?

Rhea

"I mean, you risked your bladder exploding to let me sleep a little longer on the drive over here. Not to mention whatever desperation made you pack up my stuff and insist I stay here tonight."

"Of course I insisted you stay here tonight. You shouldn't be in that house. I don't understand how you can live there. It must be full of horrible memories for you. And I'm starting to think... maybe, maybe I do care. About you. A little." I actually suspect it's more than a little, but I can't tell him that. He's already told me relationships are off the table.

Aiden smiles and moves closer to me on the couch. "You think you might care about me?" He reaches up and cups my face in his hand, brings our foreheads together, and whispers, "I think I might care about you, too. And that scares me to death." He lets out a sigh. "But I think if I don't at least make an attempt with you, I'll regret it for the rest of my life."

I feel his lips brush mine, the barest of touches, and my breath mingles with his.

"I've been thinking about you non-stop," he says, placing gentle kisses along my lips, causing butterflies to flit around my stomach. "The way you smell, the way you taste, the way you look, the sound of your voice, even the way you take everything in stride. Everything about you draws me in, and I'm so fuck-ing tired of fighting it."

Aiden's hands wind into my hair, tilting my head while he slants his lips over mine. His tongue tickles my lower lip, and I fist my hands in his shirt, pulling him closer. I try to climb into his lap, but he stops me, laying me down on the couch instead, notching his body between my legs. I can feel how hard he is through our clothes and I roll my hips, pressing myself against him. He groans and thrusts against me.

"Not so fast, Rhea. We're taking our time tonight. Last time, I didn't take the time to properly worship your body. I intend to fix that," he says against my mouth, interrupting his slow perusal of my tongue for a moment.

He teases the skin at the hem of my shirt, pushing it up so slowly that I lose patience and quickly rip it over my head and throw it across the room. "I need you to touch me," I say when he chuckles. "Now."

"Someone is a little impatient. And what's this? No bra?" He groans and drops his head back. "A guy could get used to this."

My skin is burning with the need for his touch. I want to feel his skin against mine, feel him inside me, and he says I'm impatient? I'll show him impatient. I thrust up quickly and drive my hip and shoulder into him, flipping us over and off the couch onto the floor. We land with a thud and Aiden's eyes open wide in surprise. I straddle his hips and grind against him.

"How's this for impatient?" I ask, bending and kissing along his jaw to his neck. His short beard scratches my skin slightly, promising to leave me pink after.

When Aiden grabs hold of my hips and pulls me down, forcing me to grind against the length of his cock, I can feel how hard he is for me. Fuck, he feels good. My orgasm is building already.

"I'm the one who should be impatient, babe. I've been hard for you for days. I'm so relentlessly turned on by you that I've started hallucinating that my dick talks. And he's *so* mean to me all the time. I don't think he likes me very much."

"Oh, really?" I murmur against his ear, nipping at his earlobe. Maybe it's because I'm in a lust-fueled daze, but it sounds like Aiden just told me his dick talks to him.

"Yeah, he really likes you though," he says, grinding against me again, pushing my orgasm a little closer. "And so do I."

Aiden grabs me and rolls us again, putting him on top of me once more. Suddenly, he pins my hands to the floor above and kisses me again, deeper this time.

"God damn it, Aiden. Stop torturing me," I whine, and try to rub myself against him.

"Ah ah. Not yet, babe. I haven't finished exploring." He kisses down my neck to my breasts, pulling a nipple into his mouth, lightly grazing me with his teeth. I gasp and arch my back, pushing closer to him. "You're the first woman I've ever thought I could have something with. I need time to get to know your body better."

If this is how Aiden woos a woman, then sign me up.

My skin lights up everywhere he kisses me, the heat rushing through my body.

"That feels so good," I say. "Keep going."

He trails kisses to my other breast, lavishing it with the same attention he did the first, and little shocks of pleasure shoot straight to my clit every time he grazes me with his teeth. My breath is coming faster, and wetness is pooling between my legs.

"Did I tell you yet how sexy you looked in that dress tonight?" Aiden asks, sliding a hand down my hip and into the top of my joggers, reaching around and grabbing my ass, hard. "I was so pissed at myself for making you angry enough to leave. But damn, did your back and ass ever look amazing when you walked away. Every man in there, and most of the women too, couldn't help but watch you as you left. You're so beautiful that every eye can't help but be drawn to you."

He sits back on his knees and starts working my pants and underwear down my legs. Torturously slowly, yet again, but this time I have no leverage to get it done faster. I'm at his mercy and I love it.

"We're going to have to go out again, properly, so I can see you in that dress. Except for this time, I won't fuck it up. And then after, when we get home, I'm going to push you against the wall, stick my head up your dress, and lick you until you come all over my face and scream my name. Or maybe I'll take advantage of the dark parking lot behind this building and do it against the wall out there."

He pulls my pants and underwear off and tosses them away, into the room somewhere, like he did my shirt. Still kneeling between my legs, his eyes rake over me, taking me in. I should feel exposed, lying here completely naked while he's fully clothed and devouring me with his eyes, but instead I feel... cherished. Cared for. Loved.

"Aiden, please."

"I need a taste, babe. Just a little taste of this gorgeous pussy before I get inside you." He bends and licks me from entrance to clit. "Fuck, that's good. You taste amazing." He groans and sucks my clit into his mouth, making slow circles around it with his tongue. My orgasm is building too quickly. I want to make this last.

"Not like this, Aiden," I say, pulling him up to my face and kissing him deeply. "I want you inside me."

I tug on his shirt until he reaches back and helps me drag it over his head. It gets tossed somewhere in the room to join my clothes. He pulls something from his pocket, then quickly shucks his pants and boxers, before lowering himself over me again. He takes my mouth in a passionate kiss, then lifts himself onto his elbows and looks into my eyes before leaning back onto his knees again. When he picks something up, I realize it must have been a condom that he pulled from his pocket. I watch as he sheathes himself, pumping his cock slowly while he looks hungrily at me. I lift myself up on my elbows and watch as he slides the head of his dick through my wetness, sliding it over my clit several times, and then places his tip at my entrance.

"Are you sure, Rhea?" he asks, the quaver in his voice betraying his nervousness.

I answer in the only way I can right now, by reaching up and grabbing his neck, and pulling him down to me. I glide both hands down to his ass, squeezing it, kneading it, feeling his muscles tense as he holds himself above me, and then I pull him into me fully, his name escaping my lips in a whisper as he fills me.

"Oh god, you feel so fucking good, babe," he moans as he slides in. "So wet and tight and perfect."

Aiden pumps into me, rolling his hips while he caresses my face with his hands. He looks into my eyes like they hold the answers to questions he's been asking for a lifetime, and in his eyes, I see the answers to mine.

"I want to see more of you. Ride me?"

I nod, and he rolls us again, putting me on top, and I rock slowly, dragging my clit against him as he meets every movement. Time stops, and I don't know how long we stay like that, loving each other, until I feel the orgasm coming fast. Aiden feels it too, and he picks up his pace, pumping into me faster and faster until I fall over the edge, shattering into a million pieces of sparkling white light, as wave after wave of pleasure rushes through me and I'm screaming his name. This is more than an orgasm. This is everything.

"Oh fuck, yes, Rhea. Fuck." Aiden yells, and I feel him pumping into me, filling the condom, gripping my hips as I climax around him, the pulsing inside me pulling his orgasm from him.

Exhausted finally, after what has to have been the world's longest orgasm, I fall forward and lay on Aiden's chest. I lift my hips slightly to give him access to the condom, but I don't let him up to dispose of it, making him tie it off and leave it beside us on the floor instead. I'm boneless and want to lie here for a few more moments before we go anywhere.

Aiden tilts my head up, kissing me softly, a small smile on his lips.

"How did I ever think I could stay away from you?"

I kiss him back, grinning. "I don't know, but don't plan on that happening now. I may not have a basement, but I still have handcuffs, and I think I've just decided what you can do for me while I keep you prisoner."

He laughs. "Oh yeah? And what's that?"

"Keep giving me orgasms like that, obviously." I lay my head back down.

"Well yeah, obviously."

"And probably wash the dishes or something, too. And the apartment could use a cleaning. Someone threw clothes all over the living room."

He smiles, cupping my face, and pulling me in for a kiss. Our tongues tangle languorously, our bodies physically spent. I run my hand over his chest and abs, tracing his Adonis belt lightly, marveling at his body. This is one beautiful man I've found myself with.

"You are so gorgeous," I tell him, continuing to trace the lines of his muscles.

"You're playing a dangerous game, babe," he growls sleepily at me. "You're going to make me hard again, and I don't think either of us has the energy to do anything about it."

I chuckle. So *that's* what he meant when he said that at the club.

"Hey, wait a minute." I sit up and squint at him, a thought coming back to me suddenly. "Did you say that your dick talks to you?"

He laughs and pulls me down.

"Less talking, more kissing," he says.

And that's exactly what we do.

40

Mr. Glori-ass

Aiden

RHEA CONTINUES HER DANGEROUS game until I'm hard as stone and we make love on the floor once more before ending up in her bed, cuddled up, facing each other under the covers.

Yeah, I said it.

We made love.

I'm in more trouble than I thought, and I can't think of anything better.

"Spontaneous floor sex is fun," she says. "But let's lay out a blanket or something next time. I've got rug burns in places that should never have rug burns."

I lean forward and kiss her nose. "I think some of that is beard burn, sweetheart. And I don't recall you complaining about it when it was happening." Pulling her tight to my chest, I squeeze her gently. "I know *I* enjoyed it a great deal."

She smacks me on the arm playfully. "Tell me that again when you're the one with scrapes on your knees, elbows, back, and ass. It feels like I have a sunburn."

"Yeah, I still say it was worth it." I grin at her.

She huffs out a breath, then gives me a little smile. "Fine. Maybe it was a little bit worth it."

I roll onto my back and she follows, laying her head on my chest and wrapping her leg over mine. She swirls her fingertips through my chest hair, tracing circles and spirals over and over again, and I have never been more relaxed. Even sleeping in my bed at home, I've never been totally relaxed. I wonder if maybe Rhea has a point about that place having bad vibes. The bad memories have been part of the reason I stay there, so in a way, it makes sense.

"So, know any good realtors?"

Rhea bolts upright, the blanket falling to her waist. "Are you serious?"

Now how am I supposed to have a serious conversation with her perfect tits staring me right in the face? I reach up and palm her breast, my thumb rubbing back and forth across her nipple. Maybe this conversation can wait? My dick is coming to attention again, and I'd much rather be inside Rhea right now than talking about selling my house.

Rhea takes my hand off her breast and holds it. "Concentrate," she says, smiling down at me. "There's plenty of time for that."

"Ugh, fine." I sit up and lean against the headboard, pulling her in beside me so I can hold her while we talk. For a guy who had no intention of ever having a relationship, I sure seem to enjoy having Rhea in my arms. "I think maybe you're right about my house. It might be time to sell after all."

"Are you sure that's what you want? I don't want you to make such a big decision because I said you should. Maybe you need to think about it a little more." She straddles my legs and grabs my face with both her hands. "If your house doesn't bother you, then you should keep it. I don't think it's *actually* built on an old cemetery. Probably." She shrugs and gives me a small smile.

Yeah, I'm a goner. This woman is going to be the death of me. She's sexy, she's smart, she's funny, and for some odd reason, she cares about me. I lean forward and kiss her, wrapping my arms around her and gripping her tightly to me.

"The only reason I've stayed in my house all these years is *because* it bothers me. It's full of reminders of my father and how he treated me. He never physically hurt my mom or my sister, just me, but he emotionally abused them, and I remember that as well. I stayed in the house because it reminded me of what I could become if I ever let myself love someone. Or of what any child of mine could become. I never wanted to fall for someone and risk turning into my father. And I never wanted to father any kids. The memories I associate with the house act as a constant reminder of why I've kept myself closed off." I nuzzle my face into her neck. "You've made me want to leave all that behind. Because I want to be with you."

Rhea wraps her arms around me, hugging me tightly with her whole body. "Aiden, I don't know what to say to make you believe me. You're a good person. You're so worried about becoming like your father that I know there's no way you would. A person like him wouldn't show this level of concern. Have you ever considered a vasectomy?" She looks up at my face expectantly. "You know, because you never wanted to have kids? You could always get a vasectomy and then you'd have less to worry about. And you wouldn't run the risk of popping off a woman like a champagne cork and running away screaming if you accidentally forget a condom again."

I choke out a laugh. "Okay, I know it's not funny, but what a visual. Popping off like a champagne cork." I try hard to contain my laughter, but I fail miserably. It takes several minutes for me to calm down.

"I also thought it was like when you blow up a balloon, but don't tie it off? You know how when you let it go, it suddenly starts flying erratically all over the room while the air escapes? You reminded me a little of that while you were freaking out and trying to find your clothes."

We both laugh at that, pretending our hands are balloons flying around, and making whooshing noises like air escaping.

"I know I can never take it back, Rhea," I say when I finally stop laughing, "but I want you to know how very sorry I am. I felt like such an asshole as soon as I left."

She kisses me softly. "You were an asshole, and I forgive you. But don't let it happen again. Something like that would be very damaging to our relationship," she says with a smirk.

"How did you get so smart?" I say into her hair. "And how did I get lucky enough to get your attention?"

She leans back and looks at me. "You're not the only one with Social Work classes under your belt, you know. That, and years and years of therapy." She grins. "As for you getting my attention? What can I say? You have an amazing ass."

"I really do, don't I?" I twist myself and pretend to look at my ass. "It's glorious."

"Nothing like being humble about it." She digs her fingers into my ribs, tickling me. "See if I ever compliment you again, Mr. Glori-*ass*."

I slip out from behind her, grab her legs, pull her lower down the bed, and cover her with my body. "I like the sound of that. Mr. Glori-*ass*. Think I should make that permanent? Aiden Glori-*ass* has a nice ring to it, don't you think?"

She wraps her arms around me and squeezes my butt, making little happy sounds. "Hmmm. It is a very nice ass, but on second thought, maybe 'Mr. Smartass' would be a better name for you." She smacks me on the ass before erupting into laughter and pushing me off of her. "Now, let's find something to eat so we can go to sleep. I have a job interview tomorrow that I'm excited about and I need my rest."

She leaves the bedroom naked, and if I had to guess, I'd say she's searching for the clothes we threw all over the living room.

I jump out and run after her, making it just in time to watch her pull her hoodie down over her butt.

"Damn, I missed the show." I bend over and pick up my jeans, pulling them on sans boxers. "You'll have to show me again later." I walk to her and pull her into my arms, kissing her softly, shocked at how easy this is. "For now, how about I make us something to eat and you tell me all about your interview?"

41

News at the Precinct

Rhea

WE DON'T EVEN HAVE a chance to look in the fridge before both of our phones ring. Aiden finds and answers his right away while I follow my ringtone so I can track mine down in the mess of clothes still on the living room floor. I finally find it hiding under my pants and answer it before it cuts to voicemail.

"Hello?"

"Rhea? Something came up in the Frank Martin case. Can you come down to the precinct?" Kaden's voice sounds strange like he's trying to hold in laughter. If he's calling to talk about Frank Martin, something big must be happening. Not sure why that would be funny, but I guess I'll find out soon.

"What? Yeah. Yeah, okay. I'm on my way. Be right there." I hang up without even saying goodbye and I'm pulling on my pants mere seconds later. Is he calling to tell me I can have my job back?

Do I even want my job back?

"Can you take me to the police station?" Aiden asks as he zips his pants and slips his phone into his pocket. He finds his shirt and pulls it over his head. "Ryder says Gran, Gladys, and Lana have been brought in for questioning and he wants me to help him get them all home."

I stop dead in my tracks. What are the odds that the Frank Martin case thing that Kaden called me about and this Titty club arrest are connected? With the two late-night phone calls from the precinct at the same time? Probably pretty good, I'd say.

"Shit. Kaden called me about the Frank Martin case just now, so I'm going there, anyway."

Aiden stops his search for his shoes and looks at me. And then bursts out laughing.

"Oh fuck, what the hell did those old ladies get themselves into this time?" He's shaking his head as he walks around the apartment, picking up stray socks and shoes as he goes. "They've been begging me to let them come on a 'dick mission', as they call it, for ages. *Shit*. Do you think maybe they gave up on me and went rogue? They were all quite upset about what that guy did and how he got you fired."

"You know, normally I would say that three old ladies couldn't possibly be involved in vandalizing a person's property with giant dick pictures but... I have met these particular old ladies and I wouldn't put it past them." I take my shoes from Aiden and pull them on my feet without bothering to tie them. "But how would they have even gotten his address? I doubt Devon or Johnny would have told them."

"Devon wouldn't tell them, and I'm sure Johnny couldn't tell them. Hell, I probably couldn't find my way back there. Devon is the one who got the address from Kaden and he's the one who drove us there. He knows what those women are like. I'm sure he wouldn't give them the address voluntarily."

If they'd used some kind of underhanded persuasion, he might, though. That's a different story altogether, but I don't say that to Aiden. Let him believe the best of his friend for now.

"No sense in standing here talking about it, I guess. Let's get to the precinct and get some answers."

* * *

"You guys came together? *I know what you were doing*," Ryder says in a singsong voice when we arrive at the precinct. He's waiting by the front desk with Kaden. "I can't wait to tell everyone else."

"Fuck off, Ryder," Aiden says, looking around the room. The titty club is sitting together on a bench down the hallway and Kaden waves him by so he can go talk to them. Aiden leans over and kisses me before he goes and the butterflies I'd finally gotten under control come rushing back. That man is something else.

"Where's my wife when I need her? I'm pretty sure that *fuck off* was uncalled for. It definitely falls under the purview of her wedding vow to give them shit when they say it to me." Ryder complains before walking away to join Aiden.

Kaden watches them all for a moment while the ladies appear to be telling Aiden a very animated story involving explosions and rain if I'm judging their gestures and body language correctly. I really hope that doesn't mean they blew up someone's house.

"Captain Ross wants to see you in his office," Kaden tells me. "It's good news."

I raise my eyebrows in question. "Good news? Did Mrs. Martin leave her husband?"

"Just go talk to the Captain. He wants to tell you himself. I'll go take care of the discharge paperwork for these fine ladies." Kaden walks to the bench where Gran and her friends are sitting. "Alright ladies, let's get you out of here. I'll go get the paperwork completed and then you can get on your way."

Shaking my head, I turn and walk to the Captain's office. The door's already open, so after a quick knock on the door frame, I poke my head in. "You wanted to see me, Captain?"

He looks up from his desk and smiles. "Come on in, Ryan."

42

Glitter Dicks and Dick-sco Balls

Aiden

"AND WE MUST'VE MISCALIBRATED the timers *and* the detonators because the next thing we know-*BOOM*- tiny, shiny dicks are flying out of the cannons directly at the neighbor's house. I guess we misjudged the amount of explosive needed too because the dicks shouldn't have been able to fly *that* far." Gran almost pulls off looking contrite but Ryder and I both recognize the gleam in her eyes, which tells us there's a little more to this story than she's letting on.

"Oh, don't forget the stickiness," Gladys says. "That's what made them think it was vandalism."

"Right." Gran pats Gladys on the leg, then looks back at me and Ryder. "The dicks were sticky," she adds, like that explains everything.

"Well, now, it's not that the *dicks* were sticky. We don't just go around shooting sticky dicks at people's houses." Lana explains in a reasonable tone from her spot at the end of the bench. "Imagine shooting off sticky dicks all willy-nilly." She chuckles.

"Oh no, of course not. Shooting sticky dicks would be wrong," Gran agrees.

"The foam that shoots out of the cannon with the dicks, though, now *that stuff* is a little sticky." The three ladies all nod together, because *obviously* the liquid is sticky and not the dicks. That makes way more sense.

"That's right," Lana says. "But we must have mixed up the ingredients for the solution because instead of minimally sticky foam, we made super sticky foam. Which means the dicks will take much longer to wash away."

"But they will wash away, eventually?" Ryder asks. "So what's the problem, then?"

"Well, the man who owned the house was quite angry when he saw all the glittery dicks stuck to his house," Gladys tells him.

"And his car," says Gran.

"And driveway," Lana adds.

"And flowerbeds." Gladys finishes.

"Sounds like this guy's entire property is a giant glitter dick disco ball. A dick-sco ball, if you will." Ryder bursts out laughing.

I snicker at Ryder's joke.

Dick-sco ball.

Classic.

"I don't see why that would bother him, though. Glittery dicks look way fancier than that giant dick he has burned into his lawn. You would think he'd appreciate the addition of a bit of dick glitter. No matter how sticky the foam is, I guarantee those dicks will wash away before the grass grows back on that big lawn dick." Gran gives me a pointed look while she says this.

Holy shit, she's even more devious than I thought.

How did she pull this off? And how did she know where Frank Martin lives? And sticky glitter dicks? Maybe I *should* have been letting her assist me all this time. Glitter dicks are less damaging than salt dicks in lawns, and way easier for passers-by to see from a distance. I'm making a note of this for future use.

"Gran, why were you setting up glitter dick cannons, anyway?" Ryder asks her, finally.

"Funny you should ask. We started a gender reveal party business after talking to Rhea about it last family dinner. So we were setting up at our first client's house. The granddaughter of one of our neighbors at Peaceful Pines is having a baby, so he hired us to set up for a party that's supposed to happen tomorrow morning."

"We're going to have to cancel on our first client now, though. It's too late to get new dicks, never mind the ingredients for the explosives. All we have set up is the giant dick tunnel in the backyard. And as we all know, one giant dick tunnel does not a penis party make," Lana says sadly. "I really hate letting people down this way."

Gran and Gladys both nod their heads in agreement.

"But at least they had security camera footage covering their yard, and the neighbor's yard, that they gave to the police to prove our innocence."

"Did you say security footage?" I ask Gran, worry and excitement warring for equal ground in my belly. Security footage from a neighbor could be great for Rhea, but not so great for me.

"Yes, they have footage going back months and months." Gran smiles. "All but one day. Apparently, their security system suffered a glitch and didn't record anything from this past Sunday night to Monday morning. So strange." She shoots me a little wink as Kaden gets back with the paperwork.

That devious, brilliant, wonderful woman. The night I made that dick is the one night that's missing from the footage. She saved my ass.

"Alright ladies, it's official. You are free to go."

43

Meeting the Mrs.

Rhea

"Officer Ryan, you remember Mrs. Martin, don't you?" The captain calls my attention to the woman sitting in front of his desk. "She asked if she could speak with you for a moment now that we have some new information in the case against her husband."

I sit heavily in the chair beside Mrs. Martin. It doesn't escape my notice that the captain referred to me as Officer Ryan again, but I shouldn't read too much into it. Maybe he's calling me that because Mrs. Martin is here.

"Hello Officer Ryan," Mrs. Martin says. "I'm sure you're not thrilled to see me, after everything that happened."

"Mrs. Martin came in with the group of older ladies out in the main office," Captain Ross explains.

"Oh?" I ask. She came with the titty club? Why on earth would she have come in with them? "I don't understand what that has to do with me, or even with Mrs. Martin."

"Those lovely ladies were setting up some kind of party at a neighbor's house. They accidentally shot my house with an abundance of glittery penises, which, I'm sure you can imagine, enraged my husband. The security footage shows him threatening the ladies, so he was arrested. I got the idea that maybe the neighbor had footage going far enough back to clear your name and allow me to press charges against my husband without fear of repercussions. He's always been so careful to have no witnesses for the way he treated me, but actual video recordings would be a tremendous advantage for me."

Shit. Did they have footage of Aiden and Johnny making the big lawn dick? That could turn out poorly for them.

"They have footage that clearly shows the assault of Mrs. Martin, as well as the ensuing completely reasonable, and by the book, arrest of Mr. Martin. Once the Commission reviews the footage, which I have already made several copies of, you will be reinstated and will resume your regular duties with Officer Cross as your partner." The captain looks pleased. "He is shit at paperwork. It will be nice having you back to keep him in line."

That thought doesn't please me as much as I thought it would. I'm not sure I want back on the force now. I have a lot to think about when I get home. But I tip my head politely all the same. No sense in talking to the captain about it yet.

I look at Mrs. Martin. She looks as though she's been crying, but there is a sense of calm about her that wasn't there the last time I saw her.

"Mrs. Martin?" I ask. "Are you going to be safe now? Do you need somewhere to go?"

She reaches over and pats my hand. "You are so sweet, dear. I mean, Officer." She smiles, but it doesn't reach her eyes. "I'm not entirely sure where I will go, but I would think I should be safe enough at the house tonight, at least. Captain Ross said that my husband will remain in custody tonight?" He nods at her question. "So I'll go there for the night and I guess I'll figure something else out tomorrow."

"I think I might have a better idea," I say, a thought forming in my head. "How do you feel about ladies' clubs?"

She looks at me quizzically as I stand. "Come on, let me introduce you to some friends of mine." I turn to the Captain. "I look forward to hearing from you when the police commission reviews the footage. Thank you for calling me in to tell me about this."

Mrs. Martin follows me out of the office and we join the titty club, Kaden, Ryder, and Aiden, who are all waiting near the entrance to the building.

"How did it go?" Aiden asks, pulling me in for a quick hug and kiss. I'm amazed at how easy this thing with him already feels. It's like we've been together for years, instead of only a night.

"Good, I think. The neighbor had footage that showed the arrest of Frank Martin and it proves that I behaved appropriately. Once the police commission reviews the footage, I should be back on the force. But... I'm not sure that's what I want anymore."

Mrs. Martin is standing beside me, hands clasped in front of her, while she looks at the floor.

"Hello dear," Gran says. "I'm Delores, and this is Gladys and Lana."

"Um, hello. My name is—"

"Cathy, you fucking bitch. You're going to regret this. You can't do this to me." Oh, look. Frank Martin is down the hall and thinks he can threaten my new friend. "And you old bats, you're going to regret shooting me with dick confetti. Mark my words." As I'm about to step around Cathy Martin to give that asshole a piece of my mind, the three ladies of the titty club form a wall with Cathy behind them.

"Listen here, you wrinkled, stinky, old nutsack," Gran yells. "This lady is one of us now and if you try to mess with her in any way, you're going to realize having glittery dicks all over you is the least of your problems."

I see Gladys nudging Cathy in the arm, whispering something in her ear.

"Piss off, Frank. I'm not your punching bag anymore. Have a nice life. Or don't. Because I no longer give a fuck." She smiles shyly as the ladies of the club wrap their arms around her and lead her out the door.

Aiden, Ryder, and Kaden stare down the hallway until the officer escorting Frank Martin drags him away. He's so shocked by what his wife said he hasn't uttered another word. The only sounds coming from him are sputters of indignation and indecipherable gibberish.

"Okay, that was fun. But we have a penis party to save and cocks to construct. Time is trouser snakes. Let's go people. Time's a-wastin'." Ryder claps his hands and rubs them together as he walks out of the building. "Tallywhacker-ho!"

I look up at Aiden. "Should I be worried?"

He grabs my hands and places a kiss on my knuckles. "Probably?"

44

All Hands on Dick

Aiden

"Alright cock-struction crew, listen up. Some of you will assemble skinny dicks over here at the kitchen table, some will do the fat cocks over there on the island, others will man-handle the monster dongs in the dining room, and the rest will play with the puny pee-pees will be over on the coffee table in the living room." Ryder is directing all the helpers to their stations as we prepare to spend as long as it takes making dicks out of candy and baked goods. "You all have your ingredients and you know what to do. Make some dicks and make us proud."

When Gran, Gladys, and Lana said they'd have to cancel their party because they shot their dick loads too soon, Ryder came up with a plan. Gran had given us the idea herself when she described the penis party she threw as a gender reveal for one of the staff at Peaceful Pines. She and Gladys had handmade hundreds of different-sized dicks out of crispy rice treats for that party and we are going to recreate the magic tonight, using different ingredients.

Before we left the precinct, we called all of our reinforcements to have everyone meet us at Alex and Connor's place because they have the biggest kitchen. Then we made a quick run to the twenty-four-hour grocery store and stocked up on ingredients.

Every member of Sleeping Dogs is here, along with all the significant others, friends, and hangers-on they could find.

It's all hands on deck tonight.

Johnny and Alex are doing the baking and the rest of us will work on decorating what they make and constructing dicks out of store-bought baked goods and candy. Gran saved all the gigantic, inedible dicks they had made for that other party, so we sent Devon with her to get them out of storage at Peaceful Pines.

"Is this the sort of activity you usually do?" Cathy asks Gladys while constructing a magnum dong from a whole jelly roll cake, a couple of giant muffins, and a small round cake. "Making penises out of foodstuffs?"

"Oh no, this is for our new gender reveal party business. This is the backup plan because we 'accidentally' shot our glitter dicks all over your house and yard." Gladys uses air quotes with the word accidentally, confirming for me that shooting Frank Martin's house with millions of tiny, glittery dicks was not actually an accident. "But at least the guests of the party will still be able to see them, so it wasn't a total waste."

"Usually our evenings involve a little less dick," Lana adds helpfully, a sweet smile on her lips. "Though not for lack of trying, at least on Gladys' part."

Gladys shoots me a dirty look. Rhea and I are working at the magnum dong station with Cathy, Lana, and Gladys. I'm the only one who gets the dirty look, though.

"I've been trying to see this boy's wee willie winkie for a while now and he's been refusing to show me. And from the looks of it, he's going to do the same thing as Ryder did and run off and get married before I get to have a peek. It's not fair, I tell you."

Rhea laughs. "You know, Gladys, there are easier ways to see dick than lusting after younger men of your acquaintance. You could take a trip to Vegas with the girls and hit up some strip clubs. I think Gran would probably be up for that."

Each of us has completed one dick and we're working on our second when Gran and Devon arrive with the giant dicks from the retirement community. Gran comes to join us at the magnum dong table and Devon heads to the puny pee-pee crew in the living room.

"What are we talking about over here?" Gran asks, pulling over her jelly roll and other ingredients. "Did I hear someone say Vegas?"

"Rhea was suggesting you all take a trip to Vegas to see some strippers so that Gladys will stop trying to get a look at my penis." I glance over at Rhea before I continue. "I don't think she wants to share me with anyone."

Rhea doesn't skip a beat. "He's not wrong. I'm terrible at sharing. Besides, I licked it, so it's mine now." She turns and gives me a big grin and a wink. She goes back to forming foreskin out of fondant to partially cover the head of her magnum dong. She's an equal-opportunity dick developer. Some of her dicks have foreskin and some don't.

I shake my head a little to clear it. Did she say what I think she said?

She sure did, says my dick. *Tell her she needs to do it again if she really wants to own me. Oh fuck, who am I kidding? She's the only one for me.*

Shut up, dick. This is important. I need to find out if she really meant it.

"Did you just tell a table full of ladies you licked my dick, so now it's yours?" I whisper into her ear. "Because if you did..."

"Oh, ha. Yeah, I guess I did, didn't I? Oops."

I shove my hand into her hair and pull her lips to mine, kissing her deeply in full view of everyone at the table. Rhea fists her hands into my shirt and pulls me closer, kissing me back with just as much desperation as I'm feeling. There's whistling and yelling in the background and somewhere in my mind I remember we have an audience, but I can't be bothered to care. Not when this beautiful woman told me I'm hers and now she's kissing me like it's the only thing that matters. Eventually, she breaks the kiss, but she doesn't drop my shirt. Instead, she looks up into my eyes and smiles.

"I guess it was okay," I say with a chuckle. "Besides, that same rule applies to you. So if I'm yours, then you're mine."

Her grin spreads across her face. "Well then. As long as that's settled."

"It's settled," I say, mirroring her smile.

"Ahem." Johnny clears his throat from the doorway. "Now that we've determined you two are in love or whatever, can we get these dicks finished? I've had my hands on more cocks tonight than I ever thought I would in my life."

It seems that while Rhea and I were kissing and laying claim to each other, the rest of the dick construction crew had gathered in the doorway to watch the show. Bunch of pervs. But I can't complain. I just had the most amazing woman I've ever met say that I'm hers and she's mine. If these clowns want to watch me kiss her, that's their issue, not mine.

Then again, the faster we get these dicks done, the faster we can get out of here. So, with that in mind, I yell, "Alright guys, back to work. I need to get my woman back to my place so I can lick her thoroughly to ensure my claim on her is secure."

Rhea smacks me on the arm. "Aiden," she hisses. "Don't say stuff like that." She looks upset for a moment, making me worry I took the joke too far, then she adds, "Your place is a spooky freak show full of poltergeists and pig-men, remember? You can't expect me to want to get naked with all *that* going on around me."

I bark out a laugh. "Oh yeah. Right. Your place it is, then."

For some reason, Rhea making light of the terrible memories in my house doesn't bother me. I held on to my childhood house for years as a reminder of my horrible father and what I needed to avoid. But Rhea is right. I won't turn into my father simply because I share his DNA. I've done everything in my power to avoid that fate, and I think I've done well. I can allow myself to love someone without being afraid of what could happen because I am not my father and I never will be.

"So, I'm looking for a good realtor. If any of you know one, give them my number."

45

Dick-x-hausted, But Not Like That

Rhea

"Oh my god, I don't think I'm ever going to look at cakes and candies the same again after tonight." I groan as I kick off my shoes and send them flying across the room. "Who knew you could make dicks out of virtually anything in the bakery or candy aisles of the grocery store?"

Aiden walks in behind me, toeing his shoes off and leaving them neatly placed beside the door. Huh. That's not a bad idea. It would make it a lot easier to find my shoes if I did that. I consider tracking down the pair that I just kicked off, but exhaustion wins and instead, I drag my ass to the bedroom and fall face-first on the bed.

"Pretty sure anyone with a twisted sense of humor could have told you that." Aiden rolls me over and starts getting me undressed. "Why else would Gran and her friends know how to do it?" He gently slides my joggers off and begins working on my hoodie, which proves difficult since I've gone rag doll on him. "Come on, Rhea. Help me out a little. You'll be more comfortable out of this sweatshirt."

I force myself to sit up and let Aiden pull off my shirt, but as soon as it's over my head, I flop back down onto the bed. He chuckles and focuses on undressing himself now that I'm naked.

"You're adorable when you're tired," he says. "Thanks for helping tonight. I know you probably never thought you'd be making dicks out of candy with a bunch of dudes in a band and some old ladies."

I turn my head a little and open my eyes. Aiden is walking toward my bathroom, nude, with that amazing ass on display. If I could muster any energy, I'd be up and sinking my teeth into that thing right now. I've thought about biting it so many times, and I have yet to make it a reality. But turning my head and opening my eyes is the extent of what my body can do right now. I'll have to save the biting for tomorrow.

"Hey, you get back here," I call out when he leaves the room. "I was promised a thorough licking. I demand satisfaction."

He peeks his head back into the room and points his toothbrush at me. "I don't think you're in any shape to be demanding satisfaction, baby. Just saying the word satisfaction is pushing you past your limits. If you're still going to your job interview later, you should probably try to get some sleep."

Shit, that's right. I haven't even thought about the interview since speaking to the captain earlier today. After all the mess this situation with Frank Martin has caused, I'm not even sure now if I want to rejoin the force. Maybe this is what it takes for me to finally move on with my life and find another, better way to help people?

I drag myself off the bed and join Aiden in the bathroom, pulling out my toothbrush. "Why'd you have to remind me of my interview? I liked our other plan better." I pout while I squeeze the toothpaste on my toothbrush. "Don't think you're off the hook, mister. I'm taking a rain check on that licking for later."

Aiden spits in the sink and rinses his toothbrush, putting it in the medicine cabinet when he's done. He steps behind me and wraps his arms around my waist, his chin resting on my shoulder while he watches the reflection of me brushing my teeth.

"I've avoided relationships my entire life, Rhea. If you think I won't take every chance you give me to make love to you in whatever way I can, then you're crazy." He punctuates his statement with a kiss behind the ear and a smack on the butt. "Now get your ass into bed, woman. I'm interested in trying this *spooning* thing all the kids are talking about. No relationships also meant no cuddling, and I'm pretty sure I'm going to be amazing at it."

Aiden seems serious about us, but is it too sudden? What if he doesn't really want to be with me? What if he has second thoughts because selling his house is too much for him? I wish these doubts weren't swirling in my head because whatever I'm feeling for Aiden is big. Really big. I can't help but worry about whether he's feeling the same way. I'm too old for what-ifs, though, and if I want answers, I know the only way I'm going to get them is if I ask.

I let out a sigh and hurry to finish with my teeth and then wash up before getting into bed. I'm not used to sharing my space like this, but Aiden has naturally gravitated toward the side of the bed I usually leave empty. I suppose that could be a sign we're meant to be, but I'm pretty sure the nightstand full of books on one side was a pretty big clue to where I normally sleep. I bury myself under the covers and turn to face Aiden, my worries making my stomach hurt.

"Aiden?" I ask, after I finally work up the courage. "Are you sure?"

The tone of my voice must tip him off, since the question itself wasn't very specific, and Aiden wraps his arms around me and pulls me against him. I feel his lips press against my forehead before he rests his cheek against it.

"I've feared relationships my whole life until I met you. You're the only person who ever made me think maybe I wouldn't turn into my father. You're the only woman I've ever been able to breathe and be myself around. I am completely sure. I know it's fast, I know it's crazy, and I know it's not the sort of responsible thing that I would normally do. But I am all in with you, Rhea. I'm selling my house and I want you to help me find a new place where we can be together. We can make our own memories. Good, happy memories. And hopefully a new family will buy my house and be able to make new, happy memories of their own."

I release a long, shuddering breath as the tension I was feeling leaves my body and lean in to kiss his chest. "That sounds perfect," I say dreamily. "But you know the house isn't really haunted, right? It feels that way for you, and for me, because I care about you. A new family wouldn't have to worry about red-eyed pig-men or skeletons in the yard or anything." A huge yawn escapes me and my eyes drift closed to the sound of Aiden's laughter, as I'm rocked to sleep by the movement of his chest while he quietly chuckles.

46

First Night in the New House

Aiden

"This is the last of it," the guy from the moving company tells me. "Both the house and the apartment are now empty."

"Thanks, man," I say, slipping him some money for a tip, as I'd already done for the rest of his crew. "You guys do quick work. We really appreciate it."

Rhea and I wasted no time moving in together. A few days after the penis party rescue with all of our friends and family, we called a realtor that Travis recommended and started looking for a new place right away. And while we searched, Rhea insisted we stay at her place so that the bad vibes at my place wouldn't get us.

I'm finishing putting some stuff away in the kitchen when Rhea gets home from work.

"Hey, babe. Sorry I'm late," she says, coming over and kissing me. "Winnie needed me to stay and help with dinner tonight. And she wanted me to thank you for sending me to her. Again." she laughs. "I wonder if she's ever going to stop thanking you and realize I would have gone to work for her, anyway."

Turns out Rhea's job interview was at the same shelter I've been volunteering at for years. When Rhea showed up for her interview, I was volunteering for the day already. I remember how excited I was that she visited me so soon, essentially the morning after we got together.

She was less excited, because at first she thought seeing me there confirmed that I had been following her around like she initially thought. Once I explained I'd only been hoping to get her involved in a self-defense class at the shelter, she finally dropped her suspicions. I was worried that having me at the shelter would make her change her mind about wanting to switch careers, but because of the way the police commission dealt with the Frank Martin ordeal, she had already decided to stay off the force. She was tired of the politics getting in the way of the help she wanted to provide.

When Winnie realized Rhea and I knew each other, only after she'd already offered Rhea the job, she got the wrong impression and thought that I'd recommended Rhea for the position. I can't tell you how many thank you cards she sent me in those first few weeks.

"If I can ever convince you to let me take care of you, so you can volunteer there like I do, she'll never stop thanking either of us." I pull Rhea down onto my lap on the floor and kiss her deeply. "Let me shower you with love and money already, damn it."

This is a disagreement we've been having for the last few weeks. I say she should let me support her fully and then she can volunteer at the shelter and Winnie will be able to hire an additional person. She says she wants to pull her own weight while also working a job that she loves. She refuses to acknowledge that it's money I donate that pays her salary, anyway, so it's not like she'd be taking anything extra from me.

My woman is nothing if not independent. And stubborn. She's definitely stubborn, too.

"We've been over this, Aiden. You already bought the new houses. And paid the movers. And bought all the new furniture.

I'm not letting you take care of everything. Even letting you do all of that was more than I'm comfortable with. End of discussion." Rhea scrambles off my lap and stands up. "Now what's for dinner? I'm starving."

I push aside the box I've been emptying and get to my feet. "About that," I say. "Come with me. I want to show you something." I take her hand and pull her along behind me.

"Where are we going?" She asks as she jogs to keep up. "And what's the hurry?"

Without answering, I help her on with her coat and put mine on as well. It's chilly out and I'm taking her out to the dock.

After seeing Denise and Ryder's house at the lake, we realized it was the perfect place for us too, and let our realtor know to focus her efforts here. Nothing was available, and no properties at all with a lot as big as Ryder's, so we made tentative cash offers to all the property owners with one stipulation. We would only buy a property if we could also buy the one beside it because we have plans to tear down one house and live in the other until we decide whether to rebuild from the ground up. Within a week, we had three sets of neighbors offering properties and we could take our pick. Now, only two weeks after we made the original offer, we've moved into our space and we're about to spend our first night here.

I couldn't think of a better night than this for what I have planned. If I can make it through without throwing up, everything should work out fine.

I called Winnie earlier and asked her to keep Rhea late so I would have time to set up my surprise. And so the lighting would be right. It's nearly spring now, but with the still early sunset, the sky is just now settling into twilight.

"What are those lights?" She asks when we get to the dock. I came out here earlier and set up twinkle lights all along the railings at the end of the dock. "What are you up to?" She eyes me suspiciously.

"You'll see."

I pull her along to the end of the large dock and up the stairs to the deck on the second level, where a small table for two is waiting for us. Rhea sits in the chair I pull out for her, with the cutest confused look on her face, as she looks at the table full of food and the lights wrapped around the railings surrounding us. Music plays softly through Bluetooth speakers attached to the railings, a playlist of romantic songs that I've been agonizing over since I came up with this plan.

"Our first date at Marcus ended so badly that I thought I would recreate it here. Marcus was kind enough to make this all up for us and have one of his kitchen staff deliver it."

I pour us each a glass of champagne.

"This is amazing, Aiden. For someone who has never done this boyfriend thing, you are surprisingly good at it."

"You make it easy," I say, passing her a glass. "Before you, I had no intention of ever trying to be good at it. I had no intention of ever doing it, period. Meeting you changed my life."

"Yes, well," she says and then takes a sip of her champagne. "I am pretty amazing and wonderful."

I chuckle. "You are more than amazing and wonderful, Rhea. You are everything." I take a deep breath and try to calm myself. Nervous energy has me wanting to bounce around, but I need this to be special. "Something happened to me the day I found you there on the sidewalk, sad and crying. Ever since that moment, I haven't been able to get you out of my head."

Rhea laughs. "That's probably because you saved me from being assless that day. It would have been bad if you'd left me sitting there and I had to chew off my ass to escape from being frozen to the ground."

"That's true. You assless would be a crime. I love your ass." I lean forward and kiss her before sliding off my chair and get down on one knee. "And I love you."

Rhea's mouth opens in shock. "Oh my god, Aiden. What is happening right now?"

"I love you, even though I thought I would never be free to love anyone. I love you, even though I thought no one could ever love me back. You showed me that avoiding love wasn't necessary. You taught me I am not my father, and that I will never be my father. You are the smartest, kindest, funniest, and most beautiful woman I've ever known." I reach up and wipe a tear from Rhea's face. "I know this is fast, but I've never been more sure of anything in my life. Rhea, will you marry me? Will you make a family with me?" I pull the ring from my pocket and hold it out to her, my heart beating so hard it feels like it's going to jump right out of my chest and into the lake.

"You want to have a family? With me?" Rhea whispers.

"Yes, love. I want to have a family with you. You showed me that a family is something I can have. And I only want to have one with you."

"Oh my god, Aiden. This is amazing!" She jumps out of her chair, leaving me kneeling in front of it while she paces around the deck. "We're going to have a family. I can't believe this. How many kids should we have? We should have foster kids, too. I was a foster kid and I think you and I would be great foster parents. Wouldn't that be amazing? Foster kid to foster parent? We could foster to adopt, even." She stops and looks over at me. I'm still kneeling, still holding the ring out, still waiting for an answer.

"So... is that a yes?" I ask with a grin on my face.

"Oh shit!" She yells and runs back to me, tackling me to the floor and snatching the ring from my hand. "YES! Of course, yes. I love you, Aiden. I'm so happy we found each other."

"I love you, Rhea. Now kiss me." I pull her down until our lips meet. "Thank you for changing my life."

Rhea slips the slim platinum band with three small rose-cut diamonds onto her finger before lowering her face to mine. "Thank you for having such a nice ass." She kisses me quickly and jumps up. "Now let's eat this food. I'm still starving."

I laugh as she pulls me to my feet. "Yes, let's eat. Before everyone else gets here."

47

Elvis? Is it Really You?

Rhea

"I CAN'T BELIEVE YOU guys convinced two separate people to sell to you just so you could have a big property at the lake," Ryder says. "But I think even with your two properties, Denise and I still have you beat for lot size."

I look around the open concept design of the main floor of our house. There are boxes on every flat surface, plus more boxes stacked neatly against the walls. We're lucky they delivered our furniture yesterday, because now our guests at least have somewhere to sit. Aiden also unpacked the dishes so we have something to serve food and drinks with. Maybe instead of a housewarming party we should have planned an unpacking party. Not sure I really want all these weirdos going through our stuff, though. Not telling what sorts of things they'd find, or leave, if we let them.

"I'm sure you do have a bigger property. Gran was smart to hang on to that lot all these years," Aiden says. "We wanted to make sure we had something a little larger than most of the other houses out here offered. Plus, no one was selling anyway. I figured if we were going to offer to buy places that weren't even for sale, we may as well see if we could get what we actually wanted."

"Your realtor must have huge lady balls," Denise says, "to go around the lake making tentative offers on every property."

I laugh. "Oh yeah. Finley definitely should walk bow-legged because her lady-balls are enormous. Travis recommended her. It wasn't until we'd sent her out to make those offers that we discovered we were her first clients and she really came through for us." I look around the house, scanning all of our guests. "I actually sent her a message and told her to come by tonight. We got these properties all thanks to her. The least we can do is invite her to the housewarming party."

We're waiting for the last of the guests to arrive so we can announce our engagement. Everyone is coming for what they assume is a housewarming party, but we're going to surprise them with the engagement, too.

Just then, a swarm of about twenty kids runs through the house, chasing each other and screaming loudly. Before I can ask where they came from, since I've never seen them before, they yell at each other.

"You're it."

"No, you didn't tag me."

"Uh huh, I did. Mom. Braden says I didn't tag him, but I did. He's cheating."

"Mom. Sarah is lying, again."

"You guys are both lying. We weren't even playing tag. You were *chasing* me."

"Shut up, Austin."

A piercing whistle cuts through the noise, and the herd of kids stops in their tracks. *Huh.* Would you look at that? There are only three of them.

Who would've thought only three kids could make that much noise?

"Braden, Sarah, Austin. That's enough. Come over here and wait for your mom to get inside." Travis, apparently the source of the whistle, calls the kids over to the couch. "I'm sure you know better than to run around screaming in a stranger's house. At least wait until you meet the people who own the house before you start acting crazy."

The kids walk over and sit beside Travis.

"Sorry, Travis," they say in unison.

Wow. Travis must spend a lot of time with kids if he's able to wrangle these guys that easily. Or else he spends a lot of time with these kids specifically.

"Guys, where did you go?" Finley comes running in the front door, her head swiveling until she sees the kids sitting with Travis. "Oh, hey, Travis. I didn't know you would be here tonight."

Interesting.

"Yeah, um, I do some work with Aiden sometimes." Travis runs his hands over the back of his neck. "The kids were just waiting for you to come in and introduce them to Aiden and Rhea."

Travis gets up and walks over to see Gran and the rest of the titty club. They've adopted Cathy into their little group, but they've been having trouble thinking of a new name to account for the fact that there are four of them now. I keep trying to tell them they should keep the titty club name, because they won't get a better cheer than 'go titties', no matter what name they choose.

"Fin," I say, "We're so glad you could make it. We were just telling our friends how huge your lady-balls are." I point to Ryder and Denise, and Finley laughs and says a quick hello. "How come you never told me you have kids?"

"What? oh, um, yeah. Three kids. Braden, Sarah, Austin. Say hello to Rhea and Aiden." The kids mumble hello and the one named Austin also waves to us. Finley finally turning to face me. "They're supposed to be with their dad tonight, but... well, it's complicated. But I wanted to stop in for a minute to congratulate you on moving in. We won't stay too long. I wouldn't want to put a damper on your party by having my kids running around."

"Oh please," Aiden says. "Have you seen our guests? We're surrounded by pregnant women, cops, and filthy-minded grandmothers. This isn't exactly one of those wild parties that people always assume rock stars throw. More like a family get-together than a party, really. And we'd love it if you stayed as long as you like."

"I'd watch the kids if they're hanging out with the old ladies, though. They probably will be a bad influence on them. I'd hate to see what those grannies would teach young children."

"Oh." Finley blinks several times. "Wow, yeah, okay. Thank you." She grins at the two of us before heading to the couch to talk to her kids.

Our friend circle is certainly an odd collection of people. Aiden was right that we're not really the sort of group to have wild parties. And certainly not with the particular assortment of people here right now. And really, I haven't seen much from the rest of the guys in the band in the last few weeks being around them that would make me think they like to party either. I like it. It's like meeting your favorite actor and discovering they like nothing better than to go visit their mom and eat marshmallow cereal out of a mixing bowl. Or like when I first met Marcus, and he offered to put the hurt on Aiden if necessary.

"Are we ready to make our announcement, babe?" Aiden whispers in my ear.

"I think so," I say. "Is everyone here now?" I haven't been able to keep track of everyone because they've all been touring the two properties and splitting their time between inside and outside on the back deck.

"The only people I haven't seen yet are Johnny and Becca," Aiden says. "But it's getting pretty late now, so maybe they're not coming? I don't want to wait any longer for them to show up, anyway. I'm dying for everyone to know that you agreed to marry me." He pulls me into a deep kiss. "And then I'm probably going to take you to bed so we can have our own celebration." He waggles his eyebrows suggestively.

"Well, I suppose we should try out the new bed. Plus, it's our first night in the house. Our new home." I smile up at him and reach around to pinch his butt, something I do as often as I can. "Did you get the bedroom set up already?"

"Yes, ma'am. That was the first thing I did when the furniture was delivered. I figured as long as the bed is ready to go, we can take our time with everything else."

Aiden kisses me briefly before going out to the deck to send everyone inside for our announcement. Gran notices I'm standing alone and comes over to talk.

"Well, girlie," she says as she hugs me. "Welcome to the family. I knew this would work out between you two."

"What? Aiden told you already?" That sneaky son of a bitch. We were supposed to tell everyone together. "When did he even have time? It's only been a couple of hours since he proposed."

Gran chuckles. "No, silly girl. You just told me." She kisses me on the cheek. "That move works every time. I won't tell anyone else yet. I have a feeling we won't be waiting too long for the official announcement, anyway. I'm going to go sit with Gladys to make sure she doesn't get too upset when she finds out yet another dick is forever beyond her reach." She shoots me a wink and walks away.

I'm still laughing to myself about Gran when Aiden comes back to me after rounding up the guests.

"That Gran is devious. She tricked me into telling her first by pretending she already knew." I shake my head. "I should know better than that. I was a cop. I interrogated people for a living. That's like, interrogation 101."

Aiden pulls me into a hug. "Aw, babe. She is the sneakiest person I have ever met. It's fun having her around though, isn't it?"

"Yes, it is." I'm still going to pout a little, though. I can't believe she pulled one over on me. God, I love that woman.

Aiden pulls away and gets two glasses of champagne from the counter behind us. He passes one to me, then calls out to the crowd of guests.

"Hey, everyone. Thanks so much for coming tonight to celebrate with us in our new home." He raises his glass a little and gives a small nod.

"And thank you for accepting me into your lives the way you have. I've had very few friends and family around me throughout my life, and having you all here means so much to me." My eyes are already getting a little misty. Most of these people aren't related in any way, but they're the best family I've ever had.

"There's one more thing we wanted to celebrate tonight, since we are all here together." Aiden smiles down at me and pulls tightly to his side. "Shortly before you all arrived tonight, I asked Rhea to marry me."

"And I said yes!" I finish with a slight squeal and hold my hand up to show off the ring.

A chorus of congratulations and cheers goes up, and we get rushed by everyone wanting to hug us. Several minutes of hugging and kissing go by before we have time to breathe.

"I knew this would happen," Xena says, squeezing me tightly. "This is all because I arranged for Aiden to bang your worries away. I'm such a good matchmaker."

I raise my eyebrows at Aiden. If only Xena knew it was the parts of our relationship she involved herself in that caused us the most trouble. I won't be telling her, though. She's so happy with this result that I'll let her think she helped make it happen.

"So, who's next to make it down the aisle, do you think?" Devon asks. "You two, or Alex and Connor?"

Travis comes walking up to us, his phone in his hand, and a confused look on his face. "I don't think it's going to be either of them, actually," he says, holding his phone up for us to see. "Looks like Johnny got the jump on both of you guys."

A short video plays on Travis's phone of Johnny and Becca standing in front of Elvis as he announces them husband and wife and tells Johnny to kiss his bride. We all watch, dumbfounded, as Johnny and Becca launch themselves at each and kiss passionately.

Several moments of silence go by before someone finally speaks.

"Well, shit," says Gladys. "Better get over here and unzip those pants, Travis. Looks like you're my last chance."

Aiden widens his eyes at me and we both laugh. I can't feel sorry for Gladys, though. I locked Aiden down, that's all that matters to me.

THE END

Keep Reading for a Sneak Peek of Only the Best (Sleeping Dogs Book 4)

Chapter 1 – I Call Dibs

JOHNNY

The crowd is insane tonight, rushing the stage as soon as the lights come up, screaming so loud that the floor rumbles beneath me. We've played a lot of shows in a lot of really cool places, but it's always good to be home. And not just because the hometown crowd always screams the loudest.

Being in one spot for a longer period gives me the chance to find her. You know, 'the one'. Someone to date for longer than a few days or weeks at a time. The guys like to give me shit for ghosting women after a few weeks, but when I know, I know. Why would I waste my time on a person once I've figured out they aren't the one? Plus, it's not like I disappear without telling them first. I always break up with them before I block them.

It's not like I'm a complete asshole. I'd probably call my-self a romantic, actually. I'm looking for that 'love at first sight', 'sparks and fireworks' kind of love.

That's why I pay extra attention to the faces in the crowd during a home show. I'm aware it's probably not a good idea to look for my future wife in the crowd at one of my shows, but who knows when and where fate will bring me my other half? There is always the risk of the woman I meet just using me for my fame and money, but no risk means no reward. And it's not like that hasn't happened before. Besides, she wasn't even a fan, just a model who was using me to boost her career.

We're halfway through our set list when the lightning strikes. When I see her, my heart stops and tingles run down my spine. She's not in the crowd, not really. She's in front of the fence, standing near security, and pointing a huge camera toward the stage. Toward me.

She's scorching hot.

She's dressed casually, in jeans and a tight t-shirt, her curves making them look painted on. Her chin-length, dark hair is asking for me to run my hands through it. She has tattoos up and down both of her arms, and it looks like she has a chest piece as well.

I'll need to get a closer look at those, for sure.

Fuck, I hope this is the photographer Denise was talking about. The one who is shooting the meet and greet after the show. Either way, I'm meeting her.

Tonight.

I'll make sure of that.

Somehow.

I give her a subtle wink and a little smile. She lowers her camera and looks me up and down, her eyebrows raised, a little smirk on her dark red lips.

Oh yeah, I need to meet this woman. She clearly doesn't care who I am. She's giving me shit with just a look and fuck if it isn't making me hard.

We play a few more songs and I can't tear my eyes away from her the entire time. I'm probably creeping her out, but thankfully she's working and not paying much attention to me. I know I'm coming on a little strong, but I have a limited time to make this happen. I don't want to rely on the off-chance that I'd be able to find her if she disappeared right after the show.

Suddenly, Connor announces we're playing an acoustic song that wasn't on the set list at all. My guitar tech runs out and swaps guitars with me. I point out the photographer and tell him to get Devon, our head of security, to invite her backstage. Denise said no sluts backstage tonight, but this is my future wife we're talking about here, not just some groupie.

By the time I look back at her, she's gone.

Fuck.

There's nothing I can do about it now, though. I have to finish the show.

We play a few more songs, and an encore, and finally the show is over. If that photographer isn't in the dressing room when we get there, my plan is to ask Denise to track her down. If anyone can find someone, she can. She has her hands in everything involving our shows, going way beyond standard practice for a manager. She probably already knows everything there is to know about this photographer.

Once I step into the dressing room, I realize I won't need to get Denise's help. The sexy photographer is already here.

"Who is that?" I ask, somewhat less than casually, when my eyes catch on the two women near the entrance to the dressing room. I hope my interest isn't too obvious. The last thing I need is someone giving me a hard time about my love life. Again.

We're scheduled for some meet and greets after the show we just played, but usually they give us a few minutes before letting people in. We all like a few minutes to contain some of the adrenaline coursing through our veins after performing before having to be on our best behavior. I think I'll let it slide this time, though, since it means that sexy photographer is here.

The woman with the camera is without a doubt the hottest woman I've ever seen. I need to get to know her. The other woman is also attractive, but the photographer is way more my type. Black hair, dark eyes, ass and tits to die for, and she's covered every inch of visible skin in beautifully done tattoos. I couldn't see them well from the stage but I can see now that the artwork is amazing.

As is the canvas.

I need to know where else on her body she has tattoos. Where do they stop? If I trace the flower on her right arm, does it go to her shoulder? Her back? All the way down to that sweet ass?

I tear my eyes away from her when Devon answers me and I almost feel a physical loss. Some force is pulling me to this woman and I don't even know her name.

Devon looks over at the other side of the dressing room. "The photographer? Her name's Becca. The other one is Alex." He raises his eyebrows at me and Ryder, putting emphasis on the name 'Alex'.

"Holy shit. Are you serious? Like 'Alex', Alex? 'All I Ever Want' Alex? 'Better off Dead' Alex? Connor's long-lost songwriting muse and true love, Alex?"

Ryder lists off song titles from our first album, all of which Connor wrote for Alex, his first love and first heartbreak.

"Yes, Ryder. All of those things." Devon says. "He doesn't know she's here, so this could be interesting."

Ryder cracks open a bottled water and passes it to me before grabbing another for himself. "Okay, well, dibs on the other one, then."

Anger bubbles up inside me as I think of Ryder with Becca. She can't be with someone like him. He's a cool guy, but he's a man whore. Different chick almost every night. He would never treat her the way she deserves to be treated.

I know I'll treat her right, but how can I know if we're compatible without us spending at least a little time together? I always start out with the intention that a woman could be the one. Because that's what I'm looking for. I want to find my other half. Does that make me blind to a woman's true nature? Sometimes. But I'd kiss a million frogs if it meant I'd find my princess.

"Fuck off, Ryder," I growl at him. "Stay away from her."

He raises his hands in surrender and backs away. "OK man, no problem. You got dibs."

"Shit. Sorry, Ryder. I didn't mean that. I just... I don't know, man." I run a hand through my hair and look at the floor in front of me. What the fuck is wrong with me? "I want to get to know her, that's all."

He slaps me on the back and shoots me a wide grin. "No worries, man. I get it. You're in love again." He laughs. "Now that I look closer, you seem like you'd be more her type, anyway." He leaves me and walks over to talk to Denise and Travis.

How will I get to know Becca better? I need a plan to get her alone. From the way she's talking to Alex, it looks like they came together. If Connor doesn't invite them to the after-party, then I will. I just need to make sure none of the fans hear me when I tell her. The last thing I want is to be surrounded by fans when I'm trying to talk to her. Maybe I should ask them right now, before this all gets started? I take one step in their direction when

Connor comes storming in, head down, bee-lining to the bar on the opposite side of the room.

"What the fuck? Where's the fucking whiskey?" Connor yells.

I sneak another look at Becca and Alex. Looks like the real show is about to start. It's too late to ask them now.

"You guys don't even drink whiskey, and it's not like I've had enough for you to hide the bottles on me now. Don't tell me this meet and greet is some kind of bullshit intervention." Connor looks accusingly at me and the rest of the band just as Alex shoves the whiskey bottle into his hand.

"Oh, shit. I'm so sorry. I was nervous, and I needed to fortify myself with many drinks. Um, here you go."

From where I'm standing, I can see Connor's eyes widen and his jaw drop. I see his entire life change before he even turns around to see that it's Alex. My gaze drifts to Becca, and my heart pounds hard in my chest.

I want that.. I want a love that lasts more than three weeks.

Maybe Becca's not that person for me, but maybe she is. All I know is I'm desperate to talk to her and find out.

We get busy going through the motions of the meet and greet, but I sneak looks at the sexy photographer every chance I get. When she's not taking my picture, I get to watch her work, and I love it. Seeing the way she lines up each shot is mesmerizing. I've never been that into photography, but Becca makes it look so good that I might need to add it to my list of interests.

After the meet and greet, we all go over to Rough Mix, the bar where we played our first proper show, and I snag the seat next to Becca. She's sitting on my right and we're close enough that I can feel her thigh pressing against my leg, close enough that I could easily rest my hand on her knee without stretching. And I want to touch her so badly. I'm able to restrain myself, but only just. She looked hot in the dressing room, but now that

I'm right next to her, I can see how beautiful she really is. That, and she smells amazing. Every time she turns her head I get a whiff of some spicy-scented shampoo or perfume. Whatever it is, I'm sure I look ridiculous when I breathe deep every time she moves.

Not creepy at all.

"Ha! I can tell you about that." Becca jumps up off the seat and into the space next to the table where she acts out the story of Alex catching her boyfriend cheating.

I can't tear my eyes off of her as she describes, in detail, Alex getting home and thinking there is a burglar, only to realize it's her boyfriend fucking some other chick in their bed. Becca acts out Alex's umbrella-destroying home run hit on the dude's ass, the other woman's embarrassment, and the dude's crying and whining about being sorry. A hilarious story, especially with Becca's reenactments of erratic humping, swinging umbrellas, and cheering crowds.

We're all laughing, Becca back in the seat beside me, when Connor turns to Alex and says, "So, Alex, you seem pretty okay for just finding out about this today. Are you? Okay, that is."

"Oh, she's totally used to this. It's happened to her before." Becca says, wiping her eyes and letting out a small chuckle.

Alex's face drops. "Okay, Becca. I think that's enough story time for now. These guys don't need to hear this."

"Wait," I say, my eyebrows bunching in confusion. "This isn't the first time?" Alex is a very attractive woman, and she seems pretty fun too. How does someone like her get cheated on repeatedly? She must have terrible taste in guys. Except for Connor. He's a good dude.

"Not at all," Becca says, looking directly at me, not noticing the venomous look Alex is giving her. "She's nearly into the double digits with cheating boyfriends."

Suddenly Alex shoves Aiden out of the booth and slides out after him. "Okay, cool, yeah. Thanks for the drink, Connor. It was really nice seeing you again. Nice to meet all of you," she says to the rest of us. "I need to get going, though. I need to work early tomorrow. Maybe we can do this again sometime?"

Alex turns and sprints to the exit, with Connor not far behind.

"Oh, fuck," Becca says, running her hand down her face. "I really need to learn when to shut up." She grabs her bags from under the table and stands up. "Nice to meet you guys," she says, and then she disappears into the crowd.

"Wait," I call out after her. "Becca."

Shit. I didn't even get her number. Now, how will I find her again? Because I'm sure this time, it's real.

She's definitely the one.

CONTINUE READING IN ONLY the Best (Sleeping Dogs Book 4)

Keep Reading Sneak Peek of Santa's Baby (coming late 2023)

Chapter One

PHOEBE

Of all the ways I ever imagined spending the Christmas of my thirty-first year I can say with certainty tracking down the Santa Claus who impregnated me was not one of them.

Yet here we are.

"This place is nice, Phoebe," Gavin says, walking into the living room and setting down a box marked "Lincoln." "Maybe the owners won't ever come back from their trip abroad so you can buy it. The furniture is pretty sweet." My idiot brother then flops face down on my fully furnished rental's overstuffed blue velvet couch and groans obscenely. "Oh, man. I could do dirty things to this couch."

It's not every day I rent a place sight unseen, so you can imagine the relief I felt when we got here and the place looked exactly like it had in the photos. That I could find a fully furnished place on such short notice, right before the holidays, was a miracle in itself. Finding a nice place in a safe neighborhood? Yeah, there had to have been some divine intervention involved for that to happen.

"Ew, don't be gross Gavin. And get your stinky ass off the couch. You're filthy."

"Is that any way to treat the guy who helped you move?" He dragged himself off the couch. "Speaking of which, didn't you promise me pizza and beer as payment for that help?"

"Ha! Nice try, kid. I'll order pizza but you're sticking with soda until you're of legal age. Plus, you still need to drive home so I wouldn't let you drink even if you were old enough."

Gavin is eighteen, my much younger sibling from my mom's second marriage. My bio dad left mom when Lane was born and I was still a few months shy of two years old. Needless to say, after being with such a bastion of paternal fortitude, it took Mom a long time to find another man worth taking a chance on. I was twelve when she started seeing Dennis, and fourteen when they married and Gavin was born.

Like most teenage boys, Gavin's all raging hormones and unrestrained snark. But, despite his many annoying traits, he has the biggest heart and he's one of my favorite people. When I found myself left at the altar almost a year ago no one was angrier than Gavin. He stormed around the hotel, hoping to run into my newly ex-fiance so he could unleash his teenage fury. It's probably a good thing he never found him, though. I doubt it would have been a fair fight.

Seventeen-year-old Gavin was a short, scrawny little shit. Eighteen-year-old Gavin is almost six and a half feet tall and packed with muscle. He's never said so, but I'm pretty sure he started working out after the wedding disaster so he'd be ready if he ever saw my ex again. After a year of protein shakes and lifting weights, not to mention a huge growth spurt, Gavin is formidable. It still wouldn't be a fair fight, but the advantage would go to Gavin, not Webster.

I almost feel guilty for not being as upset as he was about the situation. It was a shock when I got the text telling me he wasn't coming, but not marrying Webster Day was for the best. It was a dick move, but in the end, he made the best decision for both of us.

"No way, Lane said she would drive home." Gavin jumps up off the couch and yells down the back hallway, "Isn't that right, Lane?"

Oh, shit. Despite being one of my favorite people, I may have to murder Gavin if he wakes up Lincoln. That thing they say about never waking a sleeping baby? Yeah, that's totally true.

"Shhh. Will you shut up already?." I slap my hand over his mouth. "Lincoln is sleeping."

He looks so sheepish I might actually believe he felt bad about it if I didn't know better. There's no way Gavin would leave here without saying goodbye to his nephew, even if said nephew is barely old enough to see past his own fist. Gavin is sure Lincoln recognizes him, though, and is so proud of that fact. I believe it, too. Lincoln always seems calmer when his Uncle Gavin is holding him. And Gavin never misses a chance to hold him, even if he has to make his own chances.

"Too late," Lane says, coming out of the back hallway with a tiny baby snuggled in her arms. "Little guy was awake when I tried to sneak into his room to drop off a box. I think he sensed me because as soon as I walked in an unholy rumbling started coming out of his little rear end. You need to do laundry, by the way. I rinsed everything and left it to pre-soak." She looks down at Lincoln with a grin and singsongs, "Isn't that right, Linky? Mommy has to do laundry. Yes, she does. She's lucky Auntie Lane changed you and the sheets instead of running away and letting her deal with it."

My heart swells watching my little sister snuggle my baby and not for the first time since I came up with the plan, I second-guess my decision to move back to Westborough. What am I going to do without my family around to help me for the next three months? This was a terrible idea. But if I want Lincoln to at least have the chance to meet his father, this is where I need to be. And my sense of right and wrong won't let me entertain the thought of not trying to find his father. There's a man out there who doesn't know he has a son, and that doesn't sit right with me. I want him to at least have the choice of whether to be involved in Lincoln's life, even if he ends up being a dickhead like my father and chooses to have nothing to do with him.

"Hey, hey. I can see your brain working from here." Gavin is back on the couch, getting his sweaty teenage boy smell all over it. Whatever, I'll Febreze it when he leaves. He can't stink it up too badly in such a short time, can he? "Everything is going to be fine. Tell her your news, Lane. I can't handle seeing her cry."

I reach up and touch my cheeks, and sure enough, they're wet. "Sorry if my feelings offend you, you little twerp. I'm going to miss you guys, that's all. I'm allowed to be sad about that."

He jumps up off the couch and wraps me in a sweaty hug. "I'm going to miss you too, Feeble," he says, using the nickname he called me when he was little and couldn't quite get his little mouth to say Phoebe. "But you won't have to miss Lane."

I blink a few times and pull myself out of his embrace. "What's he talking about?" I ask Lane. "What are you talking about?"

Gavin takes Lincoln from Lane, snuggling him tightly to his chest, and takes him into the kitchen. I hear the cupboard doors open and close and the water runs in the sink. Sounds like Uncle Gavin is making his nephew a bottle.

"I didn't tell you because I knew you'd try to talk me out of it, but I'm staying with you. You have the third bedroom I can sleep in. I even got myself a part-time job at a coffee shop. I'm staying to help you with Lincoln so you can focus on finding his dad. It will be easier to track him down if you don't have to bring Lincoln with you everywhere you go. Plus, I can't be away from you guys for that long." Lane's eyes are shiny with unshed tears. "I just can't get enough of those midnight feedings," she jokes.

I chuckle. "Are you sure? You don't have to put your life on hold for me, Lane. I love you for wanting to do this, but you don't have to stay."

"I know that," she says, wrapping her arms around me. "I want to stay."

"You're the best sister I could ever ask for," I choke through a sob. "I couldn't have made it this far without you."

And it's true. The seemingly endless months of my pregnancy with Lincoln would have been so much harder if it hadn't been for the help of my brother and sister, and, of course, my mom and stepdad. I won't tell Lane and Gavin, but after living back home with my parents for the last year, and having my family around all the time, I was a little scared to be on my own with Lincoln in the city. I loved living here with Webster, but being on my own with a baby is different. The excitement of Westborough seems almost scary when I think about protecting my son from unseen dangers. I tried to play it cool, but I'm thinking I didn't do such a good job of it if Lane secretly arranged to move here with me. I've never been so happy to be such a shitty liar.

"Are you guys done with all the girly feelings out there? Me and the big guy want to come chill on that sweet-ass couch but we don't want your emotional breakdowns cramping our manly style."

Lane and I both burst into laughter. After one more squeeze, I let her go.

"Yeah, we're done," I call out. "I'll order that pizza now so you can get on the road."

"About that," he says, walking back to the living room with my son in the crook of his arm. "Mom told me to spend the night and drive back in the morning. She doesn't want me driving alone at night in the winter. I don't know what she thinks I do after work at home. It's usually pretty late by the time I get out of the market."

Lane sits next to him on the couch, her eyes on Lincoln. "There's a big difference between driving five minutes in Fallbridge at ten at night and driving on the highway at two in the morning. Especially in the middle of winter."

"Yeah, yeah. Okay, Mom," he teases. "I'm already staying the night. Happy?"

"You bet," she says while ruffling his hair, taking advantage of the fact that he has his hands full feeding Lincoln. "We just wuv you so much, Gavvers," she adds in a baby voice. "We would hate it if anything happened to you."

"Hey, no fair. Hands off my hair. Do you know how long it took to get it like that?"

They sit side by side, alternating between cooing over Lincoln and bickering with each other while I busy myself with ordering the pizzas and unpacking some boxes. The best part about finding a fully furnished rental is how little I had to pack to come here. It would have sucked if I'd had to move my furniture out of storage for such a short stay. Three months isn't long enough to justify renting a moving van. With this rental house, all I needed was some boxes in the back of Gavin's truck and I was ready to move in.

I just hope three months is long enough to find Lincoln's dad.

The doorbell rings, and Gavin hops up to grab the pizzas. "Oh, thank god. I'm starving," he says, spreading the boxes down on the coffee table and flipping one open. "I'm a growing boy, you know." He grabs two slices and stacks them.

I bring plates and napkins out from the kitchen. "We know, Gavin. You tell us every time you get even the tiniest bit hungry."

He wiggles his eyebrows, and grins before shoving the pizza sandwich in his mouth.

"So, Phoebe. Why don't you tell me how you plan on finding this guy? All you said before we came was that you're moving here for three months to look for him. Do you even have any idea where he is?"

I heave a sigh. This is the biggest problem with my plan. It sucks. When you get blind drunk after being left at the altar and hook up with someone you just met, it would be a lot easier to move on with your life if you didn't get yourself pregnant in the process. Failing that, it would be nice if you remember the name of the person or any detail about them other than he'd been dressed as Santa Claus for a Christmas party that was being held at the same hotel as your wedding. The only things I have to go on are the big red velvet coat I stole when I crept out of there in the wee hours of the morning, still drunk from the night before, and a picture I snapped of him with his face mashed so far into the pillow you can't tell with any accuracy what he looks like.

Why did I take his jacket, you ask? I guess I thought my walk of shame would feel less shameful if I covered my wedding dress with Santa's jacket. It didn't. But I made it back to the room without being seen, packed up, and headed home with no one finding out I spent what should have been my wedding night with a stranger.

Until a month and a half later when I got the shock of a lifetime, ensuring that *everyone* would eventually know *exactly* how I spent that night.

That's right.

My fiancé left me at the altar and the first thing I did was run out and get impregnated by Santa Claus.

Talk about Ho Ho Ho.

WANT TO KNOW WHEN Santa's Baby is available? Get the Roomie Review. Sign up at chantalroome.com/newsletter

Books by Chantal Roome

SLEEPING DOGS THE COMPLETE collection

The men of Sleeping Dogs have had their fair share of women, but now that they're a little older, and a little wiser, they're looking for something more meaningful than the one-night stands typical of their past.

Second Chance (Sleeping Dogs Book 1)

She's an unemployed chef afraid of being burned by love again. He's a world-weary rock star tired of being used. Can a second chance at first love heal them both?

Face the Music (Sleeping Dogs Book 2)

She's a serious control freak of a band manager. He's a jaded joker of a rock star. Will a jealous ex and surprise pregnancy tear them apart before they start?

Skip a Beat (Sleeping Dogs Book 3)

She's a disgraced ex-cop looking for a career change. He's a moody drummer trying to keep his demons at bay. Can vandalism and ill-conceived revenge plans be the glue that mends their lives and binds them to each other?

Only the Best (Sleeping Dogs Book 4)

He's a romantic, guitar-playing tattoo artist looking for true love. She's an emotionally and physically scarred photographer who keeps people at a distance. When one wants true love and the other wants one night, can friendship and a fake relationship ever be enough?

Way off Base (Sleeping Dogs Book 5)

She's a single mom struggling to rebuild her life. He's a reluctant rock star tired of being alone. Can they repair a foundation of lies to build the life they both want?

CHANTAL ROOME WRITES CONTEMPORARY romantic comedies and is the author of the Sleeping Dogs series of cinnamon roll rock star rom-coms. She loves writing love stories with just the right mix of sweetness, humour, and sex. When she isn't writing, she's drinking way too much coffee, binge reading romance, and living out her own second chance romance with her husband. She's also a mediocre mom to two frustrating, but hilarious and endlessly loveable kids, and one dog who has eaten every toy he's ever been given.

Keep in touch with Chantal on social media

Visit Chantal's website at: www.chantalroome.com

Get the Roomie Review Newsletter chantalroome.com/roomiereview

Join my readers' group facebook.com/groups/theromcomroome

f   facebook.com/chantalroomeauthor

⊙   instagram.com/chantalroomeauthor

𝓟   pinterest.com/chantalroome

♪   tiktok.com/chantalroomeauthor

𝕐   twitter.com/croomeauthor

g   goodreads.com/chantalroome

BB   bookbub.com/authors/chantal-roome

www.ingramcontent.com/pod-product-compliance
Lightning Source LLC
Chambersburg PA
CBHW061608190726
48288CB00007B/2227